# THE ACCIDENT

# THE ACCIDENT

S.D. MONAGHAN

bookouture

Published by Bookouture
An imprint of StoryFire Ltd.
23 Sussex Road, Ickenham, UB10 8PN
United Kingdom
www.bookouture.com



ISBN: 978-1-78681-256-8
eBook ISBN: 978-1-78681-255-1

To Anne – my one true north.

# CHAPTER ONE

Lawrence Court was a cul-de-sac lined with sturdy detached nineteenth-century red-brick Georgian houses, nearly all of which had been gloriously renovated and massively extended in the last decade. Inside were people accustomed to being ushered to their tables and to having their children accepted by the best universities; who avoided the Christmas rush by employing personal shoppers, and who never queued at banks but instead met with their wealth manager. Most of the driveways parked two SUVs and a slick coupé or fat saloon. Several homes had small yachts resting on their carriages across the lawns. One back garden was illuminated with the blue rectangle of a lit pool.

The indicator ticked its second-by-second pulse as David's BMW slowly cruised down Lawrence Court. It was nearly 10 p.m., and all seemed peaceful in this world. He turned off the headlights and pulled up onto the curve. In the circle of the cul-de-sac, a tall hoarding stamped with the logo MAXIMUM BUILDING SERVICES shielded one of the houses. He was greatly pleased at having pulled off the classic coup of buying the worst house on the best street and turning it into the best house on the best street. David – who taught history at Trinity College – naturally considered ancient ruins to be glorious. But hundred-year-old ruins were just sad.

In the morning, David and his pregnant wife would finally be moving in. That was why he was there: for a private moment to walk through the finished project and then to have a cigarette out the back – a very special treat, as he hadn't smoked in two years.

Then he saw it – Tara's blue Ford coupé, parked across the road. It was so unlike her to go out alone at night. And why was she here? Had she been planning the same thing? Were they *that* psychologically attuned to each other? David smiled. *Perhaps.* But just as he was about to step out of his car to surprise her, he noticed another vehicle next to Tara's – Ryan's white SUV.

Footsteps began to echo, breaking the kind of silence that existed only in the neighbourhoods of the very rich. They came from behind the ten-foot-high timber enclosure. The hoarding door opened, and in the shadows a couple kissed. *It might not be her. It might be someone else.* David knew it wasn't someone else. Crouching down in the seat, he held his breath, as if that would stop the pounding in his ears. Insects whirred about him through the opened window.

Tara exited the hoarding door alone. Just eight weeks pregnant, she appeared breezy and innocent, as if she'd just picked up a takeaway for a night in. Pointing the key at her Ford, the locks went *thunk*. As she swept her hands through her shoulder-length auburn hair, the street light glinted against the pale round opals clipped to her ears. She had bought them in Prague with David only a few months previously.

His hands were damp, his breathing shallow and quick. It was as if he'd just seen water flow upwards. David appreciated even the tiniest details about his wife's past. He knew everything about her: intimate particulars of her childhood, her family, past lovers, fantasies, previous health issues; her fears, flaws, her jealousies and hatreds. Tara didn't have secrets – except on his birthday and at Christmas.

She got into her car to return to their apartment. There she would wait for David's return from his under-12s' coaching, having no idea that he'd left early and skipped the traditional few pints afterwards with the rest of the backroom team. As she accelerated past his BMW, the tyres flattened an empty Coke can. He immediately pictured her driving the way she always did – not paying attention; singing along to the radio; distracted by songs she knew, 1990s songs; whacking the wheel in time and laughing when she got the words right – and then crashing: her body destroyed, her mind extinguished, their unborn child terminated.

David caught himself in the rear-view mirror – a handsome, forty-year-old man, abruptly suffering from the universal condition of being the unhappy spouse. A bullet of sweat rolled down his forehead. His skull suddenly looked lived-in for too long, his full lips shrinking into the lean geometry of his face. The usual vibrancy of his blue eyes abruptly deadened. Even the fibres of his thick hair felt heavy. As he leaned over the steering wheel, his body had never felt so slack, so tired.

With almost panicked movements, David withdrew a cigarette and turned the lighter's flint. He inhaled and his chest felt aflame. But after several pulls, the pure bad pleasure of it came tearing back, wafting through the healthy, moist caverns of his lungs and then blasting into his bloodstream. It was the first time he'd smoked in two years, and he was thankful for this pleasure after the shock of so many stings.

*I wish I didn't know*. How would his life have worked out if he hadn't come here tonight? Would he and Tara have lived happily ever after? What was he going to say to her? Would she try that most abject of lies: blunt denial?

*Was there something I did? Something I didn't notice?* There was nothing wrong with their relationship. Their life was exciting and interesting. Tara was eight weeks pregnant.

Except… There had been one moment, just after they'd begun gutting the house. It had been David's fortieth birthday and they'd been celebrating with friends at their apartment. Tara had seemed off that night, and when they'd sung 'Happy Birthday', David had noticed her not singing but instead looking at the carpet. Had it just dawned on her what it meant for David to be ten years older than her?

But Ryan was the same age as Tara. Ryan and Tara had dated when she'd been a student. Back at their apartment, would she be waiting to tell David that everything had been a mistake? That it had taken the process of designing a house with him, of building it, to make her realise that she didn't love him any more?

*Do I love her?* The question hit his brain like a large bug splattering the windscreen. He felt the answer in his gut: of course he did. The fact that she had just betrayed him didn't only enrage David. It frightened him. It showed him that he could lose it all. That it – the vast array of great things that was 'it' – could depart forever. David was very aware that his next few decisions were the most important he would ever make.

Stepping out of the BMW, he slammed the door. Looking around, he expected a blind to twitch, a security beam to blast exposure, an alarm to bleat. But there was nothing – just a shuffle of leaves above as the warm night took a breath.

Sucking the cigarette to its final half-inch, he dropped it to the road. Something within David, something intrinsic, needed to deal with Ryan – even though it would be easier to follow Tara back to their apartment and shout at her in self-righteous fury. But when he thought about his wife, he didn't just feel anger – he also experienced the dread that she didn't love him as much as he loved her. After all, over the years he'd willingly scorned many opportunities with awestruck students, fellow lecturers and even the safely married dean of the faculty of arts and humanities. And yet Tara had responded to the very first opportunity that presented itself. *Was this her first opportunity? Was this the first time?*

David walked by Ryan's white SUV where a hi-vis jacket was bunched into a ball on the passenger seat. He closed the hoarding gate behind him and the arm snapped down into the slot.

For the first time, David had a clear view of his home's restored Georgian facade – for months, there had been large skips in the driveway. He stared up at the windows that had been imported from Germany. It was almost impossible to believe that just six months ago, the site had been a derelict ruin.

David walked up the driveway and the crunch of gravel beneath his shoes reminded him of the marble chips on graves. He passed discarded tubes of paste, empty concrete bags and surplus sheets of Kingspan insulation. Stone steps flanked by arched handrails fanned up to the entrance of the three-storey house. The porch door was open and a faint light came from inside.

David entered the broad white hallway which was perfect for his wife's home gallery. The air smelled of varnish, sawdust and glue. A winding staircase circled the main architectural flourish – a raw poured-concrete pillar that stretched up thirty feet through the centre of the building like the toughened bark of an old oak. From up on the first floor, light seemed to be leaking from a bedroom.

David climbed the stairs, his feet making no sound on the freshly laid carpet that was already scarred by builders' boots. *I told that asshole to make sure his guys put protective mats down.* Emerging onto the landing, the floor remained in almost complete darkness; the doors to the three bedrooms, the walk-in and the main bathroom were all closed. But there was still a dim glow from the very top of the house, tinting the freshly plastered ceiling a stale nicotine-like hue. *I told that asshole to make sure his guys had finished all the internal painting today.*

He continued on up the turn of the staircase to the attic conversion that was soon to be his home office. The garret door was ajar and inside, light glowed from a naked bulb. David caught the whiff of a cigarette. He listened to the *babumph* of his heart and pushed the door further open, expecting a shrill creak to proclaim his coming. But the door silently glided inwards, revealing a low, sharply angled ceiling marbled with smoke. A shadow sketched a human shape on the opposite wall. On the bare boards, a used condom glistened like something just killed and skinned. Next to it, a saturated tissue resembled a half-melted snowball. And then there was a small, tight puddle of cotton on the floor – Tara's black panties. David had watched her step into them that morning as he'd shaved.

Ryan stood between the opened floor-to-ceiling windows where the Juliet rail had yet to be installed, his back to David. Flicking his cigarette out into the night, he continued gazing at the dark shadows of mature oaks and elms. When the breeze blew, the heavy clusters of leaves shook, revealing the lights from neighbouring houses.

'What are you doing in my house?'

Ryan turned about. His mouth pursed, lips setting tight like a turtle's. Wearing only jeans, he was tanned and muscled with a tattoo down his right arm of a Celtic spear surrounded by meaningless hieroglyphs. Inked across the right side of his chest was the script, *'Why Hast Thou Forsaken Me?'*

'Dave? Wow. How did... When did…?' Ryan stepped towards him, his forearms firm and sinewy, the kind a man gets from life rather than the gym. 'I'm just making sure that my guys have everything wrapped up for your big move tomorrow. Only the patio to fill and bits of wiring – it's all on schedule.'

In the light of the naked bulb, he was almost too good-looking. His smooth skin, tanned from the outdoors, appeared to be made out of pale chocolate, while his Brando-brown eyes narrowed evocatively whenever he smiled. 'Man, it's hot tonight,' he continued. 'No let-up to this heatwave. Anyway, didn't want any last-minute hiccups. All part of the service. You're welcome.' After a moment, he tried again: 'Bet you can't wait till you're in tomorrow and my crew have all fucked off?' Then he laughed in a what-the-hell way.

When David still didn't speak, Ryan's smile faded. His expression became vague, waiting to choose the appropriate emotion to wear. With head lowered and fringe hanging down, he said, 'It's way after ten at night. Why are *you* here?'

'I know everything.' David had spoken before working things out. It was all going to accelerate now.

'Well that's... that's a real pain.' Ryan's eyes could have burned pinholes through paper. 'But since you know everything, then at least you're aware that it was just the once. Just tonight. Never to happen again.' He took another step forward, his focus swooping, swallow-like, back to his own immediate concerns. 'Look, Dave, there are many ways this can play out. But there's only one way that is the right way – get me? It is what it is.' Ryan exhibited his smug-little-genius expression; a look that David had secretly despised for the past six months. 'Dave: go home. Go home to your famous, wealthy, young, pretty wife. Wake up in the morning, move in here and pretend nothing happened. Because outside of – what? Thirty minutes? – nothing *did* happen. Some things can remain a mystery. You don't have to know everything. That's how people live happily ever after. That's the trick.' Ryan spread his arms, as if attempting to embrace all the white space of the attic. 'Dave, we have a good relationship. Look around you. This incredible Georgian building. This piece. This art. Look at what we built together.'

'Together? Ryan, you're a glorified brickie. If you'd never existed, this house would still have been built. You won the tender. Nothing else.'

'That's cold.' Ryan sucked in his cheeks, sculpting his jawline. 'But fine. Can I leave? Do you think that would be all right?'

'It's more than all right. It's required.'

Ryan moved to the left, stepping around David as if he were an inconvenient box. But then David slammed his hand into Ryan's chest. It succeeded in halting him, but David also felt how heavy Ryan was, as if his frame had been stuffed with rocks rather than blood and guts.

Ryan jerked his head up, sensing brutality. 'You threatening me? Because if you are, let me give you the warning most people don't get. Fucksticks like you – without fighting skills or weapons – they should keep their counsel or they get a severe fucking tune-up.' Ryan looked calm, but there was a wired alertness to his eyes. David imagined the tracking of Ryan's mood on an EKG ticker tape. It was starting to spike.

David ploughed into him, reversing Ryan until his back smacked against the wall. *What now?* He'd learned from an early age that words were not always enough. They can lose their power, and it is then that you need to throw a punch. But could he remember how to fight? The last time had been years ago. Back then he'd wanted to dominate, to triumph, to protect the girl who would become his wife. A cold jolt sparked down David's spine. He could lose. *Hit him.* He needed to dig deep – find that nasty streak. *Hit him hard.*

Ryan spread his shoulders, his long neck tensing as he decided upon the most suitable retaliation. David retreated a few feet so as to be out of headbutt range. Ryan's eyes narrowed as he prepared to strike, choosing the spot carefully, intending to do the appropriate amount of damage as quickly as possible. David knew it was coming. So he struck first: jabbing his right fist forward, aiming for Ryan's nose. Ryan managed to move his head to the side and David connected with his eye socket. Appreciating the warm sting across his knuckles, David felt impressed with himself. *I remember now. Violence is easy.* He jabbed again, connecting with the chin.

Ryan staggered backwards and reached out, his face communicating what an awful feeling it is to grab for something just to find that your hand is snatching, snatching at thin air. And then he vanished through the open French doors.

A dull thump sounded three floors below.

David stared at his future life collapsing in on itself like a dying star. Slowly he moved towards the opened doors where the Juliet rail was supposed to be. Looking down, he saw Ryan lying in the pit dug for the patio's foundation. Face up, his legs rested across an orange sewer pipe. One arm was half-raised, but gradually it dipped towards the clay as if surrendering to the inevitable.

'Ryan?' David said in a loud whisper. 'You OK?'

Nothing came back to him. Not a movement. Not a sound. David continued staring down on the body, affixed by the banality of tragedy. Illuminated by summer moonlight, Ryan's face was as purple as raw liver, his tongue protruding. A cerise pool flourished around him, seeping eagerly out of his cracked skull like it had been waiting decades to do so. The flowing red curtain trickled along the grooves in the dry clay, winding its way like some biblical crimson river, pouring into the deepest part of the pit, where the marshy soil beneath the sewer pipe slurped it up. David couldn't look away. The sight was irrevocable. It would not be undone. The dead simply do not return.

David ran his hands through his hair. So it wasn't going to happen: his happy-ever-after in the palace of his dreams. He wasn't even going to get a single night in the house he'd planned and built with his wife. What would become of Tara and his unborn child? David looked up to the perfect night sky, but he didn't see beautiful stars – just distant explosions of ultra-violence.

But it wasn't too late. Ryan might still be alive. There might still be time. *Act. Do something.* All he had to do was run down two flights of stairs, cross the vast kitchen, roll back the huge slider and then save Ryan. David spun round, registered a heavy thud against the side of his skull and dropped into the relief of a great deep nothingness.

He came from somewhere cavernous and black, but his eyes remained blast-furnace-forged closed. A painful pressure was growing on either side of his brain, as if he was growing horns. It didn't feel like a hangover. *I'm lying on the floor of my new office*. He opened his eyes. Sunlight barked in his face as it blazed through the unfastened French doors. It came streaming back, the memories and feelings, like flies buzzing inside his skull. The worst possible thing had happened, and yet the world had continued to spin on its axis. Already, a slither of sunlight had made it from the wall to the edge of the floor.

David rubbed his head. There was a small lump, slightly scabbed, in the corner of his brow. To the side of the French doors, the attic roofline lowered sharply. Had he hit his head off an internal structural beam in his panic to help Ryan? He hauled himself into a kneeling position, the bare boards denting his knees.

There was noise from below. Were the police here? An ambulance? Where was Tara? Would there be time to talk to her before he was arrested for murder? It wasn't as if he lacked an ironclad motive.

His dream of building his own house and living in it with Tara had been snatched away at the very last second. This would kill his seventy-six-year-old mother. His sister would be ashamed. No, it was over. The future cancelled. Soon, the world would be as if he had never been there. He looked at the fresh plasterwork around the French doors. If he was to stick his finger into it, it would leave a mark. He stuck his finger into it. It left a mark.

David inched his head through the French doors and out over the edge. Down below, he expected to see the police, medics, yellow tape. But there was no one there. David blinked. No corpse. There wasn't even a pit. Instead, there was freshly laid limestone across most of the patio area. Some tumbled travertine slabs had already been laid.

A wave of sheer bliss crashed over him. Ryan was alive. Of course he was. While David had lain unconscious, Ryan must have dusted himself down and gone home.

David inhaled deeply the morning's summer breeze that seemed to originate from the sun itself. This was the best time of day: newly minted, before the ongoing heatwave turned everything slovenly. But the reality of his wife's betrayal made the rustle of leaves less cheerful, the sunlight less promising.

David checked his watch – 8.55 a.m. The builders usually started at 7.30. They had been working away for almost ninety minutes, oblivious to his comatose body on the top floor. A burst of conversation sounded from down in the kitchen before the noise suddenly shut off.

Unsteady on his feet, David scooped up the used condom, the flimsy panties and the dried tissue. He found a glimmer of solace in the fact that, despite Tara's pregnancy, she'd still taken precaution against disease – which considering Ryan's reputation was a genuine, if remote, risk. Had Ryan been telling the truth when he'd said that it had only happened once? *He had no reason to lie.*

Outside on the staircase, David noticed a discolouration on the wall in front of him. It looked as if something damp had been rubbed across the fresh paint and hadn't yet dried. He touched the surface stain and smelled his fingers: a vague odour, similar to that carried on a sea breeze. Above it was a cobweb, like the sail of a yacht, already woven between the skylight and the corner of the ceiling. David pulled it down and rolled it into a sticky clump. *This is my house.*

In the first-floor bathroom, he pocketed the panties before flushing the condom and tissue down the toilet. Then, descending to the hallway, he came across the electrician who was finishing up the installation of lights that would illuminate Tara's artwork.

David cleared his throat. 'Hiya, Mike.'

The middle-aged electrician almost lost his footing on the stepladder. 'Jazus. If it isn't the Prof. Where'd you come from?'

Tara had told the crew that David was a college professor, rather than just an undergraduate lecturer. She'd thought it was funny.

'Slipped by you earlier.'

'You're a ninja. What happened to the noggin?'

David rubbed the corner of his forehead. 'Just a knock.'

'And probably the first time you're on site without a hard hat. Ryan with you?'

'No. Why?'

'Cos he was supposed to be here at 7.30. No sign. But his car's outside. Weird.'

'His car?'

'Yeah. Must be gone off with a contractor or something.' Mike turned back to the light fitting. Conversation over.

David stepped around the tins of Farrow & Ball and entered the kitchen – a space big enough to house a car showroom. Drifting by all the new stainless steel apparatus, the granite countertops and the elegant spring-mounted, single-lever tap curving out from the centre of the island, David stared through the huge slider window to the new patio. Where was Ryan? At the hospital? Maybe he'd got a taxi home and was lying low there, embarrassed at what had happened last night but relieved to be alive. Perhaps he was furious at what David had done and was planning revenge. *Well, bring it*, David thought. He pictured Ryan standing in *his* house, pretending to be his friend, congratulating him on his design. But suddenly a new and more appalling suggestion occurred – could Ryan be under the limestone?

Beyond the patio were the freshly landscaped grounds that only days ago he had considered grand and beautiful. But now David thought that the just-rolled lawn looked like a synthetic turf that could be vacuumed of dirt. Even the flowers looked plastic. It was as if the entire garden was an expensive, unnatural theme park. The grass stopped at a wooded area of pines, elms and oaks. A pathway separating the trees and lawn had been laid with leftover antique bricks. Ryan had done it for free; a gift. Tara had been delighted and had ignored David when he'd muttered,

'It's amazing what they'll throw in when you spend a mere one and a half million.'

There was a man crouched down at the far end of the kitchen. It was just Bruno, pasting silicon where the glass met the timber floor. He'd pulled his T-shirt over his head like a keffiyeh, protecting his pale Lithuanian face from the magnified sunlight blasting through the window. His pinky-white ass crack rose from the sheath of dirty blue jeans. Slowly, he shifted around on his haunches and nodded without smiling.

'Good morning to you, Dave,' Bruno said, greeting him with an apprehensive face, as if David had hurt him a few years ago and he had never forgotten it. 'What happened to your—'

'Hit it on a beam upstairs. It's fine. Outside – there was a pit there yesterday?'

'This morning I finish paving patio with travertine. Got some already done. When FlexBond hundred per cent dry, I finish off.'

'How did you fill it? With a shovel?'

Bruno laughed. 'I use the three-tonne micro-digger.'

'The what?'

'The three-tonne micro-digger.' Because Bruno's responses were delayed, talking to him was sometimes like making an internet call to a developing country. 'The small digger. We can still get it in the covered side passage. Does not look wide but it's good designed. No storage problems in this place. Lots of space for kit-and-caboodle. We even got the telehandler through yesterday.'

'Did you see anything in the pit?'

'Huh?'

'Did you *check the pit* before filling it?'

'Why would I do that?'

'What if there was an animal in there? A cat, or something?'

'The engine scares them off.'

'So you looked and didn't see anything?' David knew he was putting words into Bruno's mouth. Or at least trying to.

'Listen to me – I got on micro-digger and filled in last foundation for the patio. Then levelled over with eight inches of crushed limestone in layers for freeze-thaw cycle. Just one inch of sand and travertine pavers can be dry-laid. No curing. Very smart design. That's it. If there was a deaf sleeping cat there, then it's probably still down there now. They'll dig it up one day and think it's a... How you say? A dinosaur!' Bruno laughed, pleased with his joke – then stopped abruptly. 'You are not missing your cat?'

'What? No.'

Bruno shrugged. 'Have you been talking to Ryan?'

'Why?' David replied, a little too fast.

'Everyone looking for Ryan.'

David was staring through the sliding door to the limestone-topped foundation that remained untiled. *It's impossible. Ryan is fine. He couldn't be under there.*

'Hey, Prof!' It was the electrician, standing at the kitchen door. 'We're saved, ladies. All our problems are solved. The main man is here.'

*Oh thank you, Jesus.*

Mike stepped out of the way to allow a tall, broad man with dark sandy hair to enter the kitchen. It was Gordon, the project's architect. He always dressed in a suit, even when clambering across roof tiles to examine chimney cracks.

Visibly crestfallen, David said, 'Oh, it's you. I thought it was…' His voice trailed off, as if by uttering Ryan's name it would somehow communicate to all present that he had done something terrible.

Pressing 'call' on his phone, Gordon placed it to his face and waited. Then in an educated Southside accent, said, 'Yeah, it's me. Ryan's not here. He's not at his office and he's not at home… No, *it is* important. My fucking builder is missing on the last day. Yes, *Ryan*.' Then, staring at David and nodding to the voice in his ear, he said, 'I'll talk to him.'

David quickly tried to think of all the mistakes he might be making.

Gordon closed the phone, stared at Bruno and, after finding his face in his mental card index, nodded. Then he scanned the kitchen like he owned it and said, 'Morning, Dave,' with the alertness and resolve of a forty-five-year-old who enjoyed a 6 a.m. run to kick-start every day. But despite the *swish* of his presence, he also held the bearing of a person who desperately fought to keep his weight under control. His face was unlined and his skin soft, but his jowls were beginning to sag, while at the back of his neck, flesh had started to gather in small rolls.

David told himself to be normal and say something casual, but still said nothing.

'Dave, I'm surprised you're here already. And of course, for this time of the morning, you're looking great,' Gordon said, in a tone that conveyed that David was actually looking awful. 'I love the I-don't-wash look. Very hot. The homeless are so sexy. You know, where I live they've got this incredible new technology called soap. What happened to your head? Looks sore.'

Achieving something close to sober decorum, David tried to smile but only succeeded in baring his teeth. 'Just a knock. Don't worry about it.'

'You're bleeding,' Gordon added, as if it was the worst crime in the world. He turned on his phone's camera and reversed the lens so that the screen acted as a mirror. In his other hand was an electric razor and it began to buzz its incessant one-note hymn. David wondered why Gordon couldn't have shaved at home or even in his car. Plus, he was now getting tiny hairs on the floor. However, the man did like to make a production of everything.

David couldn't put his finger on why he liked Gordon. His architect was of the privileged class he'd always despised. Gordon came from old money and a well-below-average share of worries. He'd been birthed into the security-gated quarantine of a beautiful

Dalkey home with rock stars and movie directors for neighbours. The last time David had been out for lunch with Gordon, the architect had ordered a bottle of Dasani. Not 'water', but Dasani. Meanwhile, everything David had achieved was the result of a struggle – a struggle to educate himself with scholarships while working in a warehouse; a struggle to lose his accent; to become a lecturer; to work on his PhD; to get the girl. He had never had a 'home' in the maze of the Cawley Estates when growing up – David, his parents and his sister had simply spent a few years in one council house before being moved down the road to another. He could never forget the creaks, hiss and moans of those small, jammed buildings that had caged him in. And while he didn't like people to know where he'd come from, he privately, secretly, despised the quasi-aristocratic upper-class.

Gordon placed his Prada-encased foot next to David's on the low windowsill.

'What's wrong, Dave?'

'Nothing,' David said, feeling like a student in an exam trying to hide his cheat notes.

'You're distracted. And you're not happy. It's my job to make you happy.'

'I'm just... I'm just thinking.'

Despite the fact that Gordon was David's employee, Gordon had a natural ability to intimidate him. Most of the people David had gone to school with were now addicts, incarcerated, dead or had emigrated. Most people from Gordon's school were now politicians, lawyers and even judges. At David's school, all he had learned was *fuck school.*

'Jesus, I love my job, and building your house in particular was fun. And challenging,' Gordon said, with the confidence of a man who believed in two things: that if he wasn't an architect then he would be just like everyone else, and that everyone else was an idiot. 'Smile, my friend. It's over today. You did it. *We* did it. The project is wrapping up right on time. Your furniture is on the way. Dave, this house will keep you clean, keep your body at an optimal temperature and it will protect you from the evils of the outside world.'

David forced a smile, trying to look grateful. But while Gordon had been speaking, he had suddenly realised that Tara must be worried about him, since he hadn't come home last night. *What will I say to her? Actually, why am I even thinking about this? After what she did? Has she done this before? Done it with someone else? Is the baby mine? No, wait. This is Tara. Of course there was no one else. The baby's mine. And what happened... Is it because she's depressed and doesn't know it? Something to do with being pregnant?*

David looked at his phone, expecting to see a litany of missed calls and texts to ignore. But there were no messages. *Jesus. But wait – keep your focus on Ryan.* Quickly, he checked his emails, having suddenly convinced himself that there would be something from his builder. There was nothing.

Gordon straightened his perfectly straight tie, leaned over the black granite island top and blew across its surface. A cloud of dust rose. Orchestrating a big whoosh of a sneeze, he *ah-chooed* into his hands. 'The house was meant to be professionally cleaned yesterday. Where is Ryan? And why is his car outside? Ryan doesn't go off-grid. Ever. Jesus, if I was to take him out for a two-hour lunch, he'd consider it an unauthorised vacation.' Gordon's phone rang, and he turned his back on the room to take it.

David's stomach felt as if it was working its way up through his oesophagus. He placed a firm, supportive hand against the wall. *If* Ryan was dead, what would happen to Tara? Her career would be over. Her work would never again be referenced without mention of the great scandal of her murderous husband and her dead lover. It would be the intelligentsia's equivalent to a slow gassing. David had a vision of Tara alone in their new house, living in the shell of her lost dreams. But she would hardly raise their child alone in the hugeness of a home in which her husband had killed her lover, would she? And regardless of what she decided to do, David didn't want her to waste her life waiting for his return from prison in ten or twenty years.

When Ryan was screwing her, had Tara seen herself as being injected with an elixir of life? David pictured her again at his birthday party, staring at the floor, not singing, not smiling. *Had she suddenly glimpsed the future? Was that the moment when she realised that me being ten years older than her was something she could no longer ignore – especially with a baby on the way? When the kid's twenty, I'll be sixty – closer to the age of grandparent than parent.*

And then there was his unborn child. *You never wanted a kid. You never planned for one. She just presented you with it.* David despised that voice in his head. It had a sly tone; one that tried to justify his self-doubt with the shrugged, 'I didn't ask for this.' Each time that voice sounded, it felt like he was betraying his own flesh and blood, abandoning those who needed him most, like a coward creeping off the battlefield.

'There's a problem.' Gordon's lips were inches from David's ear. He added in a whisper, 'Something unprecedented has happened. Regarding Ryan.' The architect glanced at Bruno, who was in the corner of the kitchen, squeezing his left foot into the cold tube of his wellingtons.

David touched the cut on his forehead. 'You found him?'

'Gotta finish this call. Do me a favour and wait for me on the patio. We need to talk. In private.'

David opened the kitchen door and stood at the edge of the exposed foundation, where only hours ago the pit had been. The time to come clean was now. Admit to Gordon what he'd done. Tell him there was a possibility that Ryan was buried there. It had been an accident, and David had tried to help him but had somehow knocked himself out. The police would be able to examine his head, see the wound, understand that he was telling the truth. Or, more likely, the police would believe he was guilty and if they couldn't pin the murder on him, they'd get him for manslaughter and throw the book at him.

Obeying his old Pavlovian response to stepping outdoors, David took out the packet of cigarettes he'd bought last night and lit up. He focused on shutting down the voice in his head that was screaming treacherous advice about telling people the truth. If Ryan was dead, under the patio, then no one knew. David could feasibly wait until all the furore around Ryan's whereabouts went away. It had been an accident, after all. Nothing he now did or didn't do would bring Ryan back. However, David's wife and child would need him around in the future. Tara's career was in free fall and David had already become the main breadwinner. It wasn't fair that his unborn child's reputation and prospects could forever be tarnished by a split-second mistake committed by its father. The time had come to make a choice, and choice in this situation was very dangerous. Because once a choice was made, he would have to forego all other possibilities.

From behind him, Gordon said, 'Is that a cigarette?'

Exhaling a tube of smoke, David answered with, 'You found him?'

Gordon continued towards a cast iron table and two chairs on the lawn next to the hedge. The bees bobbed and weaved on the breeze before dipping to the rows of lavender and red trumpets of oriental lilies. David tried to soak up the garden, wanting it to calm him, wanting its depths of colour and space to subdue his pulsing angst. But it didn't happen.

As Gordon sat, he asked, 'So you started smoking again? As of today?'

'I'm full of surprises.' David took the opposite chair.

'Either that, or we don't know each other very well.'

'Don't tell Tara.' *Why did I say that?* In David's list of priorities, avoiding Tara's anger was a distant second to Ryan's disappearance.

'It's been a difficult few months with the build. Now that it's over I've decided to treat myself.' Casually, he drifted away from the edge of the table until he leaned into the backrest of the chair. Trying to ignore his quickening pulse and the tautness in his chest, he forced himself to ask, 'So... Have you found Ryan?' He pictured his builder's concussed manifestation; Ryan telling everyone that David had thrown him out of the attic window. The only favourable outcome would be Ryan emerging from the streets and not remembering anything. But David had learned that life generally didn't do people favours.

Gordon placed his hands flat on the table, as if demonstrating that he came in peace – no weapons. 'All I know is that wherever Ryan is right now, he doesn't want to be there.'

There was a tremor in David's fingers. He remembered his first day of teaching, his notes rattling in his hands like he was a soldier on the brink of the terrible battle he'd been lecturing on.

Speaking almost compassionately, Gordon said, '*You* don't like Ryan. You never liked him.'

David raised his eyes, trying to convey surprise and bewilderment, as if he couldn't quite believe that Gordon had questions about his open, innocent, no-secrets-here life. 'What? *Me*? Are you crazy? Ryan is a great builder... I trust him.'

'I don't believe you.'

'Excuse me?' Everything was already wrong about this conversation.

'I *said*, I don't believe you.'

'And I don't care what you believe.' David clenched a fist and placed it on the table between them. It was time for his architect to be put in his place.

'I just never sensed a bond between you two. I saw you watching Ryan and Tara. They were once an item, weren't they? Long before you came on the scene.'

David reddened. He frowned to make it look like anger and extended a pointed finger inches from Gordon's nose. 'Everyone knows that. Jesus, Ryan and me even laughed about it. I couldn't give a damn about who my wife saw before she met me. He's a good builder. That's why I gave him the job. I was building a house – not looking for friends. And I find your tone and questions insulting. What's the matter with you?'

'That's all bullshit, Dave.'

'Have you lost your mind? I like you, Gordon. You're interesting to be around. But don't think you can talk to me like that.' *What does he know?* There must be a point to his architect's behaviour. It just hadn't become clear yet.

'We're not talking about Ryan the builder. We're talking about Ryan the man who did it all with Tara before you even met her. You hate him. Admit it.'

David didn't blink. 'No, I do not, Gordon. And you're about to be fired.'

'Here's a great idea. Maybe you should tell the truth for a change? Seriously. Try it out. You might like it.'

Gordon's conduct was burning a hole in David's stomach. He needed to know what his architect knew. *Give him something; get something back*. 'Fine, there's nothing wrong with Ryan that a personality implant and ego reduction wouldn't fix. But I don't hate him. I've known worse parasites. I just dislike him. Happy?'

'Finally.' Slowly, Gordon clapped three times.

David fell back into his seat. A tumour of exhaustion grew heavier with each passing minute and pulsed warmly behind his eyes, even though it was only 9.30 a.m. and a long day stretched ahead with its challenges and traps. Knowing that life was only going to get harder – his life *and* the lives of his wife and child – was already becoming a heavy, constant fatigue. In a low voice, he said, 'There better be a good reason for this. Because if not, then you and me – we are done.'

'Done? Is that what you think? Really? Dear oh dear – we're not done. We're just starting, Dave. Speaking the truth is only the first step to getting to the truth. See, I admire you and Tara. Healthy, successful, young-*ish*. Maybe you and Tara will beat the odds. Maybe you'll disprove the old adage that marriage is a long dull meal with the pudding served first. I can see you both getting older and handsomer. But without her, you'd be nothing much – just another mid-lifer who moisturises.'

David spotted a blue line of biro on the white cuff of Gordon's shirt beneath his Gucci suit. That sartorial slur, so unusual for Gordon, warmed him. Maybe the biro mark was just the first surface indication of a deeper fracture? *Imagine Gordon doesn't know anything. Imagine he's just having a breakdown.*

Gordon said, 'For six months, I've witnessed the work crew mooning like schoolboys every time Tara came around. As for you – they just saw you as another prick with more money than them, thus proving their working-class belief that any woman will give in to you when you spend cash on her. Of course, they weren't to know that it was Tara's money. The tits-and-footie tabloids don't review art launches at the RHA.'

David calmly inhaled, telling himself to be patient, to take what his architect was giving, because soon he'd find out just what Gordon had.

'So Dave, what's between you two? Ten long years? I'm sure that for your age you can still effortlessly conjure up world-class boners. But ever wonder what it's going to be like when you're sixty and there's a lot more salt than pepper in your hair, and she's still a hot MILF who wants to see the world and have some fun?'

*Yes*. 'No. Now why are you still here?' David stood and pushed back his chair.

'Taking all that into account, I have to admit that I wasn't *that* surprised that Tara fucked Ryan last night.'

David slowly sat back down. Every new revelation was adding a fresh layer of dust to the heavy crust already settling over his very essence.

'Oh, yeah,' Gordon drawled. 'That spooked the horses.' He stretched out his arms and yawned, his big mouth forming a circle. He was lazy and assured: as if he had the perfect plan and knew that he was smarter than everyone else. 'Look, Dave, don't blame her. Ryan has an effect on women. He knows how to talk to them. He grew up in a house full of girls – five sisters. He's lucky with women – the way any good-looking, funny guy is.'

David spoke slowly and clearly: 'You have no idea what happened between them. And you understand nothing about Tara and me as a couple.'

'Some would call you naive. But I think it's rather cute – even touching – to have made it this far without realising that you can't trust women. But hats off to Tara – she's not really like other thirty-something housewives who still present well. With most of them, there's a sense of pointlessness about the performance. But Tara's the type that has never gone unnoticed in public and is well capable of dealing with leering men, jealous women and misogynists. It's just a pity that she didn't have an old-fashioned view of how to run her marriage. You know, the way it should be: the man has his interests and the woman tries to be interested in those interests.'

'Gordon, I genuinely thought we were friends. I respected you. Admired you, even. But you actually hate Tara and me.'

Gordon smiled, made the shape of a gun with finger and thumb, aimed and pulled the trigger. 'Oh, you have no fucking idea just how much.'

'Fine. I get it. But so what? I'm supposed to care because…?'

Gordon stood and fastened his jacket. He then walked across the patio to the kitchen door. David wiped his hand across his sticky forehead. *Go. Leave.* But instead, Gordon turned about and smiled, communicating that he knew exactly what David was thinking. 'Dave, it's pointless.'

David didn't know what to say, so he said nothing. It was as if he could feel every single hair piercing into his scalp. *This can only get worse.*

'I know what you did to Ryan.'

*Bingo.*

'You killed him.'

Instinctively David rose from his seat, the movement repositioning his clothes against his skin, making him aware of the dampness under his arms. He lit a cigarette and followed Gordon to the patio, his hands clenched together, letting the oozing sweat mix in a vile sliding flesh-on-flesh sensation.

'Dave,' Gordon said. 'We'll finish this in an hour at the university. But for now you'd better stub out that smoke. *She's* here.'

David followed Gordon's gaze into the kitchen and down the tunnel of light between the French library doors, to where the front bay window looked out onto the driveway. There was Tara, in grey jeans and a white All Saints shirt, the top button undone, revealing her slender neck, bare and ready as Marie Antoinette's.

# CHAPTER TWO

'We're home, Dora,' said Tara, standing in the driveway's landscaped gravel circle, holding the handle of her tabby's cage. With the hoarding dismantled, the driveway was like a dense forest suddenly denuded of foliage. It led to the stone steps sweeping up to the front door of the three-storey Georgian. Observing their home being built over the last six months had been like watching the slow passage of an antelope through the lengthy gut of a boa constrictor. But it was truly theirs now. They had designed it, shaped it, rebuilt it. It was their personalised machine to live in. Surveying the face of the house with its cornice moulds as white as icing, she imagined that it had magically formed itself, flying together into its own wonderful blueprint, fitting itself into its own construction of lines and angles. For Tara, this was a house about to be filled with hope and adventure.

Lawrence Court was in the lethargic grip of August, the road spotted with shade, front lawns needing timed sprinklers, the sun sending shimmering waves of heat off the roofs of parked cars. Tara looked at the small yachts parked in some of the driveways. Her new neighbours had the money to be lazy. She wondered what all these people could have accomplished in their relatively short lives to become this wealthy. Someone a few doors up was practising Satie's 'Gymnopédie No. 1' behind an opened window, making the odd mistake but offering a peaceful, if melancholy sound. Across the road, a ponytailed neighbour dressed for Pilates buckled her two toddlers into the back of a jungle-conquering

SUV. Tara imagined the distractions that filled the days of all these urban gentry housewives – t'ai chi classes, am-dram, book clubs, volunteer work – all before the kids came home.

*One day, David and I will be dead and then strangers will take over our castle.* A second thought occurred: *But there'll be a lineage. Maybe our grandchildren will live here.*

Tara's pregnancy still had the ability to surprise her, like walking into glass. She glanced down, as if expecting to see her stomach round and taut like a space hopper. But of course the child hadn't even begun to suggest itself. She rubbed her flat belly. It was only the start of her third month, and so far the only symptom of her condition was that her breasts were beginning to feel tender. Sometimes Tara couldn't wait until it began to show. Other times, she dreaded it. Until just eight weeks ago she'd never wanted to feel that growth, that frantic multiplication of cells, the sense of something inside feeding on her. She didn't want to wreck her body. She liked sleep. Her cat, Dora, had been more than enough. But then her clockwork period had skipped and the pregnancy test had been taken. Tara remembered its twin lines winking like candy stripes; the designers' assumption that they would be sweet and gentle harbingers of happiness. She'd wrapped it in tissue and, shell-shocked, dropped it into the bin. When she told David, she'd found herself surprised that he wasn't depressed about it, or at least conflicted. Instead he had acted as if it was something that would be interesting, like a really cool project. A few days later, David had said, 'If Dora's OK with it, then I'm up for it too. It's no big deal. Sure, if it doesn't suit then we'll just take it back.'

Tara hesitated at the front door. The feeling that she was about to check into a fantastic hotel evaporated. Awaiting her was the initial fucked-up moment of standing in the same room as Ryan and her husband. She remembered that when she was leaving Ryan last night, he'd given her a peck on the cheek. It was a strange thing; the way people simply came in and out of your life. Because of his flippancy, Tara hoped that Ryan was the type of guy who could sail through this. *This. What is 'this'?* Thankfully, she hadn't seen David when she'd gone home. As usual for a Sunday night, she'd fallen asleep before he'd returned from the pub after training; and he'd already gone to the university when she'd woken that morning.

She deposited Dora's cage in the side passageway and then entered the house, her bag hanging off her shoulder. There, in the hallway, one of her life's ambitions would finally be sated – a home gallery of her own work. Later today she would hang her favourites: leftovers from the series that had made her – and paid for the house – *Erdős Landscapes*. Tara had always believed that a person could not be surrounded by music and poems in the same way that they could be surrounded by their pictures. It would be nice to enjoy her work without being sandwiched between socialites and dealers who would forgive her anything except for the crime of boring them.

Mike was standing on a stepladder, screwing in a wall light.

'Hey sparky, where's Ryan?'

'You're the third person to ask me that in twenty minutes. No one knows, and his phone's off.'

Tara tried to figure out what that meant. Internally, she took a step back. Of course everything was fine. Ryan was simply off on another job, at the suppliers, with another woman, out with friends, just running late. Looking through the kitchen door, she saw David outside on the patio, hands in pockets, staring at his feet. God, he was so handsome, and soon he'd be the most handsome dad on Lawrence Court. *How could I have done that to him?*

David was everything she'd ever wanted. He ticked every box for a great life partner, best friend and perfect father. She felt her brain grow when talking to him. She felt herself wanting to live her life so much more fully. She didn't even want to share him with others. At his fortieth birthday she hadn't been able to sing or clap. She'd just stood in the background, observing the contentedness he had with all those people – the weight it lifted clear and clean off his heart. She'd been jealous of them. She'd wanted him back all to herself. She wanted to be his only real friend. She wanted to be the centre of his attention. She wanted to receive the highest voltage of his energy. All those guests in their apartment – they'd been just stealing her life from her.

And yet, categorically, she'd had to fuck Ryan. There had been no choice about it. *I don't want to grow old. I don't want to grow old just like that.* Did she regret it? She listened to her thoughts: a great silence. While she'd had a final adventure, David was unhurt. He was unchanged. For them both, the world had continued to spin as always.

*Why is David staring at the patio?* Did he regret the tumbled travertine? Did he not think it was worth the extra money? *Sandstone is so vanilla.*

Suddenly Bruno rounded the corner and almost knocked into her. Tara suppressed a sigh and adjusted the strap of her shoulder bag. She had nothing against Bruno, but being stuck talking to him was like being stranded in the boredom of a non-moving queue. Bruno had met her husband back when David had worked nights driving forklifts and unloading forty-foot containers of Korean computer hardware so that he could feed his mother and sister while also studying at university during the day. But while David had moved on to lecture for his PhD, to drive a BMW, to marry a famous artist who commanded five figures per painting, Bruno had been let go and drifted into his brother's plastering and landscaping firm. Since their warehouse days, David and Bruno jointly managed an under-12s' football team in the tough working-class area of Cawley. Tara knew that David's involvement, and more importantly, the sponsorship he'd arranged for the team, was an attempt to assuage his guilt at having escaped the Cawley

Estates with a scholarship and a determination to take everything he'd ever wanted from life.

'You ready for the big move, Tara?' Bruno asked with a forced smile. 'You must have been very busy. That was why Dave left training early last night without saying?'

It was irritating, the way Bruno would always address questions to her that he should be putting to David. But then the relevance of what he'd asked suddenly hit her. 'Hold on – you're saying that David left training the boys early last night? You sure?'

'Not at drinks in pub after either.'

*That's weird. He must've been visiting his mother – making sure her new full-time carers he got are doing their job. He was probably also getting stuff done for today. To make it easy for us.* Tara reddened, thinking of how she'd spent last night. 'He's outside. Why didn't you ask him?'

'Dave not in good mood. Stressed. I could see it. So I ask you.'

Moving the subject along, she said, 'The removal truck's coming at three – so I hope everything will be done by then.'

'We'll be gone by midday.'

Tara knew that it must be galling for Bruno to have to help build the temple to David's success. His predicament often touched Tara, like he was unexpectedly revealed as an abandoned animal. But there was nothing she could do for him. David had done what he'd had to do to flourish. And yet she also knew that David had never contemplated leaving Bruno behind; after all, he had got him his current gig, a fact the Lithuanian had never acknowledged. Though over the course of the build, David had often wondered aloud if it had been wise to bring Bruno into his house – to mix the oil of his past with the water of the present.

Tara's mobile began to ring. She entered the empty white sprawl of the front room, took it out of her bag and answered it.

'I want to speak to Tara Brown.'

She'd never liked the sound of her full name: Tara Brown – that catch-all, everywoman name. She'd thought about taking David's, but that had just seemed so old-fashioned. She was who she was.

'Uh-huh. Speaking.'

'This is Christine Mulholland.'

*Jesus.* Tara's grip on the phone weakened. The silence built and accumulated, caught in the tight coils of cord.

'Hallo?'

'Yes. I'm Tara Brown.' *You should've said 'wrong number'. You should've hung up.*

'So you know who I am?' Her accent was plummy and severe; the voice of a woman who was used to not being disappointed.

'Yes. You're Ryan's wife.'

'Correct.'

*Correct?* 'I... I don't think he's here.'

'Yes. He's missing. Apparently.'

'Oh. I'm sure he'll...' *What's the term? Turn up? Don't say that.* 'Turn up?'

'Well, yes, of course. But his car is parked outside your house. So they've told me.'

'Yes.'

'So I thought that would be the place he'd... "turn up".'

'I suppose. Yes.'

'And I would like to talk to you.'

*No kidding.* 'Talk to me? Sure.' *About what? Ask her. No. Don't.*

'I know you're busy today, so I'll be around tomorrow morning. I assume Ryan will have graced us with his presence by then, but if not, I'll collect the car. Thank you, Tara.'

'Yeah. OK. Look forward to it.' *Jesus Christ!* Tara hung up. She could barely breathe. *She wants to talk to me? Why? Where the fuck is Ryan?* She needed him here, on site, now. *But how could Christine suspect anything?* She couldn't. Tara remembered Ryan saying that his wife liked to view the houses he'd worked on – at least, the more interesting ones. That must be it. She nodded in agreement with her thoughts, even though a part of her didn't believe them.

Tara scanned the blank front room and wished there was something to make her forget about Christine and Ryan and the toxic waste that threatened to spill all over her new carpets and freshly painted walls. There was a foreign weight in her shoulder bag that she wanted to relieve herself of. She took out the old clock that had belonged to her father and placed it above the fireplace. It was stuck at 10.45, its second hand trying to rise every so often before pathetically falling back to its original position. It reminded her of her home in the country – the place that, even when she was just twelve years old, she couldn't wait to leave; the place that had made her swear never to put down roots anywhere, because settling would expose her to the possibility of becoming her parents. But then, out of the blue, she'd fallen in love with David and had immediately craved a home: a palace that would contain no dark drama, a fortress she would share with a man who appreciated that a life lived privately didn't have to be secretive. This time, her home would be perfect. And now that they were having a baby, that child would grow up and one day leave with the intention of replicating its happy home rather than running from it.

She repositioned the clock face down. Tara imagined showing her dad around the house, and part of her wished that she could insert her mother into that fantasy. But her mother had died of breast cancer when Tara had been four. It had been a torturous death that tainted every memory of Tara's early years. Then one day, she and her father had stopped visiting the grave. Her mother was simply not there any more. It was just soil. And all that had remained were family photographs with her mother at the centre in a black devoré shawl, and reminiscences of the funeral, where Tara had felt like some kind of child star.

Tara imagined her father pulling up in his old Ford. He would have been shocked at the amount of space that two people required for themselves. He'd joke that he'd stayed in smaller hotels. He would have no idea what underfloor heating was. He'd think the architectural flourishes, such as the phallic concrete column, were a waste of money. But he wouldn't be unkind. He'd just raise his eyes at the stupidity of youth, as he'd still consider Tara as little more than a child. And underneath it all, he'd be proud of her. His daughter would have been the only person he'd ever known who had designed their own home.

Her father had been a forester, and dead fifteen years; a hunting accident, only a mile from her family home. Tara still wondered why she hadn't heard the shot. She must have. She'd been sitting on the stone wall when it happened, dreaming about finishing school in two years and moving to Dublin. Everywhere she went afterwards they'd talked about her father's terrible accident: at the church, at the shops, in the local paper. She couldn't even escape it in her aunt's house, where she'd then had to live for twenty-four months. Within two weeks of burying her father, her best friend, the daughter of a local journalist, had told her that her dad had been found with his right boot and sock removed, his big toe on the trigger, the barrel in his mouth.

'Tara!' Gordon announced from the hall. 'I felt a disturbance in the force, so I knew it was you. Come on – tell me: what is *not* to your satisfaction? I aim to please.'

'And I aim to be pleased,' she said affably, snapping out of her memories and glad to have something to keep her mind off Christine. She went out to greet him. 'That's why we get on so well.'

Gordon air-kissed each cheek; Tara tried not to hold back, but she just wasn't a hugger.

'Tara, this is the dream home for David and you. The two of you already have a great life. This is going to make it go supernova. Tonight you'll be sleeping upstairs in your amazing master bedroom. In the morning, you'll be having breakfast here in this bespoke kitchen that *House Magazine* wants to do a spread on. Your landscaped garden is blooming. You have it all. You've got everything you ever wanted. So tell me, why is God so damned pleased with you both?'

Tara blushed and lowered her head. She was never any good at taking a compliment. At her exhibitions she could only handle about five seconds of congratulations before passing the latest admirer on down the line like a sandbag.

Gordon continued, 'So once Mike has finished wiring up the hall, the gallery will be yours. I know I fought you on it. But it works. Now that I see it in action, I appreciate your vision. Very few of my clients have vision.'

'So much praise!'

'Suppose it's all down to your artistic eye. Pity you wasted it on actual art when you could've done something useful with it, like designing buildings. When did you realise you were an artist?'

Tara, who didn't consider herself a proper artist, shrugged. 'You don't realise it – other people tell you.'

'Jesus, can't you people just answer a straightforward question?'

'What? Did I just break your brain?'

'When I passed my exams – *that's* when I realised I was an architect.'

'It's hard to dislike you, Gordon. It shouldn't be. But it is.' It had, in fact, taken her a few months to warm to Gordon. She'd always been wary of charming people. Why did they need people to like them? Why did they want to seduce? What was hiding behind the charm? But Gordon had quickly figured out how to make Tara laugh, and she appreciated his eye for detail; the way he managed to blend artistic pretension with bullish leadership that kept the builders and budget under his thumb. The inescapable fact was that Gordon's innate self-confidence was combined with a soaring IQ, and that inspired confidence and trust. As an architect, he had the perfect balance between practicality and creative adventure. When David had wanted a beautiful library lined floor-to-ceiling with books, Gordon had designed one that was not just decorative, but that was also excellent noise insulation should the entertainment centre be on full blast. However, throughout the build, Gordon had often demonstrated a crude delight when stomping through their home, like a connoisseur allowed to ramble about a museum after closing time. Sometimes Tara had resented that, because it seemed he was taking all the credit – as if it had all originated from his genius rather than from David and Tara's initial sketches.

Gordon spotted Bruno hovering in the kitchen and asked, 'What's the story?'

Surprised, Bruno reddened like a spotty teenager who had been addressed by a beautiful girl. During the build, Tara had noticed that a hush came over whatever room Gordon graced. It wasn't that the builders would stop drilling, banging, pounding. They were just less casual about it. Gordon was feared and disliked by all on site – Gordon held the money.

Almost inaudibly, Bruno muttered, 'There is none.'

'Nice job on the patio slabs this morning. I was genuinely worried about how the travertine would turn out. But it's excellent. Looking at it actually puts a pep in my step. Seriously.'

'Thank you, Gordon. But there will be change order coming down for that. Just want you to know because Ryan not here to tell you. So no surprise.'

Gordon had already tired of listening to him before he'd even opened his mouth. 'Jesus, I'm *complimenting* you. What is the matter with... Look, I don't have time for this. I've a crucial meeting at ten thirty. Code red important. So just... Ah, forget it.'

Gordon had already moved on as Bruno miserably tried to figure out how he'd so quickly turned his moment of triumph into a dismal reprimand. Finally he just sighed, a man used to disappointment.

Tara glanced outside to the garden. Where had her husband gone? 'I noticed something yesterday. There's a stain on the wall outside David's office.'

'Uh-huh.'

'Just saying.'

'Nobody who says, "I'm just saying", is ever *just saying*.'

'Your job is to make me happy – I'm not happy. Make it go away. So where's my fella? Outside?'

'Dave's just gone.'

'What?'

'Yeah. He went out the side passageway before I noticed you. He wants to get something done at the university so he can leave early and get back here.'

A cool breeze flowed down the staircase from an open window. For a moment Tara's husband's absence tugged at something deep in her. His touch was always warm – a fact of animalistic consequence for someone who was usually cold.

In the kitchen there were four glass flutes laid out on the island counter. Pulling open the huge fridge door, Gordon removed a chilled bottle of Bollinger Rosé. 'It's a little early, but if you're going to have a champagne breakfast, today's the day.'

'Oh Gordon, that's so sweet.'

'You know, I was just telling Dave, I'm going to miss it here. The development I'm starting is about to be a disaster. I'm project-managing the renovation of an entire row of council houses in the Cawley Estates near where Dave grew up. Depressing stuff altogether. How can we make people live like that? You can hear everything. No space to work, to read, to think. No wonder Dave's dream was to design his own house.'

'Wow – is Gordon having a crisis of ethics?'

'No. Gordon is having a crisis of budget management. The city thinks they can do a million-euro upgrade for eight hundred thousand, and the builders think they can do a million-euro upgrade for one point two million. Fun times. Anyway, I'd assumed Dave would be here to share the fizzy money-water. And Ryan. You heard he's MIA?'

Tara swallowed and looked away. 'Yeah. I heard. Wonder where he is?'

'There's only 86,400 seconds in a day. My margins are tight. Why couldn't it be someone else? For example, him.' Gordon nodded to Bruno outside on the patio. 'Nobody misses a Polack.'

'He's not Polish, and his name is—'

'Don't tell me. He doesn't deserve the space in my brain.'

'Careful, Gordon, people might get the impression you're some type of xenophobic asshole.'

'Hey, I'm not xenophobic. I just stereotype. It's faster.'

'Don't be a shit. Bruno is lovely. He's just the quiet type.'

'The *what*? Like, he thinks speech is a flashy affectation?' Then Gordon called out, 'Men, down tools. Daddy has a treat.'

Gordon popped the cork and champagne blasted everywhere over the sink. As he poured, he said, 'I actually hate the stuff. Usually I just pretend to sip it because appearances matter. Plus, and I may have said this already, but I have a *very* important meeting at ten thirty.' However, he raised a flute to his lips and drained it in one mouthful. 'What the hell – today is a great day. Today is when it all finally comes together.'

The rest of the morning and the afternoon were a blur for Tara, punctuated briefly here and there by lucid moments of sheer anxiety regarding Ryan's wife. After Gordon left to make his 10.30 a.m. meeting, Tara walked through the house with Bruno, taking a snag list. Then, at midday, after she'd said goodbye to the few remaining crew, the removal truck arrived. She'd intended to slip off for her first spin session of the week, but as the day stretched on, she became engrossed as, piece by piece, her past began to take root in her new home. How she loved her house! She'd never get tired of it. Gordon had even made their walls work for them – there was a library on them, French doors plugged into them, neat hollowed cavities bored into them to mount sculptures and artefacts yet to be bought. And, of course, she treasured her walk-in closet, which was the size of a one-bed apartment.

Maximum Building Services had hired a cleaner to help her for two hours. The young woman proceeded to pull everything out of cupboards that Tara had filled, before replacing their contents more neatly. A van from the Trop Shop arrived and two guys spent hours setting up David's aquarium. By six thirty, everyone had gone and the front room had become an exquisitely crafted jewellery box, plush with red and black velvet and David's precious fish.

The corner of the room had the new 40-inch TV sitting on top of the control centre that was loaded with raging Wi-Fi and a premium cable package. Tara scanned the bookshelf, which held David's current reading pile – all military history – and his ornate chess set, the blue and red pieces representing the armies of Napoleon and Wellington. Then there was his drinks cabinet; Tara had never seen such a well-stocked private bar. There were at least ten different brands of Scotch, plus certain liqueurs that she'd never even heard of, never mind tasted. Waiting next to it was David's beautiful leather Eames chair and the Noguchi coffee table – he'd always had such good taste for a man.

The front room and the adjoining library had some of their old furniture, too, and yet everything seemed unfamiliar and exciting. Of course, Tara was aware of what was kicked beneath the sofas and flung into cupboards, but she liked that too, the fact that she knew what was behind it all – such as old love letters from former boyfriends, including Ryan.

Tara was impatient for David to get home so she could show him the result of her labours. He was due soon, but it was strange that he hadn't called during the afternoon. She'd tried him several times but it had rung out. *He's just busy – he has his students to teach, his PhD to write, my paintings to sell.*

She went out into the front driveway and opened up the side passageway to get Dora.

'Ah, Tara,' a man's voice called out. 'Tara Brown.'

Shay Doran, a next-door neighbour of their detached Georgian palace, was standing at the fence, smiling a friendly grin beneath his glasses. His presence hit Tara with the irritation of having to share a single armrest with a stranger at the cinema. After finally getting the house to herself, she just wanted to be alone with it all until David got home.

'Oh hi,' Tara said, and then asked how his wife was because she really should. The wife's name was Stephanie, but people called her 'Mrs Doran' as if she wore a name tag. However, the Dorans seemed harmless enough. They were a couple in their seventies. Shay liked gardening, Stephanie watched TV and their two adult sons now lived abroad.

'Fine, fine,' Shay said, in response to her enquiry about his wife. Adjusting his glasses, he added, 'I see you have a pet.'

She held up the cage so the unspectacular tabby could stare at him. 'Say hallo, Dora. This is our lovely new neighbour. Unfortunately, little Dora suffers from an incurable case of adorable-itis. So all we can do for the poor creature is give her whatever she wants, whenever she wants it.'

Shay blinked slowly, already picturing the cat spraying his flowers. 'I'm more of a dog man myself. Not that we have one. It's nice to live in a quiet area. Now, I know you'll be all busy moving in today, but…'

Tara put down the cage and wished he'd get to the point. Then she smiled, offering him the face of a woman who would do everything in her power to put things right in the world for him.

'… but I can't find Ryan and he needs to sort out the sewers. I think he's hiding from me. In fact, I *know* he's hiding from me. We've called him about twenty times.'

*Ryan*. Her pulse quickened. 'Believe it or not, no one can find him.'

'Ah, for god's sake, this is ridiculous. You might believe that, but I certainly don't. How can the head of a construction company be AWOL? It's ludicrous. And he doesn't even know what the problem is. Which means that you don't know what the problem is. It just happened this morning…'

Tara's eyes widened at the sudden realisation of the colossal boredom she was about to be put through. She tried to concentrate, but it was like listening to the shipping forecast. Shay began to relay each detail of what he considered to be a plumbing disaster, but was in fact just a single blocked drain outside on his decking. The piping had backed up earlier in the day and Shay had of course immediately called the emergency drains crew. But they had only been able to fix the situation temporarily by using suction pumps because, according to Shay, there was something irremovable blocking the sewer on Tara's side of the boundary – beneath their new patio. Concluding his detailed story, Shay said, 'You can understand my frustration. It's our turn for dinner tomorrow, and now our friends will have to dine indoors because of the smell. It's not too bad now. But it could get worse. And that will be embarrassing, as I'm sure you can imagine. Ah, but what do you care?'

Shay shrugged as if his troubles wouldn't, and never had, interested his neighbour. That irritated Tara – she thought that she'd successfully disguised her disinterest. 'But are you one hundred per cent sure it's our build that has caused it?'

Shay was no longer smiling. All pretences were off. He spoke softly: 'Do I sound confused to you?'

Tara's eyes widened. Where had that come from? Neighbours were supposed to behave to each other with distant courtesy. Was he trying to intimidate her? Would he talk to David like that?

'The blockage is on *your* side, Tara. It has to be. The pipe travels under your patio. The drains people have told me this. Common sense tells me this. We'll have to get rods down your access point on the patio and figure out what's going on under there.' As Tara's smile melted, Shay's friendly smile returned. 'So, if you can get Ryan to organise the sewer rods for your patio as soon as possible, that would be appreciated. We'd really like this sorted before it escalates.' Shay waved adios over his shoulder and retreated to the penance of his home life.

Back inside, Tara released Dora to the mammoth task of scenting every edge and corner of her new home. Finally, it felt that the future had arrived and that it was good. The move had come so fast, it was as if Tara had been abducted in her sleep and then awoken somewhere entirely new. She thought back to when she'd originally moved in with David, only a week after kissing him for the first time. Tara had embraced the unprecedented jolt of no longer being alone and had slipped so easily into the pockets of his life. Her belongings had simply vanished into his tiny one-bed apartment.

Tara's bare feet tested the condition of the carpet beneath her toes. The fabric's quality thrilled her. The perfect vacuum lines left by the cleaner gave the wool the look of a manicured pitch before a cup final. She remembered when wealth had meant nothing to her. It had never been a driving force. It had never dictated her life choices. But then she'd grown up, made money of her own and suddenly experienced what it could do – permit travel, build a house, allow both herself and her husband the freedom to be what they wanted to be.

Dora was curled up on the living room windowsill, pushing her head against Tara's hand before exposing her throat, demanding attention after the trauma of the move. Suddenly a car pulled in from the road and swooped round the circle of the driveway. It wasn't David. A man stepped out of the car. He was tall and broad and she knew just by looking at him – at how he surveyed the face of the Georgian, how he observed her through the front window as if *he* was invisible – that something was about to be awful.

# CHAPTER THREE

That morning, after leaving Lawrence Court, David had driven the thirty-minute journey to the university to wait for Gordon. On the way, he turned off his phone. He needed to think without Tara calling and reminding him of her great betrayal. His brain went round in circles. *What exactly does Gordon know?* How *does he know it? What does he want?*

As he pulled into the university car park, he muttered the words, 'It was just an accident.' But he wasn't sure if he believed them. There were two contradicting voices in his head: *you overreacted* and *he deserved it*. David remembered punching Ryan, watching him stagger backwards and wobbling on the border of where the Juliet balcony should have been. Could he have grabbed him in time?

Once parked at the back of the bunker-like arts block, he entered the heaving concourse encircled by lecture halls. It was like stepping into a storm. On the quiet third floor, a dark, narrow corridor led to his office. Waiting at the door were two attractive female students: one from Dublin who was struggling with the weight of her laptop, and one from Galway in low-hanging tracksuit bottoms. They were both hoping for ten minutes' alone time to discuss their thesis proposals. For weeks it had been obvious that both girls nurtured a crush on him. *See how easy it could've been, Tara?* There were so many opportunities in the everyday mix of university life that, if he paid attention to them, the world outside of its sanctified walls would seem like a miasma of drear. But he hadn't paid attention to them. *I should choose one of them now. Take her over my desk. It would be easy. It would be fun.* Instead, David thought of Ryan, before apologetically telling his students that he couldn't see anyone until at least the end of the week, and closing his door.

In effect, David's office was his fiefdom from where, amid preparing lectures and finally giving his PhD research paper – 'Discovering Resistant Opposition: World War Two in the Savage' – the attention it deserved, he also managed Tara's career. It was a sideline that he'd taken very seriously from the moment he'd conjured her big break from thin air in the lobby of the Shelbourne Hotel, transforming Tara from a weekend art enthusiast into an international attraction. From that point on, he'd handled every deal, show and global exhibition she'd had over the last three and a half years. The success of *Erdős Landscapes* had ensured that he could remain an undergraduate lecturer, taking just a few specialised classes, rather than waste his time as a full-time member of faculty who had to support his then struggling artist girlfriend and pay the home nursing bills for his seventy-six-year-old mother. His sister took no responsibility for their mother; she had emigrated to Australia when she was eighteen and hadn't visited Ireland in over a decade. Over the years, she and David had basically lost touch and anyway, with a small café to run, two teenagers and no husband, she didn't have the money to help out.

David poured a coffee from the espresso maker and sat at his desk. It was from here that he wielded his power. It was here that he made important decisions. It was from this desk that he'd got Leonardo DiCaprio to write the catalogue intro for Tara's first US exhibition – or rather, to put his name to the intro that David had written. Up to nine months ago, he used to sit at this desk, take a call and inevitably end up naming a ridiculous figure in a sentence that included the word 'bargain'. David had a gift for sniffing out the buyers with serious money and rounding them up like a sheepdog.

But these days, it was usually some rich asshole phoning him up *not* to buy something. He'd known it wouldn't last. Fresher meat had been destined to replace Tara in the corporate art sandwich. That was just the way it was. But David and Tara didn't mind. When Tara's career had ignited, David had finally begun his doctorate. But time constraints had forced him to put it on hold – he simply hadn't been able to correct papers, prepare lectures, manage Tara's career *and* write a dissertation. But now that they finally had the financial security that had come from getting his wife everything she'd ever wanted from her career – artistic recognition – they'd both agreed that it was time for David to get what he'd always wanted from *his* career – academic recognition. Until now, their plan had been simple and graceful; the way things were supposed to be when you were a solid, tight team.

He leaned over the espresso and sniffed covetously. His trembling hand sent a small tide of liquid slopping into the saucer. David lit a cigarette and watched the ceiling fan chop the blue smoke out of existence. On the computer screen was the start of an email waiting to be written to Tara's PR consultant: the kind of New York publicist who had his own publicist. The blank page stared out reproachfully, as if he was hurting it by not typing on it. David didn't have many emails to send these days.

On the other side of the door, twenty feet away along the corridor, the elevator *dinged*. David flicked the cigarette out of the window. Footsteps approached, and he looked into the white glow of the email as if it was some type of crystal ball. Knuckles rapped on the door and before he could answer, Gordon entered, his undone suit revealing a small, stowaway paunch. He dropped his body into the chair like an anchor.

David put on his sombre face, usually reserved for expressing disappointment in a favoured student. 'Look, you and Ryan are close and worked—' *Be careful.* 'Work well together. But Jesus, *me*, kill Ryan?'

Gordon's silence was galling. Each passing second felt like a step towards a cell. And still Gordon waited, because he knew there would be more.

'Why would you think such a thing? You'd want to be careful, Gordon. As I tell my students, madness is just one small step to the left of being imaginative – that's why Hitler was an artist. I mean, are you on crack? *Me*? Murder Ryan?'

Gordon's head tilted slightly. He did this when feigning confusion. 'Finished?' He was enjoying giving David the space and time to embarrass himself further. 'OK. Ryan was a mess in that pit. His head, it was…' Gordon gazed up to the narrow window. 'The only thing that didn't break in Ryan's face was his fucking teeth.'

'Jesus. So is he... Did I…'

'Ryan is dead.'

David took a sip of coffee to hide his face.

'Rigidly dead. Stone-cold dead,' Gordon explained further, as if there were degrees of deadness.

So it was true. David really had killed him. Ryan wasn't wandering the streets with amnesia. Ryan wasn't comatose in a hospital. Ryan wasn't out drinking with a friend. For a moment, he had difficulty digesting this news. David didn't have much first-hand experience of death. His school friends who had OD'd had only become junkies after David had left them behind. In fact, until his father had died, he had considered bereavement to be something like a literary theme or a sombre movie premise.

'It was an accident.' David spoke those words as if they contained a sacred truth.

'An accident?' Gordon exclaimed, his smooth, moisturised face suddenly turning red in an instant. 'I'll tell you what it was – it was brutality. Brutality above and beyond the call. Wow – you can take the thug out of Cawley but you can't take—'

'I didn't mean it. I just wanted to... You know... I had no choice. I *had* to hit him.'

'It was a crime of passion. I understand. *Flectere si nequeo superos, Acheronta movebo.*'

'What?'

Dismissively, as if answering a particularly slow nephew, Gordon elucidated, *'If you can't reach heaven, raise hell.'*

'I hit him and he staggered backwards and... The rail hadn't been put in.'

'That's better, isn't it? Speaking the truth. No more repressing, hiding, sneaking around. It's a weight off the old shoulders.'

David sighed long and deep into his hands. 'Christ, I told him to get it done last week. I told him! He didn't deserve to die. His wife's now a widow. I'm responsible for that. Look at me, Gordon – I have to live with this.'

Gordon pointed at him. 'You're talking about guilt? That's just the bullshit indulgence of the loser. You didn't feel guilt when you thought you were getting away with it.'

David wanted to say – to *insist* – that he had felt guilt from the moment it had happened. But what he really felt was massive regret. He wished it hadn't happened. And of course, he felt fear. But guilt? No.

'Dave, there are just two types of people in the world. Diers and killers. Most are diers. And despite your *humble* origins, I would never in a million years have guessed that you were the other one – the more interesting one. But I suppose you had much to protect. And a man who has much to protect has much to live for.'

David's forefinger touched the fading bruise on the side of his forehead. 'I know what Ryan was doing in my house at midnight. But what were *you* doing there?'

The architect maintained insouciance, but there was a subtle twitch beneath his cheek. He pretend-yawned to iron it out. 'I was due to meet Ryan when he was finished with Tara. He liked to multitask. We both work late – sometimes very late – and were meant to be finalising things. I wanted to know that everything was shipshape. I was on the middle floor when Ryan flew by the window and went splat. I went up to your office and saw you pawing at your hair as you looked down at the patio. So just as you turned away from the window, I floored you with a hammer. It was risky. Took expert timing. A second too late and you would've seen me. A fraction too hard and I could've killed you.'

'You hit me? I knew I couldn't have... What happened to the body?'

Gordon blinked twice. That was as discombobulated as he got. 'I scooped clay over him, and scoop by scoop, Ryan was rubbed out. Manual work always gets to feel rhythmic and almost pleasurable. I should do it more often. Soon I was walking across the shallow grave, hardening down the soil. Then when Bruno arrived, he got going with the digger to tier the top of the foundation for the rest of the dry-lay. And just like that, Ryan was gone, as if he was never here. Sunk beneath your gorgeous tumbled travertine, his life weighed down with Virginia Woolf rocks. Or rather, crushed limestone – to be precise.'

David pictured Ryan being eaten by worms, ripped apart by earwigs and nested in by beetles. 'Why have you done this, Gordon? Why have you helped me?'

'*Helped* you? What do you think this is – *Eat, Pray,* fucking *Love*?'

'What do you want?'

The conversation had finally reached the point where Gordon had wanted it to go. 'Oh, I can see your fear Dave... It's in the air, like a mist.' He waved a lazy hand like he was clearing the room of an odour.

'What. Do. You. Want?'

'It's not like I want the moon and the stars. I just want money, money and... Let me see... Oh yeah, money.'

'You're serious?'

'They're all very good reasons, Dave.'

'You're shaking me down? *You* – you're blackmailing me?'

'I'm giving you a chance to get away with it scot-free.'

David's thought processes jackknifed on his unconscious superhighway. *'Scot' was a redistributive taxation levied in the early tenth century as a form of municipal poor relief. That's where 'scot-free' comes from.*

*Focus! Stop hiding.* 'How much?'

'One point four million.'

David closed his eyes. 'One. Point. Four. Million?'

The architect smiled. 'It's just a number.'

David opened his eyes. 'Pi is just a number. One point four million is one point four *fucking* million.' On the first day of David's university scholarship, exhausted from another ten-hour nightshift driving the massive Caterpillar P3500 forklift, he'd been ticked off by a professor in front of the whole auditorium for casually saying 'bullshit' in a class discussion. Since then, he'd rarely cursed again.

'Getting away with murder comes at a price.'

'We'll be ruined.' David's finances were complicated, but not *that* complicated. One point four million was everything they had. But that wasn't the worst of it. Most of that money was there to repay the bridging loan for the renovation. If they defaulted on that, they'd lose the house, on which they had taken out a two-million-euro mortgage.

Gordon said, 'Remember my mantra during the design stage? "Sometimes you have to spend to earn." Well, this will be the best money you've ever spent. It'll keep you out of jail for the rest of your life.'

'Tara's paintings have crumbled in price. She's over. She'd be lucky to total one hundred k for the rest of her life, even if she continues to paint and sell regularly.'

'True. I don't know much about the art world, but I know enough to realise that someone like Tara will never again come up with something so zeitgeist-kissing as *Erdős Landscapes*. I suppose she's the art world equivalent of the novelty song – a one-hit wonder. But you know, Dave – don't let that diminish your pride in her or indeed yourself. You both made your strike, and it was a bullseye.'

Less than two months ago, David had been gazing down in disbelief at their bank statement. He could barely fathom that there was a number of such enormity printed beneath their names. Now it might be all about to vanish – as if it had never been there.

'If we lose the house then we lose everything,' he said. 'Lecturing here barely covers the rent of a one-bed apartment. We're having a kid. And my mother... Jesus, she had a stroke. I'm now paying for her home help. She'll be dependent on welfare handouts without me.'

'Look, what's your point? You come from filth, Dave. You come from the Cawley Estates and therefore probably still secretly think that it's cool to be poor. Therefore when the inevitable happens, you can deal with it. Or maybe you won't. I don't really care.'

'You can't do this to us. Just take four hundred thousand. Five hundred. But leave enough for repaying the bridging loan. That's our house.' David could feasibly keep the sudden loss of half a million from Tara for a few years – which could possibly give him enough time to come up with something to plug the gap in their finances. He could go back to working nights in the warehouse, which along with his university salary might just pay the mortgage, while Tara might – just might – make the occasional big sale to supply the flow of funds required to bring up their child in the manner Tara was planning.

Gordon looked at him with a vague disinterest. 'One point four million. You're going to give your architect what he wants and deal with the repercussions later. You'll have enough left to get through the next few months without Tara knowing. Then when your kingdom falls, I'll be long gone, to the States, and you'll have come up with some sorry story as to why you have idiotically invested all your money in a doomed but *very legal* get-rich-quick scheme without her knowing.'

'A get-rich-quick scheme?'

'Tomorrow I'm having a contract drawn up that you're going to sign, that says you're investing in an apartment complex I'm planning to build – but not really. You will give me the money in forty-eight hours – Wednesday morning. Your money will be legally invested in my company. Of course, the apartments will never be built, and I will move far away across the ocean. But way before then, the building society will have taken back Lawrence Court and chased you for the loan that you can't repay. You'll lose your house, end up officially bankrupt – but *free*. In other words, Dave, you'll have got away with murder.'

David thought of the account he held with Tara in KLT. Withdrawals only required one to sign. Once Gordon got what he wanted, then there would be about forty thousand left. So he could keep the unavoidable threatening letters secret from her for a few months. David paid the bills. Tara always left the statements unopened for him. And then... And then...

Gordon said, 'Let me make it simple for you. You're not going to say anything to Tara, because you can't trust her. She's already fucked Ryan behind your back. What else has she done? What else would she do? You really think that when it comes to protecting her future – her *baby's* future – that she wouldn't toss you overboard like the toxic waste you are? And even if she doesn't, you still can't control her. She finds out about this and she's a loose cannon. So, like I said, you are *not* going to say anything to Tara.

You're then going to pay me one point four million *and* you're going to lose Lawrence Court. Either that, or you're going to go to the police to tell them how you threw Ryan out the window. Now that would be something – coming clean. It always is. I just love when people cause a classic scandal by being caught telling the truth. This one has everything – murder, illicit sex, money, a *once*-renowned artist, a jealous husband. And you can also tell them that you buried the body on your property. You'll have to take responsibility for that, too, because I certainly won't. Burying the body? Try and claim manslaughter having done that. I dare you. I double-dare you.'

'If I take out that much, Revenue will soon find out.' David picked up the cigarette box and rotated it. 'Especially with the bridging loan due.'

'Don't bore me. After budgeting your house, I know more about your finances than you do. The money's in KLT. Your mortgage and loan are with the building society. KLT don't care or know about the loan. And the building society can't stop you investing with me instead of paying them. Because that's what you're going to do.'

David saw a way to buy time. He grabbed it. 'How do you think I'm supposed to get your money in just two days? Walk into the bank with a suitcase? It'll take a week to order up that much cash.'

Gordon didn't move a muscle. 'You seem to be labouring under the impression that I'm the kind of moron who would fall for a Nigerian email scam. So I'll tell you exactly what's going to happen. Tomorrow, I'm opening an account in your branch. The day after, you're coming with me to the branch, where you will electronically transfer the cash from one internal account into the other. And that will be that.'

David needed to find a hole in Gordon's plan. 'Ryan's wife, Christine. She isn't going to just—'

'I've had Christine on the phone every thirty minutes this morning. She's going out of her mind. You're responsible for that. Christine is a good woman. She doesn't deserve to be in this hell.' Gordon's fingers formed a triangle before his face. 'But look, after a year or two, Christine might realise that Ryan being missing is the best thing that ever happened to her. She'll move on to something else or someone better. Or maybe she won't. It's not my problem. And soon it won't be yours either.' Gordon gestured with his hand, flicking away the topic.

'And what about the police?'

'You honestly believe that there's even a minute possibility that I don't know what I'm doing? Bullshit – you know what kind of man I am. By taking the money, I'll have implicated myself. It will make me an accessory. So, if somehow the police find out, then we both go down. And *I'm* not going down. We're both on the same team – but it doesn't have to be "Team Fuck Up".'

'They'll have to start looking for Ryan soon. And they won't just go away.'

'Of course they will go away. Ryan's not a young man. He's not someone's missing child. He's not a gorgeous woman. He's simply another guy with no kids. They disappear all the time. Guilt, heartache, mental illness; there's lots of reasons men like Ryan walk into the sea and are never seen again. Some just get bored with afternoon TV. Others hook up with a girl half their age and they're gone. They run from problems. Jump on a plane or a boat and disappear forever. It happens all the time, and no one fucking cares. And those of us who worked with him, who saw him regularly, who even liked him, we'll have totally forgotten about him too.'

The only sound in the room was that of the breeze blowing through the half-open window. David knew the power of silence. He remembered his father saying nothing. He remembered those silences more vividly than he remembered the things he said.

Finally David said, 'But why are you involved in *any* of this?' When David pictured Gordon, he saw someone born male, rich, white and handsome – his entire life was a peaceful, comfy sleep. 'The violence, lying, blackmailing; this is not your world. What are you doing? I can't believe you're doing this just for money.'

'Think I'm being cheap?'

'For someone like you it seems a big risk – a messy business to get involved in.' He was aware that Gordon had been silver-spooned his whole life. Gordon knew what freedom was. His grandfather had designed the early air force bases for France's *Service Aéronautique*, while his father had been a favoured architect of the RAF. David had heard all about Gordon's wonderful childhood in a fantastic home in the middle of what his parents had considered permissible Dublin – a small neighbourhood into which the nation's tributaries of wealth and privilege emptied. 'A million-plus is a lot of money. Sure,' David continued. 'But successful architects who come from your type of background don't get their hands dirty like this.'

'Yeah, OK. It's a weird one, right Dave? The fact is, all I have is about one hundred k.'

'One hundred k? That's just walking-around money in your neighbourhood.'

'Used to be. Alas, Father lost it all in the crash. The banks took most of it. The government took the rest. Jesus, my father had a complete breakdown last year. And, as you know, my family have a proud lineage. Now they're only letting the old man stay in his "family seat" until he dies – which should be soon. He's already had two triple bypasses. Basically there's nothing left for me here. So my hundred k, plus your generous donation, is one and a half million euros. And just what I need. See, I've had some offers already in the US. Now I just need the capital to launch me and keep me in the manner to which I'm accustomed.'

For a moment, David was sure that something like remorse or sadness had passed before Gordon's eyes. He leapt on it. 'Gordon, we got on. I know we did. You're not *that* good a liar. Don't do this to us.'

'You mistook my professionalism for friendship when I was making all your "gimme" dreams come true. Easy thing to misinterpret. I mean, it's because of me that your house seems like a gorgeous boutique hotel rather than a draughty ghost home for a couple with zero kids. I suppose people like you – who care *that* much about money – can only be punished by losing it.'

'We don't *care* about money. Not in the way you mean. Tara wouldn't have been selling her paintings outside of a city park if she cared about money. She would've stayed in insurance. Instead, she followed her heart and—'

'"Followed her heart?" You think that's a good thing? It's just pure egotism.'

'And if I cared about money, I would've done something with a future. I wouldn't have used my scholarship to study history. I would've slaved away in a warehouse every night so I could've become an actuary or whatever during the day. We were lucky. Tara and I know that. And we decided to use our good luck to build a house and put a kid in it. That's hardly insatiable gluttony.'

'You genuinely believe that you're the hero of your own story, don't you? But what you don't realise, Mister Historian, is that it's a tragedy. A tragedy for the rest of us that you're not off in a dingy bar in Cawley, or at the bookies', or feeding the fucking pigeons in some council park.'

'Jesus Christ, just what is your beef with me and the Cawley Estates? Fine, I was born there. Raised there. Deal with it. I have.'

'What's my beef with you and the Cawley Estates? Let me tell you – if you'd never crawled out of them to fail at living like a civilised human, then Ryan – my friend and work colleague – would still be alive. You are aware, Dave, that in this society of ours, this world that you inhabit with the rest of us, that throwing a man out of a second-floor window is about as socially acceptable as – Mister Historian – toasting the Führer at a bar mitzvah?'

David stared at his architect and tried to gather in his thoughts. He had two choices – pay the money or go to jail for murder. But the more he tried to think, the more Gordon's smile exasperated him. He needed to wipe it away, if only temporarily.

David said, 'Am I being lectured on ethics by a man with a second-class degree from a pay-as-you-go college? I checked up on you, Gordon, right back when Ryan recommended you to Tara. Sure, you have the reputation, references and experience. But if we go all the way back to where you began, then you're just another indulged prick who bought his way in.'

Gordon's mouth opened but nothing emerged. There was a shift of power in the conversation and David was intent on milking it. He continued: 'You may be clever, but like so many spoilt brats, you were lazy, preferring to go out spending daddy's money rather than actually studying. So of course, you didn't have the points for university. One of your colleagues at the Royal Academy told me that. But to be fair, he wasn't bitching. He was trying to say that results weren't everything – "sure, look at Gordon". So this guy told me that when you didn't get into university, daddy sent you to London. And even then it was daddy who got you the work experience and then it was daddy who got you your first contracts.' David kept going. He was always happy to keep punching in the clinch. 'Gordon, the only reason you're not hanging shirts in Zara is because of an accident of birth.'

Gordon seemed perturbed that David's fear had vanished. He wasn't the type of predator that wanted to admire his quarry. A rich claret stain spread up his neck and flushed across his cheeks. 'Fuck you, Dave. Do you know what *real* historians call you? Do you know what *real* professors call a charity-scholarship degenerate like you? "Who the fuck is Dave Miller?" *That's* what they call you. Yeah, that's right. Never forget that you're from Cawley, one of the scummiest areas in Dublin. Because the rest of us never will. It's always you new money people who get too loud, too quickly in the restaurant. You start itching and scratching at your designer suits, because no matter how fitted it is, it just doesn't *fit* you. Jesus – *you know* you don't belong here in this university or in Lawrence Court. You belong in Cawley. You always have. When I was up there scoping out that project for the council, every time I saw a fifteen-year-old cockroach scuttle by, I saw you. Up there it's just the holy trinity of drinking, fighting, mating – eat, kill, fuck. The poor fighting the poor as they've always done. They spend their whole lives wanting and wanting, scratching "them" lottery cards, placing "them" bets. And then you come along thinking you can change the status quo because you "read real good" compared to the other inbred fuck-tards in your school. And because of that, you get sent to university *for free*. And what do you do? You fucking kill a man. With your bare hands. You get everything you ever wanted and yeah, you still have to go and kill a man. And just because he messed with your woman. Do you know how working-class that is? You are scum, Dave. Useless fucking scum.'

*So is that it? Gordon is going to destroy me and Tara because his father lost him his inheritance, and because he despises where I come from? It's more than enough, I suppose*. But there still seemed to David to be something missing from Gordon's motive. A small piece. Something as minor as a biro mark on the architect's sleeve, or his eyes blinking too quickly. But even if there was something else, then so what? It didn't matter any more. The only thing that was important was that all Tara and he had worked for was about to be taken away – either by the police, or by Gordon.

Gordon caught his breath and stretched with loud exaggeration. Calmly, he said, 'So I think we've covered all the reasons why you're going to give me the money. Oh wait, there's another. The most important one. You Don't Have A Fucking Choice.' The architect let the quiet that followed dot the full-stop. He rose to his feet and backed towards the door. 'Have the funds ready to transfer, Dave, or have your affairs in order. One or the other. Adios, *boss*.'

David watched through the opened door as the architect strode towards the elevator with the arrogance of a man who had designed much better structures than this arts block. David considered how easy life would be if one knew what to do to make people disappear. Any random examination of history reveals how man's greatest achievements have come from making violence more violent. *Is it possible to kill Gordon, too?* He was beginning to think like a murderer. David rubbed his eyes. *What's the matter with me?*

So, things had got even worse. Things had become even more complicated. David leaned back into his chair, took Tara's panties from his pocket and dropped them into the waste bin. What time was it? Could he start drinking yet? It was only ten. He needed air. He needed more cigarettes. But most of all, he needed a Scotch. He crossed the car park, his shoulders hunched and bent forward. The cost of shame – it was like carrying an old, rotting house on his back. He envied all those students who were avoiding their desks for as long as possible, lying on the grass between the buildings, storing up on the sunlight for the nearing winter. From such a distance, the heat made them look as if they'd been sprayed gold.

David got into his car and drove. *Ryan didn't deserve to die. But I don't care that he's dead. I just care that it was me who killed him. Why couldn't someone else have punched him out the window?* Immediately he remembered that Ryan had a wife. He had sisters and friends. Incredibly, he had people who cared about him.

Throughout the morning and all through lunch, David sat in a Starbucks, pondering the long drawn-out nightmare his life had become. He remembered standing in the parish priest's house with his mother, who'd volunteered to clean it once a week, and being amazed that all that space was just for one man – plus he had *two* toilets at his disposal. One upstairs. One downstairs. In each council house that his ill-suited parents, sister and himself had called 'home' there had been just one tiny, freezing toilet. That was why his father would sneak off to urinate at the kitchen sink when the toilet was engaged, not knowing that everyone else knew about his dirty habit. But then, most fathers in the Cawley Estates got a pass for their mucky diversions.

At three, David took an alcove in a Hyatt hotel bar and somehow made two Scotches and a sandwich last the afternoon. His thoughts circled and circled – jail for murder, or pay Gordon. If he went to jail, he'd lose his wife and child. If he paid Gordon, he'd probably lose his wife and child *and* ensure that they had no money, no house and no hope for their future. The best-case scenario would be that he paid Gordon and that whenever Tara found out, she would decide to stay with him. *But then all our savings would be gone. We'd be broke. We'd be parents with no home for their kid, no credit rating, no future whatsoever. My kid would be me.*

As a boy, it had never even occurred to David that it was possible for people like him to own a home. That was something only for the people who visited the local shopping centre in their big cars, who had kids who would stay tight to their mothers as they glanced at David and his friends prowling by, unaccompanied by adults. Their fear had made him feel invincible. It was true that David and his friends had been good for nothing, which was unfortunate for them. But they had also been scared of nothing, which was unfortunate for everyone else. And then one day, David had realised that it was society's fear that would keep him in the grime and clamouring violence of the Cawley Estates for the rest of his life. If he wanted to get out, he had to make society *un*afraid of him. And the only way to do that was to become part of it somehow. Perhaps it really was possible – after all, his father's stories about the Irish Rebellions were full of figures who had come from nothing and yet changed a country. His father had often told him, 'The Brits don't mind the French and the Krauts. Know why? Because they beat them. But us Micks? They'll always have a problem with the Irish.' David had realised that he just had to read more about the Rebels of yore, learn more about them and then, maybe, he'd discover their secret.

Getting into his car at six that evening, David knew he had just over a day to decide what to do. He turned on his phone, which immediately received Tara's latest message. After he'd read it, his mobile seemed to take ten seconds to hit his lap.

*'Why aren't you picking up? The police are here. Want to talk to you about Ryan NOW. I said you were only twenty minutes away. Come quick.'*

Had the decision already been made for him? The road stretched out darkly all the way back to Lawrence Court. David's knuckles were white on the steering wheel, a cigarette jammed between his fingers. Would he get to hold Tara before they took him away? Would she kiss him? Would he want her to? He closed his eyes and imagined her kiss. It was the sweetest taste in the world. Would she hate him for killing her lover? Would she wish that it was her husband, rather than Ryan, buried beneath the patio? Would they cuff him on the way out?

*Why did I go inside after she left? Why do I always have to know what's going on? I could've just gone back to the apartment. I could've just sunk into the lovely bed of her lies – and lies are harmless when you don't know you've been lied to. If I had just done that, then today and tomorrow and all the days to follow would've been the most exciting, brilliant time of my life.*

David picked up speed and the Dublin suburbs zipped past him in a torrent of earth tones, ambers, ochres. An ambulance wailed by, turning his face into a blue mask. He turned onto Lawrence Court, passed Ryan's abandoned white SUV and watched as his house expanded before him. He parked behind Tara's Ford. Next to it was a black Skoda. At least the police hadn't arrived in a marked car.

'David!' It was his neighbour, Mr Doran, who strode purposefully to the garden fence, folded his arms and napalmed the driveway with his disapproval.

'This isn't a good time, Shay.'

'Isn't a *good time*? Damn straight it isn't,' Shay said, with black-framed glasses aimed directly at David's eyes. 'Our downstairs hall is destroyed for the second time today. Worse than this morning when it started from nowhere. David, the smell inside! It's a health hazard now. Our *house*. Where we *live*. I've been on this road for thirty-five years and nothing like this has happened until you finished your build. Ryan's not answering, while your engineer just wants it all in writing and insists that it can't be your building work. But *it is* your bloody building work. For god's sake, David, there's a *smell* in our home. The problem's under your new patio. It needs fixing. Hear me? I'm arranging rods. If Ryan isn't bothered then I'll just fix the bloody thing myself. Understand?'

'I'll look into it,' David said, having no idea what he was talking about, only really registering the bit about the patio and feeling his stomach take an elevator plunge at the idea of Ryan being under there.

He let himself into the hall. Tara had already hung two paintings: *Line In the Sand IV* and *Horizon II.* Fuelled by Mai Tai cocktails, she had sketched them on a hammock in Thailand, back when they'd been plotting their future. She'd been in full flow back then, soaking herself in her life's purpose. David had always envied those who had a calling in life. Until he'd been seventeen and had begun to lose himself in the history section of the local library, he had never wanted to be anything. Up till then, he'd learned from the adults in his world – his teachers and the police in particular – that he had no future.

Dora walked out of the front room, stretched her front legs, paws fanning out prettily like petals, and glanced up at David. Twitching her nose, she sensed something and froze like a set scene from the Natural Museum of History. She dashed upstairs.

The kitchen door was ajar. David spied at what lay beyond it through the crack. He'd always liked to watch Tara from afar, observing the men around her search for an angle, reach for the clever line that would make her toss back her long neck and laugh so throatily. But then she'd slept with Ryan. Then he'd killed a man. Now things had changed forever.

Rapping his knuckles on the door, he waited for the end of his life – or at least, this phase of it. Tara smiled from the far side of the island. It sat four, but there were only two metal stools beside it, as if emphasising that all of this was just for them. David nodded at the man sitting at the dining table between the Romanesque pillars, who was clearly trying hard not to act like he was in the biggest kitchen he'd ever been in. His seat was turned away from the table so that his body faced into the room. With his long legs stretched out, David could see that he was at least six foot tall. He was about fifty, wearing an open leather jacket, and his dark brown hair was neatly side-parted.

'Come in,' the man said, in a middle-class Dublin accent. He had the routine confidence of a large man.

David half-smiled. He disliked him instantly – as he did all police. Who would want to spend time with a person who wanted to police everyone else?

'Just a joke. You knocked on the door – but it's your house. And a very fine house too. Best of everything. Top spec.' The man ran his eyes over David, lodging details of his black jeans, T-shirt, loafers, suit jacket; as if considering the fact that most people – most *suspects* – dress like who they want to be, not who they are. 'Your wife gave me a tour of downstairs. Amazing what can be done with these old Georgians. Not that there's anything wrong with the originals. Some people would pay a lot of money to get one of these perfectly untouched.'

Tara said, 'Some people intended to do that. But they all got extensions in the end. The gardens are just too big not to.'

'Have you checked up the history of this place? A house as old as this must have an impressive list of tragedies connected to it.'

Tara straightened. Critical talk about the house clearly bothered her. It was as if she believed that the house would hear it.

'What I mean is, people have to die somewhere, and a century-old house must have seen some of its inhabitants... I'm rambling. Your control room off the pantry – it's like the engine room of a nuclear sub. The plumbing involved to get that underfloor heating system, solar panels, the upstairs rads all neatly into that space...' He looked at David. 'What's your name again?'

'David Miller.' It sounded wrong to have to say that inside his own house. He put out his hand and waited for the policeman to offer his first name, but he didn't.

'*Detective* Fenton,' he said, and shook David's hand before quickly retracting his arm. 'So, a perfect house in a nice area full of two-million-euro-plus properties, with a nearby famous street full of the type of families that make the Guinnesses seem middle-class. And because this is a much sought-after neighbourhood with excellent schools, good French restaurants and an organic food supermarket, people think nothing bad happens here?'

'*Detective*,' David said, 'nothing bad ever does happen around here.'

Fenton grinned a patient, tolerant smile, communicating clearly that he didn't like his first impression of Tara's husband.

'Except for that immigrant. Remember? Six months ago? Found in the kids' playground?'

'Yeah,' David said. 'I know all about that.'

'I'm sure you do. Would've been round about when you were buying this place. Someone beat a Somalian to death. Terribly sad, and not good for the house prices.' Detective Fenton chuckled, visibly struggling to lasso his bitterness. 'Sorry,' he continued, 'it's just that I haven't talked real estate in a long time. It's not much of a topic up where I live. In fact, where I live, doing up your house involves getting a ladder and a few cans of paint. It doesn't involve diggers, cranes and closing off half the street for six months. You aren't from here, are you? Like, you're not a local boy?'

'No. The Cawley Estates. I'm sure you know them. You guys break in the new recruits up there. Maybe *you* even walked a beat up there.' David found it hard to hold Fenton's gaze – it was like looking into the power of the state. But he persevered.

Fenton smiled in a friendly, interested way – as if trying to picture David as the rough piece of work he must've been about twenty-five years ago. 'I know them well. Wouldn't say you miss it much.'

'Nothing wrong with the Cawley Estates. Made me who I am, and I had a good childhood up there.'

'Yeah,' Fenton said, clearly not believing him, his smile growing broader. 'So, Tara was telling me that you manage a kids' team – Gaelic, rugby or soccer?'

'Soccer. I just help out. Mostly on the sideline. Tactical stuff. Try and get a game for as many lads as possible without weakening the team. They're from Cawley.'

'Fair play.' Then, snapping back to business, Fenton said, 'You know Ryan is missing?'

David pretended not to notice the adrenaline in the room begin to expand like the steam from an electric kettle. 'Have you not spoken to my wife about this already?'

'No. What happened to your forehead?'

'Oh…' David rubbed the bruise. 'Hit my head off a beam this morning.'

'Uh-huh. Now, Ryan is missing. We need to find him.'

'Right – what can we do to help?'

'Wait,' Tara interjected.

Competition for David's attention was fierce.

With two pairs of eyes switched to her, Tara said, 'If he's missing... Well, fine, I mean, obviously he *is* missing – but isn't it way too soon to be calling in the cops?'

'Yeah,' David added. 'Isn't there a wait-and-see period until someone is deemed officially missing?'

'Usually there is,' said the detective. 'But Ryan has lots of friends on the force. Plus, for us he is a person of interest. He was involved in *certain* activities…'

'Certain activities?' Tara said. 'What type of—'

'Nothing to be worrying your pretty little head over,' Fenton said, standing, presenting his full height and width before quickly softening the gesture by fixing his side-parting. 'But because of *certain* activities, and the fact that he's missing, then that's enough of a red flag to get us involved.'

'Well, we haven't spoken to him since…' Tara gazed to the ceiling as if she was trying to remember something just on the outskirts of her memory. 'Early yesterday. I talked to him on the phone.'

'About what?'

'About this kitchen. The wiring for an industrial loft-like effect. It's complicated.'

David said, 'Yeah, the electrician – Mike – was wrapping up. So Ryan wanted to know if we would ever change from exposed fittings.'

'And I said, in the future, probably,' Tara added.

Like a relay team, David took her up: 'And so Ryan told Mike to put all the wiring *inside* the ceiling. Therefore, all those conduit pipes you see up there – there's nothing in them. They're just for show.'

Detective Fenton grunted. He wasn't interested in talking about the house any more. 'And that was the last time either of you talked to him? No other calls?'

David nodded. Tara did too. She was good. She was a better liar than David. There was no doubt emanating from her. She appeared to be an attractive, happy young woman who had just moved into the house of her dreams. She did not seem to be a woman who was being queried by the police in front of her husband about the disappearance of her lover.

'OK. Thanks for your time, and apologies again about having called you home so quick from the university. And that thing you do with the kids' football team? Giving back to the community – admirable. Seriously.' Fenton walked to the kitchen door, placed his hand on the handle and then released it. 'One more thing.'

'Yeah?' Tara said. The natural la-de-da casualness of her expression had suddenly dampened. It was a slight flicker in her eyes. There was something she'd forgotten, or something she'd just remembered, that might trip her up. David wondered if Tara was worried that Ryan's disappearance had something to do with her. Was she afraid that Ryan was now in love with her? The moment the thought crossed his mind, a voice in his head snapped: *He deserves to be dead.*

'Well, it's a bit tricky... A bit awkward.' Fenton made an expression as if one of his fillings had just fallen out.

'What is?' Tara asked, not smiling, no longer playing the game.

The detective looked first to David and then to Tara, his expression grave and concerned, almost embarrassed. He fixed his hair again. 'There's the problem of Ryan's phone. We have it.'

David's jaw clenched. *How?*

'Where did you get it?' Tara asked in a disbelieving tone. David was glad his wife was doing the talking. He was finding it difficult to breathe.

Detective Fenton folded his arms, making him seem like a battering ram about to lunge forward. 'He left it in his car. Though his wife, Christine, insists that Ryan would never go anywhere without it. A man of habit, is Ryan. He checks his messages last thing at night. Plugs it into the charger and goes to bed. If his phone isn't where it is supposed to be, he will rip the house apart to find it.'

'His phone…' David said slowly. 'He left it in his car?'

The detective's tongue quickly licked his upper lip. Fenton clearly believed that fact to be the least mysterious of all the facts at his disposal.

'So... His car is here. Outside. So... It seems he parked the car here early this morning and vanished. Without his phone. Christine got home late last night and the driveway was empty. She assumed he was working late. But Ryan wasn't there in the morning, either, and so at first she assumes he didn't come home at all and had left her a message on her phone. But he hadn't. And so she then assumed that she didn't hear him come in last night or leave when he got up before her.' Fenton shrugged, as if he wasn't sure if he believed that.

David felt his underarms dampening with heat. If there was a time to surrender, end it all and turn himself in, then this was it. *No – not yet. Whatever the police can throw at me now, they can throw at me tomorrow or the day after. I need time to figure it all out.* As long as he was still free, there was a chance – a slim, tiny chance – that somehow this could all work out. However, he also knew that the moment this escalated, the police would search the house. They'd talk to Mike and Bruno and would discover that David had just appeared from upstairs that morning as if he'd been there all night. And they'd check his finances. Of course they would. They'd see he gave all his and Tara's money to Gordon – *if* he decided to give all their money to Gordon. *Stop panicking*. He tried to streamline his thoughts. *Deal with one problem at a time. And the first problem is the detective.*

Fenton looked directly at Tara. 'So I checked the recent calls on Ryan's phone. There's a record of five calls between you two which were made in the morning *and* the afternoon. Three that he made and two from you. And yet... Tara, you said you'd only called Ryan once yesterday?'

Tara was about to say something but then blanked, as if not really believing that she had nothing to offer. She looked at David, a deep regret in her eyes. A sadness.

'We share the phone,' David said. 'Sometimes I take Tara's. She doesn't miss it when she's painting, and I deal with her agent and the gallery owners and all that. I'm her manager – as well as lecturing in modern European history. Those calls were from me to Ryan and Ryan to me. Yesterday, when I was last talking to him. Like I'd said earlier.'

'But you didn't "say" any of that earlier. Tara said she'd last talked to him in the morning. And you agreed.'

'Oh. Right. But I implied… that I was talking to him too. At least I thought I did.'

'OK.'

'We were wrapping things up... Like the Juliet balcony in my office upstairs. It still wasn't in.'

Tara stared at him, unable to mask her amazement. She loved her phone, and went everywhere with it. And she knew David disliked dealing with Ryan and always went through Gordon instead. The fact that her husband and Ryan didn't click wasn't a secret. From the moment work started, they'd instinctively repelled each other, despite their best efforts. Tara knew how David hated Ryan's Dickensian roguish charm, and the cad-like flirtations of the smooth-talking ladies' man as he shared reminiscences and in-jokes with David's wife, demonstrating that good memories equal events plus time.

Fenton failed to hide his disappointment. Perhaps he didn't suspect David of having anything to do with Ryan's disappearance. Perhaps he'd simply assumed that there had been an affair between Tara and Ryan and he had wanted personally to witness yet another marriage crack from side to side.

'Well that's that, then,' he said, zipping up his leather jacket. 'I'll let you two lovebirds get back to your spanking new house.'

'Wait,' Tara said. The energy in the room shifted as she suddenly became the most important of the three people present. 'What exactly were you thinking in relation to those calls? Why did you leave it until the last moment to mention them?'

David began to knead the side of his forehead before realising that he was kneading the side of his forehead. He stared at his wife, pleading, longing for her to stop talking.

Detective Fenton's smile remained in place like a limp, forgotten balloon after the party was over. He touched the parting of his hair again – it was almost like a nervous tic. 'Until we find Ryan, *everything* that connects to his life is of interest to us. I'll be in touch.'

The detective walked through the hallway, whistling quietly as he went, soundtracking his everything-is-going-my-way mood. He slowed at Tara's paintings before letting himself out. But a sense of relief from the detective's exit did not sweep over David. Where he came from, nobody's situation had ever improved after talking to the cops.

Ignoring Tara, David entered the dark of the front room and dropped a pinch of food flakes into the dim golden glow of the softly bubbling aquarium. Dora, now settling on the bookshelf, miaowed a pissed-off protest at having her world turned inside out. From the shadows, David observed the front room and the adjoining library through the French doors. With all their stuff unpacked and still so much empty space, it seemed to him as if they were in the process of moving out. And then he focused on the drinks cabinet: a beautiful skyline of bottles, decanters, glasses, mixers. He poured himself a large Scotch and watched through the window as Detective Fenton regarded David's BMW coolly and hungrily.

David returned to the kitchen. Tara sat at the island, her arms folded on the marble surface. He imagined telling her everything – punching Ryan, Ryan falling, Ryan being buried ten feet away from her, Gordon about to take all their money. He imagined her telling him that everything would be all right; that together they were invincible. But Ryan had been Tara's lover, and because of that she no longer had any right to parts of David. His secrets were not for sale.

David opened the heavy fridge door. He took a fistful of cubes from the icebox and dropped them into his drink, listening to the sound of fissures ripping through them. With two gulps, the Scotch was gone. It burned his throat and warmed his insides. He could feel its effects immediately taking grip. It was almost medicinal.

Tara's eyes closed. Usually, silence didn't bother David. He took it as a sign of their ease with each other. But maybe he'd got that wrong too. Maybe their silence was only silence. He wondered if secrets were going to become something as solidly part of their marriage as breakfast together, an hour's worth of shared TV or a glass of wine in the evening to unwind and catch up. David remembered how he'd felt sitting in his car outside this very house last night. He remembered the loss he'd experienced as Tara had driven away. And for a moment, he once again felt intense dread – that he was about to lose her forever.

'David,' Tara said, opening her eyes. 'How do you know?'

He stared at her, watching her suck in her cheeks, unaware that he could see her visibly adjusting her thought processes as she did so. There was no escaping it now.

*

Tara leaned against one of the Romanesque pillars. She was grounded with a stage performer's calm. 'Really: how do you know?'

'Skipped going for pints after training because I wanted to come here and soak it all up before the big move. And when I parked outside… Well, there you were, saying goodbye to Ryan in your special way, in *our house*.'

'I swear, last night was the only time I was with Ryan. And I don't intend to be with him again.'

'You don't *intend* to be? Really? Let me clarify the situation, Tara. You will *never* be with that prick again.' David took refuge in a cigarette. He withdrew a crumpled packet from his jacket and patted about for a lighter.

Tara's stomach sank at the thought of her husband smoking again. He was forty. Ten years older than she was. And she wanted him around forever. She watched as he lit up. He did it in the way he'd always done – as if he were in a storm rather than a highly insulated kitchen; hands cupped around the flame, eyes squinting. Dragging the smoke deep into his lungs, he absorbed the kick before evenly releasing it out into the room.

David asked, 'Why were you with him?'

'I don't know. Jesus.'

'Why Ryan?'

'What do you want me to say?'

'I want you to give me precise answers to my questions. If I'm asking, I want to know. Am I being clear enough?' David gestured at her as if she was driving too slowly in the car in front of him. 'Did you actually think he would be a... a what? A better man than me? Ryan? Are you really that stupid?'

'No. You're the best. The best at everything. It's just… You turned forty. I'm thirty. We got married six months ago. We built this place. We're probably going to die here. Don't you see,

David? This is the second half of my life. It began when I walked through that door this morning. I've been feeling it for months. And then I get pregnant and—'

'Yes, Tara. Pregnant! With *my* child. Jesus – it *is* my child?'

'For fuck's sake, David.'

'Oh, you're surprised I ask? Answer the question – like I told you to.' David stared at her, saying nothing, waiting for her to answer. When still no reply was forthcoming, he warned, 'Don't test my boundaries. It may surprise you, but they do exist.'

Tara needed to turn away and escape his gaze. They'd never had a fight like this before. David was suddenly a stranger to her. The David that she knew would try to understand; he wanted to be friends; he hated when she sulked; he avoided saying anything that might hurt her feelings, and on the rare occasions that he had accidentally done so, would drop the argument, as if it was no longer important. And so her gut instinct was to resent David's behaviour now, even though she knew that she deserved to be on the receiving end of it.

'I haven't been sleeping around. It was a one-off. You actually want a fucking paternity test? Really? Because that isn't a problem if that's the level we've sunk to.'

'It's not "we". Just you. It's the level *you've* sunk to.'

'If you want the test, then of course I'll do it.'

He shrugged, but shook his head. No. Or not yet.

'I'm sorry, David. I'm sorry. I needed to... I needed to...'

'Have sex with your builder?'

'I needed to do *something*. It could've been a stupid, expensive pair of new shoes that hurt my feet and I'd never wear and would just keep at the bottom of my wardrobe and look at every few years. It could've been a chocolate cake. But it wasn't any of that stuff. Instead I was with my old boyfriend.'

'"Fucked". You *fucked* your old boyfriend.' David rarely cursed, so when he did, it had the effect of a slap. 'You weren't *with* him.

You're with me. Now. Here. In this room. Use English properly.' The way he said it, so carefully, with cruelty in it – and pity at the same time.

'I didn't even want to. I've never wanted to. Not with him or anyone else. But suddenly it seemed like the right thing to do. It just seemed like a kiss-off to my past. It was a full-stop.' Tara felt like talking and talking because she was afraid of what might be in the silences. 'It was as if I was too happy. Jesus, that sounds mental. But I needed the experience. I needed to do the one thing that was absolutely wrong, unnecessary, contrary to everything I have and need. I was pretending that there was something else I wanted. I had to invent a hole. I wish I could explain, but it's not that simple.'

'Make it that simple.' David flicked the angry red glow of his cigarette into the sink.

Tara felt nauseous. She hated fighting with David so much that on the rare occasions it'd happened in the past, she'd felt like vomiting. The prospect of a fight grew more terrible to her with each month that passed without one. It had always been such a shock: the fact that they didn't agree on everything, that even *they* could have separate, different and incompatible wants.

'I knew that I was going to live happily ever after. So to emphasise it, I decided to be the old me. The one I was before you came into my life and made everything so fucking perfect.'

'So it's my fault now?' David smiled, almost admiring the dodge. 'You know something, Tara, I can't understand a word you're saying. Know why? Because I don't speak victim. That's why.'

There was no escaping the catastrophe she'd caused. *Everything is over*. But then she blinked the thought away. She wouldn't allow her life to be so easily destroyed. This would be a good time to cry. However, her tears were reserved for films and books. They would not pour for something real like this. '*You* didn't come into it. That... That probably sounds worse, but I'm trying to be one hundred per cent honest with you.'

David's indignation shot two clouds of crimson to his cheeks.

'Look, even though I made that decision – and at the time I thought it was the correct thing to do – I now know it wasn't.'

'Only because you've been caught.'

'If I hadn't been caught then it just would've been the stupid thing it was supposed to be. A quick, nothing fling, to be forgotten. And life would go on as if it had never happened.'

Tara waited for something in David's expression that showed his pain, his jealousy, his anger. But it was like staring into the face of an automaton.

David turned away and rolled aside the huge kitchen slider, opening the house to twilight and the expanse of spotlighted lawn. The warm night air spilled inside, bringing a few white moths on the currents. He kept going, outside to the edge of the patio, where moonbeams plunged down through the dirty-milkshake clouds. From inside, Tara scanned the depths of their garden. The distant house at the end was only partly obscured by leaves. She saw its frosted window go black as someone left the bathroom. Next door, behind the hedge, sounded the grudging scrape of a chair on Shay's wooden decking, followed by footsteps.

Tara watched as David crouched at the edge of the patio, his fingers digging between the travertine slabs into the still-setting grout, burrowing deep, as if trying to get down into the earth, beneath the cornucopia of what they'd wanted and what they'd got and what they intended to keep for the rest of their lives. She wanted to ask him what he was doing. She wanted to know *why* he was doing it.

Suddenly, Dora appeared on the lawn. She was supposed to have been kept indoors for a week before being unleashed onto the neighbourhood. But she'd snuck out and had gone hunting. Dora dropped the first kill of her new territory at David's feet: the remainder of a robin, a small detonation of matter and bloody feathers.

David bent to pet the cat, and Tara wished she could feel whatever emotion it was that he bore. There was too much kindness in him for it to be just anger. There had always been a gentleness about David that she loved. Very few men had it. But his hurt would be kept inside. That was just the way it was for men like him. Showing the pain would hurt him more than the pain itself. But there was something else there, too. She hoped it wasn't some type of regret – regret that he'd ever fallen in love with her.

*I risked all this for Ryan. I could lose everything I'd ever wanted. Ryan is such a... is such a... It's all my fault!*

For a while, in Tara's early twenties and for a few moments during the build, Ryan had been the epitome of erotic perfection to her – ideal body, a mind that was a confliction of filthiness and sensuality. When she'd first moved to the city, her friends had belonged the moment they'd learned how to look like they had somewhere to go, and fast. But Tara had needed something more… of the flesh – to make her feel rooted and at home. When she'd met Ryan – also a small-town boy – there had been a way that he would look at her; as if by holding her gaze for more than two seconds, he had the ability to make the earth, moon and stars revolve around her. Ryan had seemed to crave every inch of Tara, feed on every word and consume even her half-formed thoughts. It had taken a while for her to realise that a ladies' man does not just look at you that way – he looks at all women that way.

David, still with his back to her, and still crouched with Dora, asked, 'What do you think happened to Ryan?'

Tara did her best to sound casual. 'He's probably on a session with a buddy who got into town late last night. It's just the type of stupid, irresponsible thing he'd do – messing his work colleagues around, and his... his wife. He'll be back tomorrow.'

'The detective called him a "person of interest".'

'Maybe Ryan was selling leftover building materials on the black market or something. But I'd say it's just that he has a few buddies on the force and his wife got them involved. Nothing more than that.' Tara didn't want to talk about Ryan. What had happened between them was supposed to have been a bookend to her youth, her freedom, her irresponsibility. But Ryan wasn't a bookend; he was a virus, infecting the exciting possibilities of the future and withering them into failure. While David was cerebral, Ryan was all show. David planned ahead and strategised, while Ryan was so impulsive it was as if he constantly believed that tomorrow might not come. David had read *GQ* for as long as she'd known him and would always hold up a top against his jacket to ponder its suitability, while Ryan was habitually dishevelled: half-moons of dirt under his fingernails, plaid shirt untucked and jeans speckled with paint. Ryan was a Scorpio, David a Virgo.

Tara suddenly remembered that Ryan's wife was calling in to see her tomorrow. Should she say anything about it to David? No – she'd put this day to rest first. She stepped out onto the patio and whispered down to the back of his head, 'Are we OK? Is everything going to be normal again?'

'I don't know what normal is any more.'

'I'm sorry. Forgive me. I want my husband back.'

He stood and faced her. 'Don't be childish.'

'Is it childish to know what you want?'

'You wanted Ryan.'

'Just once. A stupid once. You're my husband. We're married. We're in this together. Forever. Like we agreed.'

'Marriage isn't mystical. It's a form you fill out. Sometimes it works. Mostly it doesn't.'

'Please, David. Don't say things like that. This is not you.'

'Just go, Tara. Go to bed. I can't even look at you right now.'

As Tara retreated back into the house towards the stairs, she knew that even if David had said, 'Yes, we are OK', what he really would have meant was that he *wished* they were OK and that he *wished* things were going to be normal again. Tara knew that the sacred balance of their relationship had been disturbed. No matter what she said or did, even if David could finally forgive her, the spirit-level of their relationship now showed an askew horizon.

Hours later, David stepped onto the landing. He paused, as if facing a fork in the road. Before him, the staircase wrapped around the central concrete pillar and continued down to the hallway gallery and up to his unfurnished office. On the wall, halfway to the attic, was the stain. It almost seemed to throb, its darkened contours bulging out from the wall as if it had been stencilled there. Perhaps because the house had been showered in only high-end finishes, this one flaw leapt out. But something else told him that it was the type of stain that just wouldn't go away; that it was the type of stain that would make a man renovate the entire stairwell just to get rid of it.

As he undressed on the landing, he replayed the argument he'd had with Tara. How much of his anger was an attempt to blame his wife for the fact that it was he who had punched Ryan out the window? *How would I have reacted if Ryan was alive and well? Would I have found it easier to forgive her? Am I being unfair?* He pictured Tara's face, her eyes glazed with hurt. Instinctively he just wanted to take that pain away. But then there was that voice again, loud in his head: *She started this. She let you down. She pulled the pin.*

Quietly, he entered the bedroom to join his wife. In the darkness they lay side by side, Tara's eyes closed, arms folded across her breasts like a pair of bat's wings. There was a ceiling fan above them – another extravagance – that David had clicked onto its lowest setting just so as to use it. The blades rotated slowly: *wuh-wuh-wuh*.

While lying there, hoping for slumber to come and restrain the nightmare, David still tried to uncover the secret way out.

He now had only one day left to decide what to do. His brain churned, struggling to make sense of it all, but its only conclusion was that if he paid off Gordon then Tara would leave him, hate him, wish that he was dead. Of course she would. He would've taken her future, and that of her child's, away. There was a limit to everything – even love.

So the alternative was to go to jail for murder. *Can I do time?* Images rolled across David's brain – homosexual rape; prison yard beatings ending with eyes hanging from stalks; an exploding cell light showering molten liquid onto his orange uniform. His brain – how he'd like to take it out and run it under a cold tap – could only come up with a singular brutal truth: before you have your world blown to pieces, you first have to endure the struggle and toil of creating a world that was worth losing.

And then there was Tara's betrayal – he was trying hard to put it behind him, to let it go. It was just the once, she'd claimed, and he believed her. *Even Tara's not that good a liar.* He tried to see what life would've been like if he hadn't confronted Ryan, if he'd just waited out on the street and then followed her home. They'd have had the same conversation they'd had downstairs this evening about her betrayal. How would it have ended? *Would we have just moved into the house today as planned? Surely I would've wanted to punish her somehow?* But by punishing Tara, he would've been punishing himself – denying them their house, ruining all their plans.

But the image of her with Ryan returned again and again. *The prick deserves to be dead. But no one throws a single punch with the intention of killing. That objective requires a knife, a gun, a rock – or at least a carefully aimed kick to the skull. But it was just a punch. Only a thump.* However, something inside David refused to accept that point. The fact was that he'd imagined killing Ryan. The image of his hands on the builder's throat had warmed him. *Feelings become thoughts and thoughts become words and words become deeds*. David hadn't felt so stuck in a mind loop of self-condemnation since his father had passed away twenty years ago. *It's never going to be the same again. You've run out of luck. From here on in, it's all compromise.*

David looked at his watch to see how many minutes had dripped by. He sat up naked on the side of the bed. As the cool night air on his skin infused his bones with cold, he thought, *I'm the worst father in the world.* His child wasn't even born, wasn't demanding anything from him and all he had to do at this point was provide a safe foundation for its arrival. Even the most primitive beasts could do that. His child. Tara had shown him the printout from the hospital. It was like a bad photocopy of a photograph depicting a grainy creature swimming at the bottom of a murky underground lake. *My child.* It was less than two months ago that the idea of a baby had suggested itself, yet remembering that time was like stealing someone else's memories. David no longer recognised himself from that time; the him who could dare to look into the future and imagine a world of happy ever after.

Just six weeks ago, David had been standing at a long bar in a members-only nightclub, on the phone to Pete, Tara's New York art dealer. The whole area was chintzy in a Victorian way. Dark wood panelling was everywhere, the walls covered with oil paintings and hunting trophies: deer heads, a huge pike, a sow. All that was missing were cobwebs. In the middle of the hunting lodge vibe was a so-tacky-it's-chic glass dance floor with 1970s disco lights that clashed with the contemporary dance hits.

David, totally at ease with his surroundings, had tried to catch sight of Tara on the dance floor. She liked him to watch her. Despite himself, he'd grown to like private members' clubs. Even this place, where, on the ground floor, there was a Bollie's – a Michelin-starred restaurant where one k was just dinner for four with wine. The fact was, private clubs were the only slices of nightlife remaining that no longer made him feel past it. In fact, most of the men in these places were older than him, and the few that were his age looked worse than he – and that was reassuring. David also liked the glasses in which they served his drinks. It was a psychological fact that food and beverages tasted better when served with heavy, expensive cutlery and tumblers. But most of all, private members' clubs were the only territories possessed by the rich in which the rich didn't aggravate him. Despite the clienteles' effort towards a laissez-faire demeanour, their unobtrusiveness projected disquiet. It was as if they felt that while money was enough to feel relaxed in an expensive restaurant, here you also had to *do* something or *be* somebody interesting. It was as if, despite having growing up with all this splendour and exclusivity, they'd remained as awkward with their surroundings as he was. Therefore, this territory was somehow neutral.

Holding his mobile tight to his ear to muffle the music, David said, 'Look, Pete, call me on Monday. It's Friday night. I'd love to say that Tara and I are busy. But we're not. We're having fun. As we always do when we're not busy. This call is making me busy.'

'I'm *sooooooo* happy for you guys,' Pete's New York drawl slithered down the line. 'It must be *soooooo* super-fantastic to be able to la-de-da yourselves over that line between carefree and gross stupidity and still not give a single flying fuckity-fuck. And I get it, man. I really do. Seriously. You're an historian – an archivist for those in the future. But I'm an art dealer – an archivist for those in the very fucking present. And *presently* the recent reviews have been *soooooo* "meh".'

'I don't read reviews, Pete.'

'David, I need an answer now.'

David threw back his Bushmills, tapped the empty glass on the bronze-plated counter to attract the barman and said, 'OK, quickly give me the question again.'

'Can we put them three onto the—'

'*Those* three,' David automatically corrected, just to annoy him, while simultaneously thinking what a waste of money and resources Harvard had been for that prick.

'Jesus! Can we put them onto the auctioneer circuit and see how they move or not?'

David grunted. He was trying to avoid that market for at least another year. When a new artist had their work peddled too early by auctioneers, it was the equivalent of having their wares appearing on second-hand market stalls. Basically, Sotheby's was the rich person's skip. For a moment, David had a dark vision of all their savings shrinking like ice caps over the coming decade or two. But then he glimpsed her. His wife. Tara, on the dance floor, in the middle of about ten people, moving to the music as if she was eighteen. The sight of her wiped his mind of all the boring responsibilities that Pete represented, making him feel as if, until that very moment, he'd been swimming in static.

David said, 'Look, I've got to go. Talk to you on Monday.'

Hanging up, he smiled as Tara continued dancing, oblivious to all around her. Her lips moved to the lyrics of the latest songs that David had never heard before. His tastes centred around music that was at least ten years old. And more recently, his dial had been stuck on classical. How did she do that, always remain aware of what was currently cool?

Shortly, Tara appeared beside him and he passed her a fresh vodka martini. She stared down into the glass as if it were something distasteful and took the tiniest of sips. Earlier, in another bar, she'd barely touched the vodka and tonic he'd placed before her. There was something very slightly off about Tara tonight, David thought. A little bit of distance that usually wasn't there. They hadn't really talked recently about her decreasing value in the art world. He'd explained to her a long time ago that it would only be a matter of time before she might be persona non grata, and Tara had replied, 'As in "persona-not-a-on-da-lista"?' before giving a so-fucking-what shrug – they'd already cashed their chips. David had believed her. But maybe she'd been fooling both herself and him.

'Come on Tara, what's up?'

'Nothing. Why?'

'Just tell me.'

'I don't know what—'

'You're not drinking. And *you think* you're not drinking because of whatever's up.'

'Bullshit.'

'But the real reason you're not drinking is so that you can show me that there's something up. So now that you've shown me, what is it?' David smiled sympathetically, looking to be taken back into her confidence, where he belonged. Always.

'Hey, you want another glass?' Tara knew how to distract her husband.

'Yeah,' he turned to the bar before immediately changing his mind. 'Nice try. Talk.'

'It's delicate.'

'Good – scandalise me.' David smiled, making light of the sudden ominous mood.

'I'm pregnant.'

David took a step back from the bar as if she'd shoved him. Tara suddenly looked strange holding the stem of the martini glass – like she was an adolescent trying too hard to be an adult.

'I've done the test three times. I'm pregnant.'

'How?' was all he could manage.

'Probably after the last time we were here. Remember, I had too many of these – after Vanessa's launch downstairs in Bollie's? I puked all night? Well, the pill must have been... *ejected* from my person.'

'Jesus…' David muttered. *Jesus! Jesus! Jesus!* 'Well, don't worry about it.'

'So what are we going to do?' She tried to lean casually against the counter, but her body was too tense to pull it off.

'…Jesus.'

Tara said, 'OK, I know you're not happy about this. I'm sorry.'

'It's not your fault. It's... no one's fault.' David was very aware that upstairs there was a rooftop bar with a fine smoking area. He'd been off cigarettes for two years and Tara had no idea how hard he still found it. He'd smoked since he was ten, and giving them up had been like losing a limb.

'David, what do you think?'

'I don't know. I'm as shocked as you are.'

'But I'm not shocked.'

'Well, you were hardly planning it?'

'Of course not. But I can't explain it. I can just feel it. Jesus – not the foetus or any sentimental earth mother shit like that. I mean, I can just *feel* what I feel. And I *feel* calm. Not shock. Kind of like... This is no big deal. Like... Jesus... Don't get scared, but more like, this was, maybe, supposed to happen.'

David picked up his drink, swirled the ice but couldn't bring himself to throw it back because he wasn't sure if he could swallow. He'd imagined something like this happening, and it was always followed by the certainty that they'd just 'take care of it'. Many of their friends had done so. David and Tara's lives were rolling along nicely, following the path that they'd carefully planned. A kid was *not* part of that plan. Neither of them had ever wondered what it would be like to be a parent. Both of them actually pitied their harassed and stressed colleagues who had families to think about rather than just themselves.

Tara said, 'Christ, I do sound like a sentimental earth mother asshole. Right, that's me told. C'mon – let's catch the morning flight to London before it's too late.' Tara laughed at her own dark humour, but only her lips and throat laughed. Her eyes remained the same – staring, observing, waiting.

David had to look away, and so pretended to scan for a waitress. Sometimes his wife's attention was uncomfortable, like the surgeon's stare just before you go under. David believed – or thought he believed – that there was so much life in this world, people were prone to exaggerate its sanctity. Tara had agreed. But had she really? It was easy to feel that way when it's not your finger that has to turn off the machine, press the syringe, pull the trigger. David was surprised that something in him was dismayed at his initial eagerness to correct course quickly and set this error to rights. After all, this pregnancy was asking questions of him. And by ignoring all the questions and just inventing certainty – wasn't that just the syntax of the righteous?

Tara said, 'I mean, I may be the one who's pregnant but I know nothing about being pregnant. I never had a mother, remember. I've no role model.'

David thought of the house they had just designed and were building. It was huge. It would enjoy nourishing, warming, protecting a child. The environs of Lawrence Court – the schools and friends – would be like a preschool for success. The fact was, he and Tara could afford to give this baby the life that neither of them had ever had. He remembered the road he'd grown up on. All the houses had had two normal bedrooms and a dreary, small box room. That had been cramped but manageable for his parents, himself and his sister. Across the road, however, there had been a family with eight kids aged three to seventeen. When they were going to school in the morning, their front door would open and they would emerge like clowns exiting a tiny clown car.

'I skipped my period,' Tara continued. 'And now if I don't do something about it, I won't bleed for nine months. That's it. That's what I know about pregnancy. I switch off when the girls who have kids talk about being fucking mothers.'

This time David managed to sip his drink. *Does having a kid ever get boring? Aren't they supposed to surprise you in both good and bad ways forever? Wouldn't it be an adventure, the way clubs, bars and restaurants one day won't be?* He and Tara would be great parents. He just knew that, the way he knew that the sun would rise.

*What the hell am I thinking?*

Tara continued, 'Like, when I'm out with Joan and she's loading her kids into the car, I think, "Joan used to be cool. Now she listens to EasyRock104 while pulling on her slacks. She's planning a *great* day out to Ikea to get feathers for the nest. She pretends to get excited over the new menu at the local Italian." But now I'm thinking: "Fuck – I don't think her life is so bad any more. Fuck – I don't think I *ever* really believed it was so bad. I'm beginning to think that I just *told* myself that. Fuck – what is happening to me?"'

David's feelings continued to seesaw from a sense of potential great adventure to impending certain doom. *I have everything I want – Tara, our new house and finally, somewhere in the future, scholarly recognition. A kid would ruin all of that.* And suddenly he had two revelations: that life is dull when you know exactly who you are, and that it is terrifying when you don't. In this way, the potential of them being parents was both thrilling and frightening.

A botoxed wannabe model approached and began to list an array of special cocktails on offer that night. David politely waved her away. He and Tara picked up their drinks and walked from the bar, passing between the tables until they reached the middle of the club and stopped at the same time. As if they'd rehearsed it.

Tara neutralised her expression and said, 'This conversation isn't going the way I expected it to.'

David lowered his head. He hated to disappoint her. He wanted Tara always to assume that he would be there for her. 'I'm sorry. I genuinely didn't mean to give you the impression that I'm not in this with you. We'll always be, no matter what, team Tara and David – Masters of *our* Universe. Anyone who gets in the way of you and I doing what we want will tremble and weep under the might of our unapologetic self-centredness.'

Tara laughed. 'No, of course I know you're with me. What I mean is, I thought you'd be horrified, and that right now you'd be even more horrified at the realisation that I'm... kind of... open to it.'

Were they actually going to do this? Were they going to have a baby?

Tara said, 'So are you? Are you open to it as well? Before you answer, realise that there is no wrong answer. A yay or nay is the direction we'll take. Team David and Tara forever! So, your answer is?'

David was almost afraid to say yes. It was as if she was daring him to be as brave and adventurous as her. Instead, he leaned in and kissed her and kissed her and kissed her.

How long had David been sitting on the side of the bed? Five minutes? Twenty? His feet, resting on the wooden boards, were numb. Why was the room so cold? It had been another day of the summer heatwave. For weeks now, people young and old had been wearing short sleeves and no jackets at night. He glanced back to the bed. Tara, always so aware of the cold, had at some stage kicked off the duvet and was only half-covered by the light under-sheet. *What the hell's wrong with me? I can't sleep. I can't get warm.*

David walked over to the window. Sitting on the sill, he lifted the edge of the curtain and gazed into the darkness of his garden. *This could be my first* and *penultimate night here, in my bedroom, with my wife who is now as distant to me as an old fling. I lost it all before I ever had time to get used to it.*

David remembered just about three years ago, when the first of the big money had gone *ker-plonk!* into their account. He had felt like a gangster who had pulled off the perfect crime. Within a week, he had finally discovered why a Boss suit cost so much money, and had bought a BMW and meals in three fantastic restaurants. Quickly they'd booked a break to the Caribbean. How they'd embraced the sheer unimaginable joy of flying first class, the wonderful trashy opulence of it, the magnificent vulgarity.

As David squinted out into the night now, something suddenly moved at the end of the garden: something real, something solid, something that was definitely not a figment of his exhausted brain. A man emerged from the forested area, stepping over the red-brick pathway and onto the grass. He moved across the lawn, heading directly for the house. Was the kitchen door locked? Yes. Was the alarm on? Yes. Were the outside security beams wired? Yes. The entire lawn abruptly blazed into light and David half-shielded his eyes.

The intruder stretched his arm and pointed up to the bedroom window. With raised thumb, he mimed a fired sniper shot. Then he retreated back into the shadows and the woodland closed behind him like a gate.

David listened to his own breathing, wanting to convince himself that what had just happened *had not* happened. But the evidence remained from the security light blasting down from the roof, bright enough to illuminate half a football pitch. Who had it been? What had he looked like? David closed his eyes and tried to focus on what he'd seen – but all he'd perceived was a faceless figure, the outline of a man in blinding light, miming a gunshot. *I should call the police.* David listened to the thought and had to stop himself from laughing. Tara would never let him go out there. He felt like waking her just so that she could make the decision for him, just so he could feel brave by staying by his frightened wife's side.

David stared down at Tara as if about to identify her body. Sometimes he found it a relief to look at her when she was sleeping.

When she was awake, her eyes seemed to have a particular view of the world that granted her insight and deductive force when dealing with men. It often disturbed him. Sometimes he was afraid that she could read his mind.

Silently, he left the bedroom, and on the landing quickly stepped into his trousers and loafers. He descended the stairs and moved towards the kitchen slider. His body was heavy – soggy with lack of sleep. A damp, pale light had already begun to seep into the air; the opposite of the rosy-fingered landscape dawns of romance. A force was tugging at his shoulder, trying to turn his head and focus his attention back into the hallway/gallery where a door led to the bar. *Have a primer first.* Five fifty a.m. Last night, alcohol had grounded him, solidified his thoughts. Now there was just anxiety and a woolly fatigue behind his eyes, the empty cavern where hope had been. But alcohol could bring the heat of that back. It could get him in touch with his primitive emotions once more. *No. I'm not* that *guy. I can deal with this alone.*

David stared through the glass to the woodland. He knew he was being watched. But by who? It definitely wasn't Gordon. The mere idea of Gordon standing in his garden at five fifty in the morning was beyond ridiculous. And anyway, Gordon had no reason to spy on him, to harass him. However, David was reminded of the unease he'd felt earlier in his office with Gordon – the feeling that there was something else going on. Something that was contained in Gordon's slight twitches and rare hesitancies. Something that was behind the scenes. Detective Fenton had mentioned that Ryan had been a 'person of interest'. What did that mean? Why were the police so interested in Ryan's disappearance after only twenty-four hours? *Everything is connected. It has to be.* It was beyond a coincidence that after David had killed a man and had begun to be blackmailed by his architect, a lone nutcase could trespass on his land at 5.50 a.m. and gesture ominously at him. *Whatever is going on down there in the woodland, I'll find out.*

Whoever the intruder was, he could be hoping, praying, that David would leave the sanctuary of the house to do something stupidly brave. But in twenty-four hours, David might leave this building for the last time in a police car. In twenty-four hours he could lose his wife, and his child before it was even born. Before any of that happened, he had the chance to act like the man he'd always assumed he was; the man who could protect his family, his home. *This is my house. That is my wife upstairs. It's my child inside of her.*

He flicked off the beam-activated security lights. Then, opening the kitchen door, he stepped out onto the patio and quietly closed it behind him. He was surprised at how calm he felt and wondered if he was simply getting used to trauma – the way people in unlucky parts of the world get used to air-raid sirens. David walked forward, onto the lawn, towards the trees, without any fear that he would never return. Even if there was only one single night that he would ever spend in his house, he would defend it, he would protect his sleeping wife, he would keep his unborn child safe. It was as if he'd always known that this moment would arrive.

# CHAPTER FOUR

It frightened Tara, how close she was to losing everything. On top of what had happened last night with David, Ryan's wife was now due to arrive within the hour. And so, after sleeping in till ten, Tara quickly began to apply mascara, concealer, cherry lip tint and a subtle blusher to finish over her cheeks. She'd only started wearing daily make-up in the last year, and it often made her feel like a little girl raiding her mother's vanity bag – which was strange, because she hardly remembered her mother.

Since last night, life had taken on an intensely hungover quality as she staggered about through the debris of her marriage. Why couldn't Ryan's attentions have been enough for her? Why hadn't it been sufficient simply to know that she *could've* had him? Instead, she'd needed to step back into the past, to when the secret of a well-lived life had only encompassed two things, lust and learning, and nothing else.

Tara put herself back in Trinity and remembered being amazed at how David had brought more light into the classroom than the windows did. She saw herself outside the Shelbourne Hotel, standing at the top of the steps beneath the portico, David embracing her, lifting her up, squeezing her, and her looking to the sky and feeling as if he was going to fling her into the sun. David was the one irreplaceable object in her life. After the next personal or professional victory, there would be more victories. After you make money, there would be more money to make. But after true love, there was just bitter, salty grief.

Would she be able to continue her pregnancy without David? Would it be possible? Tara contemplated the effort that would be involved in keeping the child safe, healthy and happy if she ended up alone. Children were in perpetual proximity to brain injury, dehydration, drowning, sunstroke. Tara sensed how little she understood about what was coming next. For weeks, her pregnancy had mostly just seemed like the anticipated arrival of a cool new piece of kit. She had a vague feeling, like a divination, of her approaching powerlessness, when her child's needs would immediately take priority over her own. Recently, her friends had been trying to become involved with her pregnancy, already buying her dinky little socks, tiny pants, doll-like shoes – which for Tara often felt like they were preparing her for some imminent catastrophe. One had told her, 'Tara, I don't think you have a clue. When it arrives, you'll realise that babies are real work. It's not like painting or your old insurance job. It's going to turn your life upside down. It'll be a high-wire act just to get through the day. Motherhood is permanent. It's there. It's there. It's there. But there's one other thing – I've yet to meet a mother who regrets having children.'

Tara looked down at her waist. From the moment she'd known she was pregnant, it had been her stomach that had drawn all the external attention. Soon the bump would begin to show. Most pregnancies became visible after twelve to sixteen weeks. About a month after that the 'quickening' would occur; the first faint fluttering movements of the baby in her womb. Apparently, for some parents, that was when the baby finally became alive.

'Become alive,' Tara whispered. She imagined the baby moving inside of her, growing stronger, getting ready to appear into the light. 'Make things better with me and David.'

As she went downstairs, her mobile buzzed. *Is it Christine – already?*

'Tara? It's Pete in New York.'

'Oh.' Tara had met Pete a few times, but had never spoken with him on the phone. He was just like any twenty-something American stockbroker, except that instead of being a stockbroker, he was an art dealer for private collectors and high-end commercial galleries.

'Yeah – "oh". Sorry to be calling, but obviously it's important otherwise I wouldn't be calling. There's those contracts – David probably told you about them – they needed to be OK'd by the end of last week. We delay any longer, and Soho & Lanes are going to start pounding you with subpoenas like they're predator drones.'

Tara blushed as if it was somehow possible that Pete knew how bad things were between David and her. 'I'm sure David's dealing with it – call him.'

'That's just it. He's not answering at his office. And he's not picking up his mobile. And that's odd. Dave always takes my calls. So where's Dave?'

*I wish I knew. And I wish he was here with me now. And I wish he'd forgive me. And I wish we were still indestructible.* Brightly, she said, 'Today my husband has arranged to be unreachable. Hence, I cannot reach him. Can I help?' Unexpectedly, a gripping shudder ran through her. What if David was missing, too? Then she relaxed into the relief that her husband was not like Ryan.

'OK – basically I'll give you the news that I was going to give him, which is: I don't get those contracts back, like yesterday, then we all get fucked in the eye sockets.'

Tara looked about the front room. Next to the TV was a media centre with a flashing modem, the DVR and other assorted lumps of equipment – one of which looked like a fax. She said, 'Send them again. I think there's a fax machine here.'

'You want me to *fax* it to you? How about I send it in Morse code? Or use smoke signals? Fuck, I'll just staple it to a pigeon's chest. Jesus Christ – do you guys still get your porn from magazines?'

'I was just trying to help.'

'There, I emailed it. Check your inbox. And show it to David. Later.'

Tara lingered in the hallway gallery. While the success of *Erdős Landscapes* had come out of nowhere – or rather, David had conjured its triumph from nothing – it wasn't necessarily the scale of the success that gave Tara the most pleasure. It was the fact that she'd stayed true to her ideals – that popular art didn't have to be commercial art. She'd also succeeded in an art world that was almost by definition masculine. Tara believed that most of the male painters she'd met were in love with being an artist, rather than with the work itself. They were the epitome of Renoir's observation that too many painters spend their time fucking beautiful women rather than painting them.

As she soaked up her work, Tara again experienced the sensation of being past her prime. It had been happening a lot recently. She was simply too old to start again. She'd never be able to do what she'd done so effortlessly just ten years ago – hustle her way in among the Dublin youngsters, get a first class degree, leave a pensionable job just because the city had felt alive and vibrant, as if it had a real arts scene – Paris in the 1920s, New York in the 1970s, London in the 1990s. Where had that Tara gone? For the last few months, she'd been so involved in designing her house that she'd rarely even thought of painting, never mind actually taking the time to lose herself in the private language of her work. But now that the house was finished, the old hunger had still not returned. Was that what pregnancy did? Gave you something else to fight for? Revealed all the other things as the baggage they were?

Sometimes, the free-floating anxiety that had hovered above Tara since she'd discovered she was pregnant threatened to collapse on her like an avalanche. Even if she was still painting, she'd never land another bonanza like David had managed to secure for them. And even though the museums were still interested in her, they didn't pay much, merely slowed down the extinction of her reputation. But it had been this art, and the year she'd spent making the rounds of all the openings, galas and launches – catching the light of every flash – that had got them what they'd wanted. Now most of their money was about to be gobbled up by the building society's bridge loan. After that, the remainder would be incinerated with school and medical fees and all the other expenses that would come from being responsible for something other than themselves. That was assuming David would stick with her. The mere idea that he wouldn't was almost impossible to imagine. But if the worst did happen, would she eventually accept his absence and drift back into insurance? Would she disappear into the countryside and live in solitude with her child? Would she move back to her home town? Without David, all these nightmares suddenly became her only options.

Until recently, Tara had never been one for reminiscing. As far as she'd been concerned, old times were only good when you were there. But in the last year, Tara had found herself scrolling back through her Facebook page, digging out old photos, exploring the online street maps of her home town. She'd even taken a trip back for the weekend, but had found the questions unending once she'd arrived there. Was the journey down OK? *It was.* How is the painting going? *It's fine.* Is Dublin fun? *It is.* Have you got a man? *I do.* And that was just the shopkeeper. This was also the first year that she'd hated the idea of her birthday: preferring not to tell her friends that she was thirty, to let it blow by, only checking for the damage in its aftermath.

Tara looked into the front room and decided against bringing Christine in there – too formal. She tried to superimpose her father sitting in the Eames chair, reading the paper with his big black glasses perched on his nose, relaxing after a day's work, waiting for his daughter to finish frying the kidney and onions in the tiny kitchen. He had regarded his widower life patiently – as if it was simply a long moment that must be endured. Was that why he'd decided to place a shotgun in his mouth? Had the years since her mother's death become so leaden and weary that it had been as if a single year was just repeating itself over and over? Maybe he'd seen nothing ahead of him that he would enjoy, and when he'd looked back he'd seen nothing that he wished to remember? A child was meant to be enough to make a parent carry on, but Tara's existence hadn't been sufficient for him. She accepted that her father had failed in his responsibility to her. But his death meant that she had somehow disappointed too.

She entered the kitchen and began to make her breakfast shake. Moving around, she enjoyed the smooth quality of the drawers as they opened and closed like the doors of expensive cars. Bundled in the corner was an antique throw – a present from the curator of the New York Soho Gallery – that had, initially by accident, become Dora's favoured bedding.

'Dora, honey – *pussss-pussss-pussss*. Come on, sweetie. Brekkie.'

Tara sat at the counter and sipped her smoothie. She was now waiting for Christine, and she couldn't think of anything else besides waiting for Christine. She knew very little about this woman, except that she had no kids, and Tara assumed that both she and Ryan were happy with that. Tara felt that, like most durable marriages, Christine and Ryan's was a comfortable habit neither wanted to break. However, she'd never spoken to Ryan about his wife or, in fact, about anything of real importance. Even when they'd been dating all those years ago, he'd rarely discussed his dreams, ambitions or his secret thoughts. It was probably why, in her early twenties, she'd become briefly infatuated with him – she'd seen Ryan as an exasperating crossword clue that she just couldn't solve and couldn't get out of her mind.

*It'll be fine. After last night with David, you're due luck.* The doorbell sounded. *Jesus.* For a moment, the colour went out of everything. Tara took a deep breath, walked through the gallery and opened the door.

Christine wore an open summer coat, a knee-length black skirt, teeter-tall heels and a tiger-print Prada top that showed lots of cleavage. Silver necklaces dangled beneath her throat. But what surprised Tara more than this medley of odd clothing was how old Christine looked. She was only in her early thirties but looked well into her forties, with a face that promised interesting stories in a hotel bar. The sides of her chin were grooved like a ventriloquist's doll, which emphasised how her botoxed forehead was as smooth as polished clay. With thick, straw-blonde hair, dark eyeshadow and brown lipstick, the overall effect was of someone who used to have money and now struggled to maintain the appearance of being an aristocratic bohemian.

'Christine, how are you?'

Christine attempted to raise her botoxed eyebrows. 'I'm fine. Well, not really. But it's good to be here, to be doing something, you know?' Her plummy, moneyed accent was sprinkled with BBC inflections, which Tara assumed were also counterfeit.

'Well, come in.' Tara ran her tongue around her lips. Her mouth was dry. *This is good. This is not violent. This is not a terrible scene.* She suppressed a grimace at the harsh echo of Christine's heels on the reclaimed floor; she half-expected to see actual footprints forced into the maple wood. So this was Ryan's wife. Tara pictured her over a decade ago as the type of ambitious twenty-year-old blonde who, after doing a six-week fashion and design diploma, got a job behind the make-up counter of a high-end store and within a year was the shop-floor supervisor. It was a lot to infer from just one minute of Christine's company, but Tara trusted her first impressions.

As Christine passed through the hallway, she stopped to admire one of the paintings.

'My art,' Tara said, redundantly. One just like it had been bought two years ago by an internet mogul for ten thousand euros. It was probably only worth one thousand now. The mogul kept

Tara's painting with the rest of his collection on his yacht – fifty million dollars of art, anchored in the Gulf of Mexico.

'When Ryan told me that he was working on a famous artist's house, I googled you.'

'Not really "famous".'

'You *are* famous. Like I said, I googled you.' Christine was briefly annoyed, clearly believing that modesty was one of the more boring traits a person could have.

'Well, I suppose I was on *Sky Arts* once for all of two minutes. They just needed a face rather than art – a kind of artist-itute. Jesus, "artist-itute". That's awful. And hence why I shouldn't ever be put in front of the camera.'

'Well, no matter what happens, you'll have done this.' Christine nodded at the nearest painting. 'That's your mark. Your thumbprint on the world. The rest of us – we will never be known.'

'God, I don't care whether I'm remembered. My moment has passed. The art world is cruel if you're not producing.'

'Just because you're having a baby doesn't mean you can just quit. Who do you think you are? A till operator at Spar?'

Tara forced a smile. *How often has Ryan talked about me to Christine? I can't believe he told her I was pregnant. Only a handful of people know. It's not public knowledge yet. The prick.* She tried to picture them having dinner together at home, but couldn't. In almost a whisper, she said, 'I hope we're mature enough for the responsibility. For the baby, I mean.'

'Ryan and I wanted children. Didn't happen.'

'Shit, I didn't realise that.'

'It's no big deal any more. Hasn't been for years.'

'Still, sorry – I shouldn't have been so blasé about mine. But it's just early days in the first trimester. It's all still so new.'

'No worries. It's me who asked. Honestly, it's not "a thing". I find the best way not to be always full of regret is to be bitter about it.' She smiled broadly. 'Kidding. Sort of.'

Something about Christine didn't make sense. Her eyes were deep mahogany and stared with a self-assuredness that was at odds with her appearance. The nebula of worn-out, downmarket glamour that haloed her did not tie in with her composure. Tara wondered if Christine really was just all smoke and mirrors. Had there been something else to her once – something before her marriage to the ladies' man Ryan had ground her down?

Christine got up close to another painting and said, 'What is it about me and kids, huh? I don't have any, but I work with them and I basically married one.'

Tara laughed awkwardly. 'Ryan. He's impossible to imagine as old.'

'Yeah. Me and Ryan go way back. We grew up in the same small town, you know? Went to the same small school. Though I was a few years ahead of him.'

'That's so romantic,' Tara said, forcing a big smile.

'Not really. I hated everything about my life until I was eighteen and got out of there. Clunnard is so hillbilly, the KKK would be the liberal party. You're from the country as well, aren't you? Ever go home?'

'Not if I can help it.'

'What about your family? They must be pleased with your success? After all, they created the artist. So people like me would presume you had a... an *interesting* childhood.'

'My family isn't interesting.'

'Every family is interesting.'

'My mother died when I was very young. I can't remember her.' *Why are we talking about my family? I need to lighten this. We haven't even got to Ryan yet.* 'Then Dad died when I was fifteen.' *Jesus. I said, lighten it.*

'That's sad. How did he die?'

'Just suddenly. One of those things.' Tara didn't like people knowing about her father. When people knew, they tried to draw her out, bond with her maybe, show her how empathic they were. She placed a hand on Christine's elbow now and gently nudged her forward.

As they entered the kitchen, Christine's face warped as if she'd just swallowed a mouthful of salt.

Tara said, 'We mixed styles for the kitchen: industrial meets farmhouse. You hate it that much?'

Christine laughed: an unpleasant burst of nasal noise. 'Oh, that's my thinking face. Ryan hates it. Everyone does.' She clapped her hands, and as if addressing students visiting a museum, proclaimed, 'It's just like Ryan described. Very classical noir and industrial. Just love the pop-up plug in the island.' Christine pressed down on the spring-loaded pad and up jumped a hidden socket tower. 'Nice range, too – ye olden world holler-back. It's all very pretty and very clever.'

Tara, a country girl, a woman who had had to work hard and take risks for everything she'd ever got, bristled with the awkward inability to take a compliment casually. 'Well, it was a once in a lifetime opportunity.'

'The house a talented artist deserves. You're obviously someone with discriminating taste *and* money. My mother would've loved this place. She loved the rich but she didn't know anyone rich besides Father. I suppose she loved them from afar.'

*Of course*, Tara thought. So that was where a building developer's wife got her plummy accent, her lavish mishmash bohemian style, the rocks on her fingers. She came from money. But she certainly didn't have any great wealth now. When had she lost it all? Or perhaps she had never been given any of it in the first place? *I wonder, was it Ryan's fault? Did her parents disapprove of him? Did he spend it all?*

Tara was now beginning to wonder what Christine was doing with a man like Ryan. Confidence and magnetism were two of her defining characteristics. She was clearly someone who always deserved to be in the room. On top of all that, Christine was three years older than Ryan. Tara simply couldn't see a woman like her deciding to settle down with a builder, even one that managed his own construction firm. She seemed too articulate, too pretentious, not to have seen through him the way Tara herself had done.

It had only taken Tara six months to realise how Ryan's mind operated. He'd simply had the astonishing arrogance of a young man who knew that he wasn't very brilliant, but must convince the world that he *is* brilliant – at something, at anything. So the gift he portrayed himself master-commandant of was seduction – and he aced all the tricks. Ryan never told a beautiful woman that she was beautiful, assuming she would already know that. Instead, he hoped she'd notice it when he went on talking to her without acknowledging it. That she'd find it interesting. Many beautiful women are rarely told they're funny, so he would always make sure to laugh during the conversation. On the other hand, he *always* told more ordinary women that they were beautiful, anticipating that they hadn't been told that before and their gratitude would have no frontier.

Christine grimaced as Dora passed by and rubbed against her ankle. 'Sorry. I have a rule concerning cats – anything smaller than a lion is vermin. No offence, of course.'

Tara smiled. *Fuck you.* 'No problem,' she said, and shooed Dora into the library.

Both women sat side by side at the island and folded their arms on the marble counter. Tara cleared her throat and just as she was going to ask about the latest on Ryan, Christine enquired, 'So I take it you're happy with your new house?'

'It's exactly what we wanted. Everything about it is fantastic.' Tara blinked, warning herself not to use inappropriate adjectives around Ryan's worried wife.

'Yes. Lucky you had a genius for an architect. I mean, of course Gordon can be a trial. But you just have to remind yourself that it's nothing personal – he's like that with all humans.' Christine looked back out into the hall, almost as if she was expecting Ryan to come down the stairs at any moment. 'So Tara,' she continued. 'You were happy with my husband?'

*Here we go*. 'The whole crew were fantastic.'

As Christine opened her coat and shrugged it off, Tara almost gasped at the sight of her large chest, now mostly exposed by the deep V of her tiger-print top. She tried not to stare, but it was like trying not to squint into direct sunlight. By shedding one layer of clothes, Christine had gone from faux-bohemian aristocrat to busty middle-aged barmaid. Tara could certainly see what Ryan had appreciated in her. He'd always liked the bad girls, especially the older ones.

Christine asked again, 'But were you happy with *him* – Ryan?'

'Of course. You do know we're old friends?'

'That's why I'm here. Besides collecting his car. At least, I think it is. The truth is, it just feels like I'm doing something. It feels like I'm trying. You know?'

'Trying?'

'Trying to get him back.' Christine delicately removed a tear without smudging her eyeliner. 'I know he hasn't been gone long, but I want to see what he saw before he vanished.' For a moment Christine smiled, showing off straight teeth that were slightly stained from decades of coffee and red wine. But then her eyes welled again and she placed a forefinger horizontally beneath her nose. 'It's like, one day he was just taken from the earth. Literally.'

'It must be awful for you. Not knowing anything. All kinds of things must be going through your head. You must be so worried.'

'I passed "worried" yesterday. Now I'm at the "out of my fucking mind" stage.'

'So when did you first... notice?'

'I was out at a meeting in St James' Home... the Future is our Youth centre?'

Tara shook her head and shrugged. She'd never heard of it.

'I'm a counsellor there. It's a special needs school for kids who never had a chance; kids with drug issues and the like.'

Tara suddenly remembered vaguely overhearing Gordon and Ryan chatting about Christine's exalted reputation and sway in the world of the social services, and so nodded solemnly in acknowledgement of her good work.

'Anyway, the meeting went on late and then we had to tidy up. No out-of-hours cleaners with the cutbacks. So I didn't get home till one. Ryan's SUV wasn't there, but sometimes he works very late. And when he comes in, he stays up gaming to unwind. In the morning, Ryan usually gets up first, makes me breakfast, leaves with a sausage and bacon roll. But not yesterday. He just wasn't there. So I phoned him and no answer. He was supposed to be here at your house to wrap up, but no one had a clue where he was. When did you last see him?'

'It must've been the day he went missing. We just chatted briefly. He was in good form.' Tara remembered his brown eyes drilling into hers. She pictured his smirk. She could smell his minty chewing-gum breath, the vague scent of stale but manly sweat on his work clothes. She remembered his touch – firm, knowing, wanting. She remembered the damp heat between her legs. She remembered experiencing a type of shame that she reckoned a clean junkie must feel when about to shoot up for the first time in ten years. She remembered Ryan lying across the floorboards, his naked, muscular body stretching to yawn. She'd liked that he was shaved of all pubic hair. Despite being the same age, it had made her feel like the older woman. *Jesus, when did I learn to think so darkly?*

Tara felt herself blush, and the more aware she became of it, the redder she became. 'Anyway, you mustn't think negative thoughts. Wait till you see. Everything will be fine.'

'Do I look like a woman who jumps to conclusions?'

Tara was startled by the blaze in Christine's eyes. So she was angry. Tara wondered if underneath it all she ever felt any other way. 'No. I'm sorry. I just meant that... I *guarantee* you, Ryan is fine.'

'And you know this how?'

'Because I've worked with him closely over the last six months. The guy is earthed.'

'So Ryan is sane and therefore can't be missing? Bad things cannot happen to him? Is that what you're saying?'

Already the conversation was going exactly where Tara didn't want it to go. 'No. Sorry. I'm just…' She suddenly had a brainwave. 'Oh, a detective called in last night to ask about Ryan.' Tara smiled, almost triumphantly. Christine could now feel secure in the knowledge that while she was sitting there being difficult, the police were working away at finding her husband.

'A detective? *Here*? Asking about Ryan? *My* Ryan?'

'Yes.' Tara abruptly sensed that there was something she'd overlooked. Something that she hadn't taken into consideration. 'Detective Fenton. He'd mentioned talking to you.'

'What did he ask you?'

'He didn't have much to say, really... Just that Ryan was a person of interest.' And suddenly Tara reckoned that she understood Christine's guarded behaviour – her husband was obviously mired in an embarrassing legal investigation that she'd hoped to keep private.

'Right…' Christine looked as if she was fighting against the urge to lose herself in her thoughts.

'Have you any idea as to what's going on?'

'Yes, I have my suspicions. There are *things*... There are *people*... whom Ryan didn't like. People whom he had *difficulties* with. I know I'm being all wishy-washy, but…' Listening to Christine talk was like drowning in euphemisms. 'I can't really go into it.'

Tara failed to suppress a trace of annoyance in her expression. *If things are private, then don't bring them up in the first place.* But not wanting to embarrass Christine any further about her husband being a 'person of interest', Tara put the kettle on and asked, 'Coffee? Tea? Or a glass of something?'

'I noticed the impressive bar in the front room. Like, I *really* noticed it. And with all this stress, I could murder a drink. So if you're partaking, I shall too.'

'Oh, not with my pregnancy. Boring old herbal tea, I'm afraid.'

Christine looked as if she'd just experienced the downer of having met someone for a night out and the first thing they'd said was that they were 'taking it easy'. Her fingers, all ten of them, were on the edge of the island counter. 'God grant me the serenity to accept the things I cannot change, to change the things I can, and the wisdom to know the difference. Just kidding. Red, please. I know it's before noon… But with all that's happening, what the hell.'

The cork creaked and then popped. Tara placed the full glass and the bottle on the counter next to her own herbal tea, the bag still wrapped in its paper envelope at the edge of the saucer. Christine visibly struggled not to lick her lips. She lifted her wine glass with one rock-encrusted hand and downed half of it like she was necking a pint. Then she topped up her glass, raised it in a toast and announced, 'So, here's to you.'

Tara filled a bowl with crisps, then raised her herbal tea and clinked cup against glass.

Christine continued, 'To Tara Brown – the cunt who fucked my husband.'

# CHAPTER FIVE

David spent the morning wandering the streets near the university, drifting by shop displays containing all the things that people wanted him to want next. He was exhausted. Six hours ago, he'd chased a man over the back wall of his garden and watched as he'd disappeared between two houses to the road outside. For a moment it had felt like a real victory; David had gone down there to the woodland and successfully expelled the intruder. But who was he, and why was he sending a message that could only be read as, 'You're gettable'? Throughout the morning, David had returned again and again to the possibility that Gordon had sent him. But the architect had no reason to, and anyway, that type of intimidation just wasn't his style. But there had to be a connection. Ryan was missing. The police were already looking for him. Why?

*Does it even matter? Tomorrow, I'll be in jail. I can't give it all away – the house, our future, everything we'd ever got. I can't do that to my wife and child. But... but...*

David scanned through his address book and pressed 'call'. As he waited, he looked up at the face of the Shelbourne Hotel. Despite passing it by several times a week, he hadn't been inside it in over three years. *How close had Ryan come to picking Tara up that day instead of me? Maybe there hadn't been that enigmatic spark between me and Tara after all. Maybe there had only been good timing.*

Listening to the options, he pressed the required number and a human answered. 'KLT Deposits. Sandra Mahony speaking.'

Sandra had first met with David and Tara when the money had begun falling from the sky. Now, after David gave her twenty-four-hour notice of a *possible* transfer, Sandra said, 'Of course we can do that. But it's a highly unusual request.'

'I have plans. It's an investment. If I'm going ahead with it, I'll see you tomorrow morning. I'll call you if I'm not. I'll decide today what I'm doing. Talk to you then.'

*What have I just done? Wait – it means nothing. It's just an option. That's all. To have an option you'll never use is better than having no options at all.*

He walked on, leaving the Shelbourne behind. It surprised David, how alone he felt. All he'd really ever had was Tara and now she wasn't there for him any more. He suddenly realised that she hadn't yet set up her easel in Lawrence Court. In fact, he hadn't seen her paint in months. David had always liked Tara's tripod and trestle by their apartment window, where she would use her narrowest brush to sprinkle subtlety across the swathes of colour, as if tapping out the Morse code of the zeitgeist. But there was also a small part of him that had been relieved Tara was no longer painting. A critic had once told him that the existence of art and literature was proof that life was not enough. Did Tara believe that? Was *he* not enough?

Outside of Cawley, David had managed to live without conflict or enemies. But now he suddenly realised that having no enemies was not the same as having a lot of friends. David's family couldn't help him either. His father had died when he was eighteen and he wasn't even Facebook friends with his sister, who hadn't bothered to come back from Sydney for his wedding. Yet suddenly David was missing her as if she'd always been there but had recently vanished. As for his mother, it amazed him that people like her still existed: going to Mass, praying, walking the earth as if man had a soul and there was real hope. His mother lived in a world of community meetings, church groups and coffee mornings, and David wanted to keep her in that happy land of la-la until her final moment. He thought of the bills he'd recently settled for her nursing care, her meals on wheels, the minibus that packed her up off to the community centre three times a week. *How am I going to do that now?*

On his way back to the university car park, he glanced over at the fast-food joint where it had all really begun. He took out his mobile, dialled and after two rings, Gordon picked up.

'What do *you* want, Dave? I said that *I'd* be in touch. Why are *you* calling *me*?'

'You said the police wouldn't care about Ryan being missing.'

'Yeah?'

'Well, the police seemed to care when they were round with us last night.'

'The police? How many? What did they say?'

'A detective. He asked us about Ryan.'

Silence.

'Gordon, you still there?'

'Who was he?'

'As in his name? It doesn't matter.'

'Of course it matters.'

'Jesus, I don't know…' David immediately knew from Gordon's tone that he knew nothing about the man who'd been in David's garden aiming an invisible rifle up at his bedroom at five that morning.

'Maybe he gave Tara a card,' David suggested, though knew he hadn't. 'Detective Fenton, I think. He said Ryan was a "person of interest". His absence had been noted and they were concerned.'

Gordon's tongue loudly probed the marshy floor of his mouth as he sought a way to take control of the conversation again. 'Don't worry about it. They're just going through the motions. They'll be in touch with me next. I'll just waffle the shit out of it. Look, I'll text you tomorrow morning – just before we meet at the bank.'

David could feel Gordon's impatience to hang up, his desire to get his thoughts in order. So David disconnected first, denying his architect the opportunity to carry out one of life's great joys – slamming down the phone.

At 1 p.m. David left the university car park and drove to the Cawley corporation pitches, where he was due to patrol the sideline for his under-12s' crucial league match, and to try and give game time to all the substitutes on the panel, most of whom were beyond useless. St Augustine's, his team of under-12s from the estates, were gathered inside the concrete bunker that was the changing room. David remained outside smoking, watching his shadow stretch before him like a beanstalk as the blaze of the sun hit his back.

Out of pure habit, he checked his voicemail. 'Dave, it's Carla. There's a package couriered over from University College Galway for you. And the dean still wants to know if you'll speak at the symposium. No hurry or anything. But when—'

*MESSAGE DELETED. NEXT MESSAGE.*

'David, it's Tod in Boston. The Soho Gallery ain't biting. Not interested. And Solar have three returns outta four. Gotta say, that's disappointing. But I suppose, if we manage—'

*MESSAGE DELETED. NEXT MESSAGE.*

'Davy, it's your mam. A mad thing, really. Just read somethin' in the *Indo* about that auld pop singer you liked back when. Ya remember? With his awful orange hair and make-up. All those posters – you were a gas one, Davy. I've cut it out and kept it. Will give it to ya Sunday. Make sure to remind me. Ya know what I'm like. All my love to lovely Tara.'

*MESSAGE SAVED.*

The kids jogged out, their studs clicking on the concrete like stilettos. Their jerseys were emblazoned with the Downey's

Warehouse Importation logo; an honour for which David had ensured that the company he'd slaved nights for supplied the club with their entire kit.

Some of the kids passed without acknowledgement, others offered a gruff, 'Gaffer.' David nodded at his favourite kid: a shy, gangly Somalian whose father had been stabbed to death a year ago on a day trip to a playground. His name was Arthur Lord. It was the type of masculine name a young black lad needed to get by in a white-ruled working-class estate.

Today's fixture was a must-win match, as they'd already lost their first three games. David watched the opposition – Foxrock Rovers – disembark from their bus, most of them plugged into MP3 players. St Augustine's had to rely on volunteers to taxi them to away games. The Foxrock players were bigger than David's team. They were better conditioned and had cooler haircuts and leather gym-bags. Their parents gathered round the bus, clapping the boys as they landed on the asphalt. 'Attaboy, Ross,' a father shouted, like he was cheering his own racehorse. 'Do your best, Marcus,' called out a mother in jodhpurs.

Bruno emerged from the bunker adorned in a Downey's tracksuit, the rolled-up sleeves revealing pale hairy skin. He handed David his red coaching vest and then sighed. 'Did you hear Gordon yesterday?' asked Bruno. 'He does not know that men like me have to work hard to be this poor.'

David wanted to agree. He wanted to add his own condemnations to Bruno's. But he knew he had to play it smart. 'Gordon's fine. He's just a perfectionist. The fact that he chooses you to do stuff over the others means that he likes you. It means that you're great at your job.' *Could it have been one of Bruno's mates who was in my garden this morning? An attempt to wank off some of his resentment?* But David looked into his old friend's eyes and saw only the decency that had always been there.

As the team gathered round Bruno, David stared down the pitch to where the Foxrock Rovers were warming up. He counted seven members of their backroom team. *They're better than us because they don't know how to mess up like we do. Their factory settings don't permit them to put their future at risk by doing something insane like throwing a man out of the top window of their home. People like me are cautionary tales to people like them.*

David was suddenly very aware of the background he shared with his own team of young boys. With them, there were no holidays abroad or family meals out. With them, their parents greeted every windowed envelope with a dismal sigh. David's mum and dad had never owned passports or contraceptives or illegal narcotics, seen pornography or imagined life without betters. When David had informed his father that he wanted to be a historian it had been like saying, 'I've decided to be a ballerina.' His father had actually got chest pains. He'd almost literally had a heart attack.

'Lads, we all good?' David asked.

His question was met with stony silence. They were still wary of him. They refused to believe that he was of their tribe. Even now, as their coach, David's contributions on football were greeted with the raised eyebrows and smirks that he gave undergraduates whenever they dared offer a personal opinion rather than referencing the source material. But David didn't blame them – he had done everything in his power *not* to be like their parents, to leave them far behind for a university life where having an ordinary mid-level IQ consigned you to the bottom of the class. He was sure they all bitched about him when he wasn't around. A gang of twelve-year-old boys – they were already as bad as the Borgias.

Bruno shouted, 'We came here as team, we train as team and we play as team. We ready to take it to them? We ready to go the best?'

There were nods and the odd exclamation, but David knew that the kids were merely responding to Bruno's volume rather than the content. Bruno tried again, but David interjected with, 'Listen – because I'm going to tell you something very important; a fundamental truth. And if you understand it, then it'll help you, not just in this game but for the rest of your lives.' He pointed down the field to the Foxrock Rovers. 'When playing against their kind, in football or in life, you're all to forget about luck. Luck is for the rich and the connected. Luck is for those dicks.'

There was an audible gasp, a few sniggers and a 'Dave, that is enough' from Bruno. But David, who was very aware that this could be the last time he would ever address his team, wasn't finished. 'People like us don't have luck to rely on. We never did. We never will. For people like us, there is only work, discipline, talent and courage. That's all we've got. So use it. Use it all.'

As the boys disbanded, Bruno said, 'Dave, what is the matter with you? You can't talk to the children like that because... because they are fucking children!'

David strolled off down the sideline, passing a streak of about fifty parents, mostly from Foxrock. One of the fathers shook his hand because he was wearing the red vest of officialdom. The parents of his own team didn't acknowledge him. Many were his old schoolmates, but they rarely talked to him any more. Once they had discovered that he'd won a scholarship to the city's most prestigious university, they'd responded with an immediate unaccountable sense of distrust, which some rapidly nourished into a pathological hatred. But David reckoned he'd probably have felt the same way in their situation. They'd called him 'College Boy'; a nickname that had stuck with him in Cawley to this day.

As the game kicked off, someone behind him shouted, 'Will ya fuck'n move it, College Boy? You're not made of glass, ya prick.'

There was a rising roar. Foxrock Rovers were powering through St Augustine's defence, annihilating their backline before – *boom*

– top corner of the net. Less than a minute of play and they were one–nil down.

David's thoughts flipped through his crisis. *If only there had been a secret camera in the attic that had filmed everything. Then the world would know that it had been an accident. I didn't push Ryan out the window. I just punched him.*

Another roar from the sidelines. Foxrock attacking again. One-two. One-two. *Bang*. A ricochet off the crossbar and back out into play.

'Jazus, ya here to pick daisies?' shouted the husky, phlegm-pasted voice. A hand landed on David's shoulder. It felt like being hit with a block of wood. David turned round. The hand belonged to Fred – an almost bald, six-foot thug squeezed into a grimy tracksuit. Fred had been the fiercest street warrior when David had gone to school. At the base of his neck was a tattoo – 88. David had told Bruno that it was the numerical equivalent to HH: Heil Hitler. Bruno had tried to disbelieve that. 'People aren't *that* stupid,' he'd said, though knowing that *of course* they were.

'We're being murdered,' Fred said now. 'I don't have Bernard out training twice a week to be part of this shite. Here's an idea – take off that lanky monkey at midfield. That string of piss is barely off the banana boat and already you have him taking our kids' places in the club.' Fred inhaled a final drag on the stump of his rollie and flicked it past David onto the pitch. He was directly in David's face now, his neck bent, his gaping eyes protruding in outrage. 'Do something, College Boy. That's my lad out there, getting a second asshole torn into him by a bunch of fuck'n ponces.'

'Stay classy, Fred.'

Fred grabbed David by the throat, positioning his bald face at perfect headbutt distance.

'Jesus, Fred, your kid's out there!'

Fred made a phlegmy growl through gums housing only a handful of teeth and hoisted his apron of fat upwards. 'About time he saw what a real man is.'

David pushed forward, driving his aggressor backwards. Suddenly, from behind, Bruno's hands gripped his shoulders before an arm locked into place beneath his chin. The referee ran to the sideline, his whistle shrill. Everyone was shouting: parents from both teams, even some of the children. *This isn't me.* David registered expressions of disgust. He registered their disappointment and shock. In the midst of it all, he had a logical thought: *How can I claim that killing Ryan was a moment of madness? That I'd acted outside of reason? That violence is not part of my personality?* The mother in jodhpurs now stood between David and Fred, arms outstretched to separate them, a beseeching woman in an ageless story.

Bruno, sweat making a skullcap of his hair, led David away from the crowd. As the dressing room approached, he said, 'I heard what you say to the kids. I see you fight with Fred. You forget what it's like. You don't understand any more. Or maybe you just don't care any more. So go away, Dave. Go back to your big house and your big deal wife and your big deal university.'

'Jesus, Bruno, I didn't mean to... It was self-defence. I wasn't going to touch him. Look, I've too much on my mind.'

Bruno offered a universal shrug – the one that said, *Leave me out of your shit* – and released him to his own devices. David retreated towards his car, his back bent, shoulders rounded against the day's unrelenting artillery. His eyes hurt. The sun illuminated everything too harshly – the tree bark, the shining metal of the dressing room roof, the hedge leaves, which twinkled as if their edges were dipped in silver. There was a roar behind him. Another goal had been scored.

In the car park, a black Skoda flashed its headlights. David recognised the vehicle. The front passenger door clicked open.

‘Get in, buddy.’

‘Why?’

Detective Fenton smiled broadly. ‘Get. The fuck. In.’

David looked up to the blue sky and wondered if he would ever again take this familiar walk from the park to his own car. Sitting in the passenger seat, he closed the door. ‘So what’s the story, Detective Fenton?’

Voices sniggered behind him. Two men in tracksuits were in the back seat. One had a shaved head, the scalp thickly sown with moles; the other’s short hair was wet-gelled forward into a straight fringe. Both had eyes disappearing in the quicksand of their own sockets. David assumed that they were working undercover.

Fenton asked, ‘Gordon was meeting with you yesterday – why?’

‘He’s my architect. Architect things.’ David swallowed, but wasn’t concerned about trying to hide his anxiety. He assumed that all cops knew that people with any kind of interesting life were unable to be normal in front of them. ‘Anyway, how do you know?’

‘Did he mention Ryan?’

‘No... I mean, yeah. But just that there was no news. We simply have to get on with it. Like, finalise the snag list without him and all that. You’ve talked to Gordon, right?’

‘*I’m* asking the questions,’ Fenton said softly, making it clear that he didn’t like David, but also that David wasn’t important enough to make an issue of it.

‘Right you are, Detective.’

‘You’re still calling me that?’

‘That’s what you told me to call you, *Detective*.’

‘How did someone like you ever get to own that house of yours?’ Fenton asked, his accent changing, subtly but noticeably. It was harder, more Dublin city, less suburban estate. ‘*And then*, stick a hottie like your missus into it? Shit, man, are you like, retarded or something? I’m not a fucking detective.’

'Who are you then?' David's voice was almost a whisper as he suddenly realised that he was looking at a new shark from yet another sea.

'Believe me, you prick, we are your worst fucking nightmare. We are the guys in your garden at five forty-five in the morning. We are the reason rich fuckers like you have security systems. All those scary stories you hear at your posh dinner parties or read in the paper over breakfast in your *grand* fucking kitchen – yeah, that's us.'

David grabbed the door handle but Fenton placed a firm hand on his elbow. Everything was suddenly different now – a gun pointed at a man can do that.

# CHAPTER SIX

'I'm sorry,' was all Tara could manage. She heard her voice. She heard her statement. She'd never believed she could sound so pathetic, her voice so paltry. *This is a nightmare. The worst possible things keep happening.*

'No. *I'm* sorry.' Christine patted Tara's wrist with exaggerated earnestness. 'Here am I in your house, looking for attention like an I-don't-know-what.'

'Look, you've made your point. You've seen me. You hate me. I get that. I don't blame you. I'm sorry. And that's all I can say. Over and over again. Now leave. Please.'

'Ha! You think it's that easy? I will go when I've said what I want to say.'

'Look, you know it now. You found out. And you've made your point.' *What if David returns? Would he throw her out? No – he'd throw us both out.* 'Whenever Ryan turns up, sort it out with him. But until then, you can't take it all out on me.' *How did she find out? Ryan's been missing since he was with me.* 'How did... How did you find out?'

Christine laughed. 'It's amazing what a wife knows about her husband, Tara. See, Ryan and I have gone through so much over the years... More than you would believe. Did Ryan tell you that he got me pregnant back in school?' Christine waited for confirmation, but Tara just stared through her. So she continued, 'God, he was just so gorgeous back then. So I'm eighteen, pregnant and obviously I can't tell anyone. So I mark it return to sender. I mean, Ryan *is* a teenager too. So I sneak off to London…'

Unexpectedly, Christine suddenly forced herself to be quiet, as if she desperately wanted – *needed* – to talk, but was bound by confidentiality, like a priest in a confession box. The longer she remained silent, the more Tara wanted to hear. She had enough of her own secrets to have learned that the things really worth hearing are the things people absolutely refuse to speak about.

So Tara – both wanting to hear more, yet smarting from the fact that Ryan had never told her any of this – said, 'If you want to talk about it, talk about it. Or don't. I'm not your therapist.' *Ryan never told me he'd got a girl pregnant. He never told me that his child had been aborted.*

Christine smiled – acknowledging, perhaps even reluctantly admiring her foe's audacity. She piled three crisps on top of each other and crunched them in her mouth. After swallowing, she said, 'Up to then I'd grown up a little princess – the type of rich where it would be insane to have ever expected to *have* to get a job. So my parents found out about my abortion and threw me out. I never got a cent from them. The Church got it all. So, kicked out of home and school, I moved to London and did a social worker cert. Then I moved to Paris and worked for a homeless charity. Then back to Dublin, where I ran into Ryan again when he was renovating St James' Home. Four years ago. It was love at second sight. We married and tried for a kid, but it turns out that because of my earlier abortion I can't have children any more. But we stuck with each other – for a while. Because we were a team. We were partners.' Christine dipped her hand into the crisp bowl, but her fingers grasped at space. 'So, a four-year-old marriage and it was good for about two of them. When the economy booms, my god does it boom, and my god did we have a comfortable life for a while. And it's useful having a handyman around. But now I'm in love with someone else. And Ryan knows. He's always known. We're well past that drama at this stage.'

'So why are you here? Ryan and I was just the once. But you – you're *in love* with someone else.'

'And that's my point. I have standards. I wouldn't ever be with a *married* man. Do you understand, Tara? Is that making sense to you?'

Tara, who didn't need to hear a lecture, said, 'And you still expect me to feel sorry for you because I slept with your husband? Really?'

'*Sorry* for me? Oh, no – I don't expect that. After all, you're the type of woman who sleeps with married men, and therefore knowingly inflicts wounds on fellow sisters. Why would you do that? I mean, you had no idea that I don't love Ryan. You didn't know that at this stage we don't have a conventional type of marriage.'

'You don't have *any* type of marriage.'

'Oh, I have a marriage, Tara. And do you know how I know?' Christine sipped from her glass. 'Because you're the kind of woman that a wife does not want to catch her husband staring at.'

'Look, it's never going to happen again.'

'Yes, but only because Ryan has had his fun with you. I hope you liked being used? But I suppose I should be understanding – Ryan only tolerates reality because it allows him to screw unhappy women who are stranded there.'

'Fuck you,' Tara snapped. *I was happy. I should be happy now. I will be happy again.*

'Oh, don't be defensive. I'm not saying you're one of *those* unhappy women. You're unhappy in an entirely different way. In fact, that's why I'm here. You're nothing like the others have been over the years. So I was curious.'

'Curious? Christine, it's not a mystery. It was just the once... I don't know what I was thinking.'

'But Tara, you did know what you were thinking. And yes, it was just the once. But it *was* something. To him. To Ryan. See, my husband screws women. Lots of women. Women that are all the same. The type that think a peek up their little skirt will get a man to follow them around the world. But you – you're an oddity. You're something radically different to the usual sluts he sticks his dick into. And it's not just your money, though of course he likes being around it. Being close to it. Being *in* it. As I said earlier – you're not a cash girl in Spar. So that's one of the reasons I'm here – to witness for myself what he saw in you. Someone who is rich and successful and therefore should be content. And yes, I can see it now. Your distinctive type of sadness. It's the little-girl-lost eyes. The fear behind the courage. I finally get it. Because, of course, all men want their whores to be fundamentally unhappy.'

Tara straightened on the stool and stared at the countertop as if it were a desk and she was being scolded by a teacher. *Take it. You deserve it. Then she'll leave.* But she couldn't help but ignore her own advice. 'Look, let's not do the whole slut-shaming thing.' *What am I talking about? Why am I even talking? Just let her vent and leave.* 'I told you already that I'm sorry. But it was nothing. Just something stupid.'

'Just like the song.'

Tara didn't know what song she was talking about and now felt foolish as well as miserable. She wished Christine would go. Why wouldn't she leave? Christine had humiliated her – surely that was mission accomplished? Mortifyingly, she felt her eyes glaze with the threat of tears.

'So now that I've figured out what Ryan saw in you,' Christine continued, 'it still leaves me wondering what a woman like you saw in a married man like Ryan. As I've already said, you're not the vacuous type of slut like the others. No. Sluts like you don't sleep with a married man for no reason. You already have everything you've ever wanted.'

'I. Am. Sorry.'

'We're both women – experienced women. We both know that if you're lucky, you'll find a few men during your life that you're attracted to. Maybe you'll fall in love with one.' Christine picked up her glass and drained the red down. 'But women are not *into* men. Jesus. No woman in her right mind *likes* men. Look at them. Take a glance out your front window. Most of them are disgusting. So you chose him – carefully.'

*Take control. Get rid of her.* 'Right, we're done here.'

'So why did someone like you carefully choose a married man like Ryan? Wait. I think I know. Ryan is handsome and sensual and you have history. So you know Ryan very well – in that you know that there's nothing thought up by man or beast that he has *not* been into at some time or another. Sexually, I mean. And of course, you're an artist – the wild, creative type. So I'm sure there's a part of you that refuses to live peacefully in the very spellchecked and autocorrected world that is Lawrence Court with Dave the professor. So, tell me, is that it? Was *that* the reason? Is it that obvious? I would've thought an artist with all this—' she gestured to the sprawl of bespoke kitchen '—would be less predictable and boring.'

Tara stood, and gestured for Christine to do the same. But she remained sitting.

'What about your marriage, Tara? How does that work again? You pretend to be faithful and your husband pretends not to care? It's a cliché, no?'

'You're right to be angry. It was probably the worst decision I've ever made in my life. But you must leave now.'

'No, it's not the worst decision you've ever made in your life. You don't know what that is yet. But you will soon.'

Tara made a 'huh?' expression.

'You know what?' Christine continued. 'Until a few minutes ago, I still felt sorry for you. I still felt that you didn't deserve what's coming. I mean, no one innocent at heart would deserve that.'

'What the hell are you talking about?'

'But after seeing you in your natural habitat, and listening to you, and seeing you with everything you've ever wanted, and seeing how you smugly decided that even *that* wasn't enough, then yes – you deserve what you're going to get. You deserve the shitstorm raging down the line towards you. I just wish – I *really* wish – that I could be there, right beside you, when it happens.'

'When *what* happens?'

Christine finally stood and stepped away from the stool. 'Well, I think I've already taken up too much of your time. I have to run. Thank you, Tara. I'm happy to have seen what has preoccupied Ryan for the last six months.' Then she sharply slapped Tara across the cheek – a quick cuff that came out of nowhere.

'Jesus. You bitch!' Tara shouted. Christine's nails had slightly nicked her when Tara had abruptly turned her head. She could feel the contours of whitened scratches already rising, the skin swelling, breaking and leaking beads of blood. Swallowing back tears of frustration and pain, she said, 'I'm pregnant.'

'And I care?'

'Get out of my house before I call the police. You nut. You mental case.'

Christine picked up her coat, tucked it under her arm and calmly walked into the hallway. Tara, still rubbing her face, shouted after her, 'You should've heard what Ryan said about you. It must be terrifying to realise that the one who knows you best actually pities you? You sad, pathetic, stupid fucking bitch.'

The front door slammed. Tara wished she didn't know how things had got to this point. She wished it was a sad, unknowable mystery. Instead, she was cursed with the knowledge that just two nights ago, a fork had appeared in her journey and she had taken the wrong turn. From the living room she watched now as Christine crossed the road and swung open the heavy door of Ryan's SUV.

'Where the fuck are you?' Tara muttered. A man like Ryan didn't simply disappear. It had only been two nights ago that his life had radiated from him with such unrelenting energy.

The landline began to bleat. She plucked up the receiver and snapped, '*What*?'

'This is Sandra in KLT; can I speak to Tara, please?'

It took a couple of moments, but then Tara placed her. 'For fuck's sake, don't tell me – you can't reach my husband?'

'Excuse me? Is this a bad time?'

'You think? Look, what is it?'

'Actually, I was talking to your husband this morning. But I wanted to check with you – as joint account holder – if there is any way we could convince you to keep your money with us? We have very competitive rates, but your husband wasn't interested. I can call back at another time if you'd prefer.'

'Sorry – but what now?'

'David's transfer of one million, four hundred thousand euros arranged for tomorrow morning.' Sandra spoke a little too slowly, her pronunciation a little too clear. 'I'm *officially* calling to run our most competitive rates by you. So, is there something you want to ask me, now that you have me on the phone? *Anything*?'

Tara's breathing continued down the line for a few moments. Then she said, 'Sorry, but David has arranged for *what*?'

A deep inhalation through the mouth. A loud exhalation through the nose. After that: 'He has arranged the transfer of one point four million euros from your joint account.'

'Sorry Sandra, I need a moment.' Tara lowered the phone to her side and carried it to the kitchen. She poured what was left of the wine into Christine's empty glass and drained it in two gulps. This was the beginning of something that she couldn't see the end of. 'OK Sandra, start again. Because obviously there's been a very *big* fucking mistake.'

# CHAPTER SEVEN

In the driver's seat next to David, Fenton's rictus smile revealed two perfect lines of white teeth. Even now, with the pistol swaying confidently in his grip, he looked like a kitchen appliance salesman.

'Let me guess, David: you've been so long living your new life that you're now the type of man that generally hates violence? I get that. I really do. Violence is no longer the source of your power. Instead, it's a threat to your wealth and to your handsomeness. But in life, we are all at some time confronted with what we hate so much. My friends in the back, let me introduce them. They're from Zagreb. The skinhead is Viktor. He is the Mozart of ferocity. The Picasso of gouging out people's eyeballs. Am I connecting with your hard-earned university degree temperament yet? Am I being under-fucking-stood?'

Viktor smirked obligingly, but from his expression David could tell that he hated being paraded around as Fenton's 'isn't that so, Viktor' dancing monkey. Presumably the money was good, and he had the self-assurance of an employee too indispensable to be fired for bad attitude. Viktor picked sleep out of his eye now, revealing blue prison tattoos slinking down his fingers, while his palm looked dipped in ink.

'The other fella is Pejo. He has a reputation for being the most dangerous, ruthless and psychotic fucker that ever unsprung a flick blade.'

Pejo nodded in agreement; a man of importance had given judgement.

'In their world,' Fenton continued, 'you can't build that sort of brand overnight. Believe me.'

David believed him. He recognised a certain deadness in both Viktor and Pejo's eyes. The study of war after war had shown him that conflict doesn't just kill off a few hundred thousand men. It murders something that can never be brought back. And if a man lives in a zone where there's many wars, then soon all that is left is the raw beast that had originally stumbled out of the jungle.

'Here's an interesting fact, David – you and me, we're from the same side of town. The Cawley Estates are just up the road from where I grew up. Isn't that amazing? I couldn't believe it when you told me that last night. I'd assumed you'd be just another ponce who'd got everything from his da. And when I met you, you even looked like a ponce who'd got everything from his da. Fair fucks, man. You did it. You pulled yourself up by the bootlaces. I've what – ten years on you? So while you were still kicking a ball around the street with other scumbags, I probably walked by one day with my mates: older, cooler and meaner than you. You must've looked at me and thought, "I want to be him one day".'

'Yeah,' David said, trying to show no fear. 'That could've happened.' Cawley and all the other neighbouring areas for about five square miles had produced many men like Fenton: men who decided that the world would only stop hating them when they beat it.

'Considering the shitholes that we crawled out of, we've done quite well for ourselves. I did what I've needed to do to get myself here. While you did the impossible and weaselled your way into college, got learned up and never looked back. That must've took some doing when most of your mates left school at thirteen. It was hard enough just to ditch the accent, huh? Don't I fucking know it. But it had to be done. No one who speaks like we did can have any success in this life.' Fenton laughed and play-punched David on the shoulder.

'What do you want?' David asked.

Fenton checked his hair in the mirror. 'I want Ryan.'

'Why?'

'*Why* is not relevant. What is relevant is that sometimes shit happens that I just can't ignore. That's when I gotta stand up and strike out and make sure the scum know their place, which is at the bottom of the shit pile. That's why I'm going to cut Ryan's balls off, dip them in soy sauce, put them in his mouth, tape his lips shut and wait till he swallows them.'

Trying hard to be nonplussed, David said, 'And again – why?'

'He stole merchandise from me.'

'What kind of merchandise?'

'Narcotics.'

'Ryan doesn't sell drugs.'

'Uh-huh. He imports them. For me.'

'Ryan? He's a builder. From the country. He likes... housewives and bottled beer.'

'OK, I exaggerate. He imported them just the once. Well, he was supposed to.'

'Look, you got me in your car. You've threatened me with a gun. You can presume that I now know what you're capable of. So explain. Cawley boy to Cawley boy. *Mano a mano*. What the hell is going on?'

Fenton rubbed his chin in an exaggerated pose of thought while his other hand relaxed its hold on the pistol in his lap. 'Yeah, all right. Knowing where I'm coming from just might help you focus more fully on what I require from you. So basically, Maximum Building Services import a lot of their building materials from Eastern Europe. When Ryan ordered steel for some council houses he's due to renovate any day now, he arranged to have hollows bored into the beams, and my connections stuffed them with Siberian gear. It was then trucked through the Ukraine, Slovakia and the Czech Republic before, in theory, crossing the border at Germany and into France to be shipped to Wexford and trucked here. Ryan gets his steel, I get my delivery, Ryan gets paid. Everyone is happy.'

'So how did it inevitably go wrong?'

Fenton crossed his leg. He was enjoying David's drollness. 'Ryan claimed the shipment was stolen. The whole lot. Steel and produce. Jesus, does he really think it's that easy to rip me off? Davy, you worked with him. Did he strike you as *that* stupid? He didn't strike *me* as that stupid.'

'So you're upset.'

'Not too much at first. I mean, obviously he got a better deal somewhere. So I told him that bygones will be bygones in that I'll just accept, from him, the price of the merchandise I'd purchased, plus a percentage of the mark-up of the profit I would've made. Therefore I still make my money but without having the bother and expense of getting it onto the streets. In effect, the merchandise becomes just another cross that someone else has to bear instead of me. And in return, Ryan not only remains alive, but he keeps the difference that he made from selling it to whoever gazumped my deal. Jesus, Davy – that makes me a fucking saint. So I gave him till Monday morning to have it for me. But on Sunday night, he just vanished. Into thin air. *Puff*!'

'But Ryan's just a builder from the country who did all right for himself up in the big smoke. He doesn't import smack from the East. How did he get mixed up with you?'

'His wife, Christine – know her?'

'Never met her.'

'She's an interesting one,' Fenton muttered as he looked out of the driver's side window. 'The way that people are interesting when they lose everything and will do anything to get it all back. So, Christine was working with one of my little helpers that a judge sent to that Future is our Youth centre for troubled teens.' He paused to give a big sitcom sigh. 'Boys will be boys, eh? But instead of helping him, she got him to help her. See, through him, she had Ryan make a deal with yours truly.'

'So ask his wife where he is.'

'Like, "duh". But she doesn't know where the fucker is, either. In fact, she thinks we killed him. See, Ryan has gone into hiding and he is the type of prick that will leave his friends and family in the shit while he sails away into the sunset. Well, that is not going to happen this time. I want my merchandise, or my money, or Ryan's head on a plate. Which brings me to the point of our little tête-à-tête.'

'I don't know where Ryan is. He's just my builder.'

'The thing is, David, the only lead we have is that the last place Pejo saw Ryan was when he was driving towards your house the night before you moved in.'

'Jesus, I don't know anything about that.'

'And then there's Ryan's phone we took out of his car, with all those calls between your hot little missus and Ryan on the day he vanishes. Weird, huh?'

'We told you about that already.'

'Yeah... You did. And I hope you're not telling any porkies, Davy. Because if I was to discover that you interfered with my business model in any way, then—'

'I'm not a dealer. How could I interfere with your "business model"?'

'If you were to come between me and Ryan – say for example you helped him, hid him, hindered me getting to him in *any* way – then it will be you who I will hold responsible for all of Ryan's crimes. And believe me, I won't show you the mercy and kindness I had originally offered Ryan. I will come down and introduce myself to dear, lovely Valerie, your seventy-six-year-old mother in her single-bed apartment, Unit 6, in the Belmont Retirement Home. I hear your ma is a devout Catholic – that God is her happy pill in her grand old age. That's lovely. I'd like to have a chat with her about that. See, I'm an atheist. And not because I like being a smug prick. I'm an atheist because God doesn't exist. And believe me, when I'm through with your ma, she'll be one too.'

David leaned into Fenton, pressing his chest into the barrel of the pistol. 'You even think about touching my mother—' But the arrival of Pejo's flick blade against his throat floored his threat.

Fenton poked David in the chest with the pistol. 'You won't do anything, David. Like most people, you're a sheep – and sheep don't eat meat.'

Pejo slowly withdrew the blade.

'So, I'm being totally honest when I say that I don't want to hurt your ma. Valerie's obviously a fine woman, to have brought up a son like you against all the odds. But I will if you make me. And when I'm finished with your ma, I'll have Tara raped with a broken bottle. Viktor knows what to do. He can cause maximum damage very neatly. Oh yes, we heard that Tara is with child. Christine let it slip. Lovely. Congratulations.'

David visibly tensed. *Jesus Christ.*

'If you want a Caesarean, Viktor is the man for the job. He studied medicine a long time ago, back in Croatia. I'll have Tara's belly opened up and let her bleed out your kid into your spanking new bath over three or four hours. Tara wouldn't dare scream, because we'll already have pulled out her tongue and kicked in her teeth.' He gestured to the back seat. 'For example, just like that.'

David glanced over the headrest precisely as Viktor smashed Pejo in the mouth with a tattooed fist armoured with the chunk of a stainless steel knuckleduster. Blood splattered against the side window and broken teeth ricocheted around the car's interior like wood chippings. A gush of blackish liquid broke from Pejo's mouth, dumping onto the leather interior in wet clumps. David recoiled against the dashboard, shouting, 'Jesus!' and frantically brushing broken enamel off his shoulder. Pejo issued a high-pitched squeal before a second blow into his eye socket shocked him into silence, though his hands lifted pointlessly as three more blows pounded into his skull.

Fenton, holding up the bloody stump of an incisor, said, 'Tragic. He had two implants in his mouth – two works of art – each one more expensive than a mid-range car.' He gave his eyebrows a Groucho waggle and, miming a drum roll, added, '*Ba-dum-psh!*'

'Why did you?... You didn't have to…' David raised his hand before his mouth, feeling that he was next, thinking of all the countless hours he'd spent flossing and brushing. In the back seat, Pejo coughed: a ferocious rasping hack dragged from the depths of his lungs.

'It was Pejo's job to follow Ryan. It was his job to know where he was at all times. But he lost him at your house. Ryan went in and, according to Pejo, never came out. But Pejo didn't wait long enough. He left, thinking Ryan would do what he'd always done – go home, play video games and sleep. But by the morning, Ryan had either disappeared or he was still in your house. But I've been there and we've been watching it. I don't know where he is, but he isn't your house guest. So Pejo disappointed me. Do you intend to disappoint me, Davy?'

David didn't reply. He just glared into Fenton's eyes.

'Of course not. I mean, you've such an amazing house. All I could think of when I was walking around it was what fun it would be to watch it burn down. Jesus, Davy, there are just so many ways I could ruin your life; it's like you're a chocolate box. Now – are we clear on what happens to the man who gets in the way of me getting Ryan?'

Dispassionately, David said, 'One hundred per cent clear.'

'Good man. We're watching you, always – as you will have noted this morning in your back garden. And if things don't change for the better, then we'll be in touch again shortly. Next time, we'll leave a message. Now, why don't you fuck off and make yourself a protein shake, or whatever it is people like you have for lunch? Get out.'

As David opened the door, he glanced to the back seat. Pejo remained upright and groaning, his bloodied skull nestling in the headrest, his left eye exposed and bulging, its lid half-torn off. His other eye was closed, the socket the colour of a kidney. He was alive, if not aware that he was alive – less a man, more a collection of pulsing wounds.

When the Skoda drove off, David looked across to the football pitches where the parents and kids were making the most of the heatwave before autumn swallowed up the blue skies. He used to tell his students that the only thing history teaches us is that history teaches us nothing. *I've committed the same mistake over and over again.* The mistake was in believing that there was a way out of this; that it would all somehow go away.

So, it was Fenton who had sent David a messenger that morning. And the message was: We're Here. You're Gettable. Fenton's men originated in places where a person would pull the trigger for a can of Coke, never mind whatever it was that Ryan owed them. And when Fenton was finished with David, he was the type of sociopath who would go on to damage Tara just because he could. David trusted his instincts. Some things didn't need to be scientifically replicated under laboratory conditions and reported in a peer-reviewed journal to be true. David had seen enough of the world to know that it was populated with individuals who just wanted to pour acid into life's spring water.

Climbing into the BMW, he powered down the window and tried to breathe normally. There was an emptiness in his stomach but he wasn't hungry. He felt as if he'd never eat again. It seemed like something people only did in films; something decorative, that whole charade of raising fork to mouth. He cruised away from the park with nowhere to go but home. As he drove, the red lights turned to green like doors being opened by attendants. Before the events of this week he would have seen that as an omen of good fortune.

David pulled into Lawrence Court and almost clipped the orange Dyno Drains Service van parked in the circle outside Shay and Stephanie's. As he slowed before the driveway pillars, there was a rap of knuckles against the bonnet. David lowered the glass and tried to smile at Shay.

'David, I need access *now*! We can't live like this. We'll have to move out. It's an impossible situation.' Shay was beginning to get emotional. 'The piping has totally backed up and hit critical mass. And do you know what the point of least resistance is? It's our hall toilet – which has filled, overflowed and ruined the hallway with soiled water. Know why? Because there's something blocking the pipe on *your* side of the boundary, beneath *your* patio.'

David tried to focus, tried to get with the conversation, but it was pointless. '*Now* is not the time. OK? I'm sorry, Shay. I really am. Just give me till tomorrow.'

Shay's lower lip puckered. He wasn't a man used to being denied anything. But David just pressed the accelerator and entered his driveway. Whatever was annoying Shay would soon be nullified by the stories he would be able to tell his friends and neighbours after David was arrested tomorrow. He parked next to Tara's car. It was a twenty-foot driveway, but it stretched five years into the past. David walked up it, his life with Tara racing by him.

The hallway smelled of mint, his wife's signature tea. *It's her fault. If she hadn't... If she could've just...* David entered the front room and for a moment couldn't help but be touched by the scope of Tara's ambition; the style and taste she'd conjured up in just one day. He grabbed a bottle of Bushmills and poured a triple measure. He toyed with his drink, watching it, trying to resist it for a moment longer. He looked at his hands. There was the beginning of a slight quiver. Then he drained the glass and poured again. He threw it back, expecting it to taste better than the first one and was immediately disappointed. The alcohol wasn't hitting him. Fear seemed to consume it before his system could. How he longed for that perfect but all-too-brief state of drunkenness where you wonder why anybody would ever want to be sober; that brief period when you are simultaneously clear-headed and uninhibited.

He inhaled deeply, entered the kitchen – and there was his wife. Tara stood with her back to him, looking out through the opened slider that let in the water-patter sound from the lawn, where the sprinkler was helping the new grass to take. She called down the garden, 'Dora honey – *pussss-pussss-pussss*! Come on home, sweetie. Treat time.' Her top dipped a few inches at the nape of her neck, exposing the first few freckles that descended between her shoulder blades, mapping out a constellation of exquisite russet dapples.

*How can she be so casual? How can she presume it'll all blow over? After what she did with Ryan?* David wondered when the bump would begin to show. Would he ever see it? *By being with Ryan, she's effectively taken my child from me.* Her pregnancy was suddenly like a ritual that David was excluded from, and always would be. He steadied his voice to say what he'd been waiting hours to unleash: *I fucking hate you right now.*

But the very second he was about to speak, Tara turned about. Her face was glowing with the extra blood that makes pregnant women look so happy: her skin full as it was of healthy nutrients, empty as it was of abusive substances. Then David noticed the cigarette in her hand. He hadn't seen her with a cigarette since she'd been his student.

Without warning, she screamed, 'You treacherous fucking bastard!'

He ducked.

Tara's wine glass exploded against the wall behind him.

# CHAPTER EIGHT

Five years ago, Tara had been one of a dozen students crammed around a table in a tutoring room of Trinity College. At the head of the table sat David, pointer in hand, a map of Europe unfurled behind him, and next to him, colour slides of MacArthur and Truman. Thirty-five years old, he was dressed in the ageing-hipster attire of suit jacket, T-shirt and Converse sneakers. There was a festive feel to the tutorial, as it was the last class of the semester. The oldest of David's mature students – ladies in their sixties – had brought in cookies and expensive unseasonal strawberries with whipped cream, which seemed to have the effect of alcohol, making the group boisterous and rowdy as the treats were consumed. But David was disappointed at how distant Tara remained. Perhaps he'd only imagined that her gaze had often lingered on him a fraction of a second more than was necessary over the past few months.

'OK,' David announced. 'Time's up. Our semester is over, and I'm adjourning to O'Neill's for a farewell pint. If any of my brilliant students want to accompany me, I'll be getting the first round.'

As chairs scraped against boards and a few students rose to their feet, Tara finally spoke, loud and assured, from the other end of the table. 'You keep mentioning that we'll be fine out here in the West as long as we have these "perfect wars". What are they again?'

A hush spread as the few standing bodies plopped back into their seats. Tara rarely spoke in class, but when she did, it was always worth listening to. There was also the fact that most of the young men wanted to sleep with her, so whenever she made a contribution it meant that they could stare at her without self-consciousness.

David examined a small dollop of cream on his finger. He wanted to suck it clean, but thought that would make him look sleazy. Instead, he dropped his hand beneath the table and rubbed his finger back and forth on the side of the chair. Matching Tara's gaze, David tried not to be obvious in his admiration for her curious brown eyes, her full lips and healthy, free-falling auburn hair.

'When missiles, planes and drones do their job, it's a perfect war – no infantry required,' he explained.

'And you *honestly* think that's a good thing?'

Her classmates steeled themselves for a show. Up to now, Tara had kept her counsel in David's tutorials, but he was aware of her difficult reputation from her mainstream lecturers. They considered her dangerous: looks, sharp intellect, plus don't-give-a-fuck confidence in a twenty-five-year-old student meant that she could have whatever she wanted in this world.

'I didn't say what *I thought*.' David picked up a strawberry and pondered eating it, before returning it to the table between his perched elbows. 'I'm here to tell you how it is – or rather *was*.'

'So instead of solving things, we come up with machines to keep the status quo as the world spins on to its stupid end. It's like deciding not to recycle because we've discovered that the human race is already past the point where the environmental devastation of the last century can be undone. Because: That Is Not The Point.'

*But surely it is?*

Emer, a nineteen-year-old, jumped in with: 'And that's the repetition of history right there. In the *male* attitude of choosing submergence in a carefully constructed fake world of insulation instead of – Making A Difference. The Generation Xbox. Those who expect interactivity, immediacy and immersion – the three 'I's of the twenty-first century first-world life. That's why we're so nauseatingly at ease with the "gamification" of war.'

'Nicely put, Emer,' Tara said.

David pretended to tie his lace so he could roll his eyes. When young women got sisterly with each other, he thought it was best not to say anything.

Tara continued, 'But David, you didn't answer my question: the perfect war – do you think it's a good thing?'

David picked up the strawberry again, took a bite and chewed, pretending to enjoy it even though he wasn't pushed on strawberries. Swallowing, he said, 'In 1939 – and for thousands of years before that – twenty-year-olds were queuing up to die for us. Tara, do you know many twenty-year-olds who are willing to die for you?'

'Of course not.'

'Then I think it's a good thing.'

'You're being vague. That could be pro- or anti-war.'

'It's not vague. It's precise. You didn't ask me if I was pro- or anti-war.'

'I'm asking you now.'

He shrugged: maybe yes, maybe no. 'I'm pro-survival.'

There was a ripple of laughter. Tara stared at him, then smiled – was it coquettish? – before causing a sensation with: 'Fuck you, Mr Miller.'

David ate the remainder of the strawberry, glad to be able to chew on something to hide the panicked tightening of his throat. *What do I do now?* If anyone else had said that, he would have immediately kicked them out, before reporting them. Being thirty-five suddenly felt so ancient. He was a decade older than Tara. She was his student. He was a cliché.

*Get a hold of yourself, David. You are the tutor. She is the student.* Drolly, he said, 'And on that bombshell, I'm off for a pint.'

Half the class accompanied him across the road to a popular bar on the late-night student scene. The split-level pub was slowly filling up with Thursday-night revellers as grungy rock pulsated from the speakers. David managed to sit next to Tara in the alcove his class occupied. As he waited for her to notice him, he wondered if there was a way to sit in a trendy bar which demonstrated that he regularly sat in trendy bars when he no longer did – all his free time being now consumed either by correcting essays or organising lectures so that he appeared to be a teacher worth listening to. Tara was animatedly talking to two young men whose names David could never remember. None of his students, besides Tara, interested him. Their papers were mostly half-hearted, with paragraphs trailing off without conclusion as if they were incapable of holding a thought long enough to do anything with it. But Tara was different. Her work was singularly focused.

David soaked up the smooth jawline of her profile. She was about five foot ten, but she held herself with such poise that she seemed taller. Her navy skirt matched her jacket, which covered a blouse with the top buttons popped to expose just enough cleavage. It was impossible to tell if she was wearing a bra. David didn't think she was. He had no doubt that she would be spectacular naked.

Suddenly Tara turned to him. 'Hi David,' she said, waiting for him to start it all.

He hunted about for a topic of conversation but failed to come up with one.

'Thanks for a great semester,' she continued. 'Didn't think I'd really like a module of Modern European War History – but I did.'

There was no flirtation in her eyes, so he adjusted his own. 'Why pick it, then?'

'To challenge myself. I didn't know anything about history.'

'What are you majoring in?'

‘Psychology.’

‘What are you going to do when you’re finished?’

‘Hopefully something interesting. Hey, is it really true that you still haven’t even started your PhD? How is that? I mean, they’re letting you teach.’

David shifted on the sofa. It actually hadn’t been a huge surprise that David had become a lecturer, despite being the only member of staff in the history department not to have a PhD. Even though he’d just finished his Masters on Modern European History, he’d already been published in one major journal and several minor ones. In contrast, most of the older senior lecturers had come to their current positions by producing turgid, overwritten dissertations on the Persian-Grecian war of the classical world. Nevertheless, despite David’s individualised brilliance, the dean had still needed to pull in favours to trump the institutionalised reservations against his lack of doctorate.

‘I’ll start it next year,’ David said. ‘Right now, I’ve got to teach rather than do research. I need the money.’ Just three short sentences were all he required to inform Tara that he was broke. The fact was that after his mother’s recent stroke, she was close to requiring full-time care and David needed as many classes as possible to save up for that inevitability. He hurried the conversation on. ‘I was editing an article I’m writing for a journal all day yesterday. I spent the entire morning working on the introduction and I took a comma out. In the afternoon I put it back in.’

Tara laughed: a deep, raspy, sexy laugh. ‘Very good. Wilde. I get it.’

‘Yeah, good old Oscar,’ David said, pretending that he’d intended to adapt the quote rather than steal it. ‘Tell me, what’s your story? Introduce yourself, madam.’

‘Born in the arse of County Roscommon to a mother who was a barmaid and a father who was a forester. Only child. Happy adolescence. Hurling fan. No serious illness. No allergies.

Moved to Dublin at nineteen. Pulled pints in McDaids for a year. Then did a degree in art. Dropped out after two years. Pulled pints again. Signed up for this degree. Ambition to become financially independent and successful without wasting my life as a worker-drone. I like cats. Occasional smoker. Favourite meal: penne rigate.'

David let her words wash over him, loving the velvety tone of her voice, the calm intelligence contained in it. His senses immersed themselves in her warm breath, the soft pant of her voice, the tickling feel of her out-of-place hair brushing against his cheek. Then he said, 'Well, that leaves me with much to assimilate. So I'm going to the bar to figure out how to best that. Want anything?'

She shook her head.

David walked off, his heart hammering away, and ordered another double Bushmills and Coke. He felt that the young men queuing next to him sensed how old he was. Anyway, the fact that he was drinking Scotch rather than a craft beer meant that he might as well have been wearing a Davy Crockett hat.

'You would like something more, sir?' the gorgeous Latvian barmaid asked as she passed over his drink.

*You bet.* 'Nah, I'm OK.' He sipped his drink, feeling it fuel his courage, loosening his tongue, spreading his shoulders. Alcohol rooted him. It put him in the moment. He understood how it had the power to change anything boring into something better. He drifted back towards the alcove, where Tara was talking to some guy in denim jeans and a black leather jacket. His fringe hung fashionably over one eye. He looked like the drummer in a shoe-gazing band of pretentious pricks; the kind of guy who tells you that he's a 'musician' before much later explaining that he's 'in retail' six days a week and in a pub band on the seventh.

As David hovered near the table, Tara introduced him to the group. 'This is Ryan – my boyfriend. I may have mentioned him once or twice…' She trailed off, laughing. Ryan was also about twenty-five, by the looks of it. He was probably her first serious boyfriend. That meant that this was big, that this was the relationship that all future relationships would be measured against.

David backed away, finishing his drink in two swallows. He made towards the exit, his shoulders a little hunched. The way Tara had said her boyfriend's name – protective, terse and burdened with consequence – it was as if *Ryan* was a unique species unto himself; one that she had discovered.

Outside, David fumbled out a cigarette and managed to light it after five strikes. He then walked among herds of roaming young men as they hunted for alcohol. Scanning the luminous signs, he decided that he was hungry. Otherwise, he had nowhere to go except home to a tiny rented one-bed apartment on the ground floor of a docklands sky-rise.

As David chose a hamburger joint, he noticed a junkie huddled next to the entrance, his eyes rolling as he drifted into the black hole of his addiction.

*Right now, he's happier than I am.*

After collecting a cheeseburger, David took a two-seater table and scanned the panorama. The lads were scattered in boozy groups, while the young women marinated in the indoor heat, eager for the months to pass until another bare-limbed hedonistic summer arrived. After a single bite, David put aside the burger, dolefully reflecting on how his youth was no longer fading – it had, in fact, already gone.

And then, through the glass, he saw Tara. She was smoking elegantly, making arcs with her hand as she raised the cigarette to her lips. She pulled on it deeply. David took in her curves, the shortness of her skirt as it hitched up her thigh, her black ankle boots. She blew out a funnel of smoke and ran her fingers through her deep auburn hair, pulling forward strands so that they fell over her eyes. Next to her was Ryan.

They entered and walked down the central aisle. After collecting fries and a Coke, Tara led the way to the table in front of David, who pretended to check his phone. Ryan slipped in beside her and sucked from his litre cup, his throat expanding and contracting like a snake's. If David did that, he reflected, he'd be popping antacid tabs for a week.

Suddenly, without having said a word, Ryan stood and walked away. Tara called after him, but he just kept going, and exited to the damp city night. She looked down at her chips and mouthed, 'Prick.'

They'd had a fight. *Excellent*. Sometimes life *does* do you a favour. The build-up was perfect. Should David cross over to her? *Of course*. When? *In a minute*. He was amazed that a young man would just walk away from a girl like Tara and not even look over his shoulder. Was Ryan *that* good-looking? Was he *that* cool?

Tara nonchalantly finished her fries. There were no tears, no panicked phone calls, no desperate texts being tapped out. There was just a frown and a pertness to her lips. She wasn't heartbroken; she was just pissed off because she was used to getting what she wanted. Tara was probably spoilt, but that was OK. It would be a pleasure to give her whatever she wanted. David imagined being able to afford to order Tara cocktails between courses at Michelin-starred restaurants, and having a grand time as the money slipped away.

Another guy sat in beside Tara. He was tall, and despite the weather wore just a football top that hugged his muscles like body armour. Leaning in, he muttered something that made Tara recoil.

She responded with, 'What's your name?'

'Kev,' he answered, in a hoarse Dublin accent. 'But we don't need names.'

'Well, Kev, I'm not your type.'

'You look my type.'

'But I have the capacity to think.' Tara slid out and moved between the grazing diners, and then down the stairs to the basement where the toilets were. Kev waited a few moments before dumping his tray and following.

'Damn,' David muttered, and he too made his way towards the stairs. Down below, a fluorescent-lit corridor led towards the toilets. Kev had managed to overtake Tara and now stood in the middle of the passageway, making himself a phenomenal plug to seal off her advancement. As Tara tried to squeeze by, Kev nudged open the door to the men's toilet and dragged her inside while simultaneously copping a feel – multitasking. The door closed behind them.

David, from the other end of the corridor, stared with incredulity. Had that really just happened? It was as if he'd witnessed an alligator snap a person from dry land to the river bed and a second later nothing remained, not even a ripple. He rushed to the door and pushed it open. Inside, opposite the two unlocked stalls and a row of urinals, Kev was holding Tara by the throat, pressing her spine against the wash-hand basin.

'David!' Tara's eyes widened as she twisted free of the thug's grip.

Kev's pinpricked pupils sized David up.

He was in this now. How long had it been since his last fight? A decade? There were those times back in the Cawley Estates when he'd woken up with an eye closed over and dried blood gluing his cheek to the pillow. Even when he'd won, though, it had felt like he'd lost. But all that had mattered in the gang was that you'd fought a good fight.

'Get out,' David ordered, maintaining eye contact, speaking loud and clear as if he was trying to control a dangerous animal.

Kev laughed. 'Fuck off, cunt, before I stab ya.'

David recognised the coked-up jitteriness of his movements. *Take him out quick*. Kev lunged forward and David punched him in the face. Globs of blood erupted from both nostrils and splattered against the mirror.

'Oh my god!' Tara exclaimed.

David's fist was daubed in red. He thought of diseases.

'You're fucking dead!' Kev roared, spreading his legs to balance – and to inadvertently divulge – the swinging punch that was about to be thrown. The tip of David's trainers connected perfectly with his balls. The force lifted Kev an inch off the ground before he dropped to the greasy tiles. He rolled over like a large round log: his eyes shut tight, hands jammed between his legs, his entire body shivering. A hiss escaped his lips, slowly and agonisingly.

'Is he gonna be OK?' Tara asked. Kev was in a foetal position, taking short breaths.

*I hope so*. 'Yeah. He'll be fine.'

Tara was clearly shaken up, but she tried to restore her daredevil, whatever-happens-will-happen demeanour, and said, 'Thanks, Prof.'

'Lecturer,' David automatically corrected her. Wired with the rush of adrenaline, it was beginning to dawn on him what he'd just done – beaten a young man in the company of his twenty-five-year-old student. 'C'mon, let's go.'

They made for the door, and moments later escaped into the street like drowning sailors plucked from the sea. They kept going, walking with an icy wind that had dislocated several brollies and made Dubliners struggle against it like mime artists. Finally, they stopped at the River Liffey boardwalk. Leaning on the wall above the black, fast-flowing water, they looked at each other. Tara pulled up her collar against the knife-sharp wind. David noticed graffiti on the wall behind her – *ONE NATION UNDER CCTV*.

Looking over the wall to the murky river, Tara asked, 'David – are you really pro-war? The others say that you are.'

David was stunned that she wasn't talking about what had just happened. Then, just as suddenly, he was disappointed. After everything they'd just been through, they were already back to the old tutor/student conversation. Quietly, he answered, 'No, I'm not pro-war. As you suspected.'

'*Knew*.'

'Yeah, knew. The others should listen better.'

'I read your essay on The Modern War in the *Journal of Twenty-First Century Studies* – which, for the few days it took me to get my head around it, was much more interesting than the talks going on in the Baltic States and the Middle East. But I gave you a chance to correct the others in class today. You didn't take it.'

David smiled. 'It's bad form to dishonour a good story. Honestly, I couldn't care less about politics, and since I'm a history teacher, that's a concept many people find difficult to understand. But it's always the same – the centre right will rule until we get tired of them and replace them with the centre left. And so it goes, just two rival gangs, power-sharing.'

Tara laughed. Then she said, 'What happened tonight was... I don't know what it was... But if you hadn't been there... Look, this is our secret.'

David stared into her wide eyes, her broad smile, her white teeth. Time had stopped. He imagined her as everything he thought a perfect woman should be: smart, funny, interesting and hot. After a full semester of seeing her once a week, he still knew so little about this Tara Brown. Only tonight was he beginning to see what she was like, bit by bit. And each new bit he liked. Each new bit invigorated him.

Tara continued, 'And by the way, it really was a great semester. Thanks for everything. See ya – OK?'

David swallowed the sound of his deep, dismal sigh. Down in the river, a pleasure cruiser rumbled by. With one-way glass and not a sign of a crew member on the decks, it radiated a ghost ship isolation. Tara stepped away from him, and it felt like Velcro tearing from Velcro.

*

Eighteen months passed before David saw Tara again.

He'd taken a shortcut through St Stephen's Green – a city park anchored by a landscaped pond. He was holding a plastic bag filled with water and the three neon tetras he'd just bought at the Trop Shop. His smaller fish had been disappearing one by one over the last few weeks, and he suspected it was because of the baby Siamese fighter that had recently become an adult. At night, he liked to sit by his aquarium to unwind with a book. However, recently his tank had no longer been the altar of respite from his mother's deteriorating health, the pressures of taking so many classes and the new unpleasant sensation that he was beginning to recognise as loneliness.

Walking through the park, David deeply inhaled his cigarette. He wasn't enjoying the metropolis the way he used to because the summer was making his gloom so much more uncomfortable. The long stretches of daylight offered little cover, and other people's happiness felt aggressive, in his face. *I'm thirty-seven, damn it.* Recently David had got into the habit of reminding himself how old he was. Sometimes he wondered if he was suffering from depression. Other times, he reckoned he'd simply become a grown-up.

Standing beneath the park's arched exit, the bag of neon tetras by his side, David was drawn towards the artists lining the fence with their canvases. He drifted along, looking at the mostly slapdash still lifes and inexpert landscapes. But then he happened upon a row of paintings themed on atlas pages. The largest frame contained a map of the world with each country painted a different colour to its neighbour. The smaller frames held just one continent each. David found maps to be totally compelling. He appreciated their perfection; the assuredness that an exact map was uncontaminated verity with no room for estimation or dispute. And of course, every map contained history. In fact, maps *were* history. Power created territory and territory needed to be marked, carved up or amalgamated. Precise records of these changes needed to be taken and—

Then he noticed her. Tara was only ten feet away, wearing a plaid shirt, jeans and brown hiking boots. Her straight fringe was high on her forehead, almost goth-like. It emphasised the smoothness of her forehead, her composure. She was talking to two men. One of them was a construction worker in a hi-vis jacket and hard hat. With hands on hips, he gave Tara his full attention, as if he could see through denim – and she radiated in it. The other man was in a grey suit, his face the colour of cereal sat for too long in milk. He flicked through his texts, disinterested. The large scroll tucked beneath his arm made him seem important.

David flicked away the cigarette like a speeding bullet into the road. He didn't need distractions. So this was what Tara was doing now. He didn't know whether that was thrilling or a disappointment. Over the past eighteen months he had never been able to walk by a certain burger joint without thinking, *That's where* we *had our adventure. What adventures is she having now?* Since he'd last seen Tara, David had dated three girls, but he'd only allowed the third one to last more than a few months.

The construction worker kissed Tara on the cheek and David immediately resented another man enjoying her when he couldn't. Tara was waving goodbye and saying, 'OK then, see you around sometime. Miss me.' David watched the handsome builder and the suit retreat into the throng of lunchtime office workers.

*It's your turn now.*

David moved on to the next canvas, pretending to study the painted delicacy like it was an algebra equation. Then he turned, manifested a look of astonishment – as if he'd only now recognised a favourite pupil that he hadn't seen in over a year – and said, 'Hey, it's me.'

Tara's eyes widened. 'Oh, wow. That's so weird. I mean, great too. But... Hi.'

*She doesn't even remember your name.* David felt himself reddening. *She has no idea who you are. You're Cicero, not Mark Antony. You're Laertes, not Hamlet. You're Lodovico, not Othello.* 'It's me... From...'

'I know exactly who you are, Mr Miller. Are they fish? *Live* fish?'

He squinted through the clear plastic. 'A few neon tetras. I've got an aggressive Siamese fighter that has whittled down my tetras and guppies over the last few months. Gotta restock.'

'How fabulously nerdy of you. I wish I had a fish tank.'

'Well, they're hard work. You have to keep an eye on the alkalinity and the hardness of the water.' *Stop talking about fish. No one besides you and the ten other loyal customers of Trop Shop care about fish.* 'Anyway, I'm getting in the way of you selling your work. I saw you with that builder and the other guy. They were probably buying your—'

'Ryan? *Buying art*? Ha! No chance. He's just an old boyfriend. What is it about today? I haven't seen him in ages and then, bang – you come along too.'

'Ryan? Your old boyfriend? That was him?'

'Uh-huh. Has his own construction company now. Takes lunch with architects with boarding-school names – like that dick, Gordon, who thinks he sweats expensive cologne. They're renovating a private members' club on The Green. Hey, you actually remember him? Jazus, I didn't think you'd met Ryan.'

'I just have a knack with names and when you mentioned "Ryan", it came back.'

'Forget Ryan. Because here we have David the historian, the scholar so bright a major university let him teach without having even started his PhD. I can't flick by the History Channel without thinking of you.' She smiled, demonstrating either the generosity of her praise or the subtleness of her sarcasm.

'Ah, it's a loser's game; at some point there's going to be too much history for anyone to keep up with. I really should bail from it.'

'Bullshit – you were the academic dog's bollocks. We all loved your class. Seriously. It was the only class where every time it was over I'd look at my watch and think "Already? *Noooooo!*"'

David looked to his feet. He wanted to say, 'Really?' He wanted to hear more.

'So how's uni going? Professorship yet?'

'Still lecturing. Still haven't started the PhD,' David muttered, as if admitting he'd been in jail on sex offences. He wanted to lie. But he had no lie to tell. There was nothing in his life that he could grab onto and exaggerate into something that it wasn't.

'No way.'

'Way.'

Tara laughed, and David wondered if she was laughing because she recognised that old-school riposte, or because she'd never heard it before because she was too young to have seen the movie that his generation stole it from. 'See, my mother had a stroke a while back, and just as I was settling down to give the PhD a lash, her health deteriorated further. She needs twenty-four-hour care now and... Well, I've got to keep teaching and taking the classes to pay for that. And I'm giving extra tutorials and whoring myself to every society and Ladies' Club talk night that'll take me. See, there's only me. My sister's in Australia and is basically useless.'

'Wow – fair play,' Tara said, almost disbelievingly.

'To be honest, I find the situation less than super-great. But, you know…' He inhaled and sealed his full lips into two straight lines.

Tara said, 'After Trinners, I was stuck in an office for nine months. An insurance company. Nothing happened there. Ever. And I hated everyone. Know why? Because they were just like me. And I was just like them – a bland, mass-produced, Styrofoam office drone. But they were happy and I wasn't. And that made me feel spoilt and pretentious. And it took me almost a year to realise that I really *was* spoilt and pretentious. I wanted more from life. I felt I deserved it.'

'You're not spoilt.'

'Would've preferred if you'd zoned in on the "pretentious" adjective.'

David gestured to her art hanging on the rails. 'You want to be an artist, so of course you're pretentious. Not that you aren't yet an artist. I just mean that you aren't *yet* on the cover of *Modern Painters* or *Frieze*. But I'm seriously impressed, Tara. It takes balls to proclaim a creative profession – the in-your-face narcissism of it. Respect!'

They both laughed, and David felt a ripple of freedom blow across his face, an adrenaline rush of pure pleasure that he hadn't enjoyed in months.

'So tell me, why are you drawing maps? Miss my class that much?'

'Of course I miss your class – but these aren't snapshots of war, or records of hostile powers at a moment of suspended animation. That's what you said about maps, I believe. But this is different.' As Tara gestured to her paintings – like they were hanging in the Guggenheim and not on a park fence – her easy-going expression transformed into an illustration of gravity. Her smooth forehead creased as she told him about the series she was still working on called *Erdős Landscapes*.

After a while David said, 'Wow, that's amazing.' He even managed to sound amazed, despite the fact that he was barely listening as he watched her lips move, her eyes widen, her neck contract and expand.

'Since all countries on any map can be identified individually with just the use of four different colours, the mathematician Paul Erdős thought... Oh, no. Rain!'

Drops began to fall – big ones that went *splat*; not the usual summer's drizzle. It was seconds away from a torrential downfall.

'Shit, shit, shit,' Tara said, beginning to untwist the metal twine pinning the nearest frame. David set the neon tetras gently on the ground and set to work on the largest painting – the one of the entire world. The rain was getting heavier and starting to shake the leaves above their heads.

Tara said, 'If you can, take it across the road to the pub. Buy a drink if you have to. Just don't let any water get onto it. I'll be over in a minute once I undo the other two.'

David stepped onto the road, ignoring the horn blare from the nearest car. The painting was almost too big for his hands to grip each side of its width. In seconds, the rain would begin to splatter the frame and dribble down the canvas. *What pub?* The painting was blocking his view and the drops were coming faster now. He kept going straight, up the broad steps to the porch of the Shelbourne Hotel, where the porter must have thought he was somebody else and opened the door for him.

David continued into the swish lobby, which was packed with tourists, business people and lunching Dubliners. His arms aching, David lowered the painting to the thick carpet and leaned it against the flock wallpaper. Bending to regain his breath, he glanced back at the entrance. It was raining hard outside – a burst of a downpour that fell with a religious conviction. Did Tara see where he'd gone? He hoped so.

Suddenly, someone squeezed between David and the painting. *Hotel muscle? Already?* But instead of security, David was faced with the back of a man's head of tight grey hair as he stared down upon the painting.

David cleared his throat and the man reached behind him, making a 'with you in a minute' gesture with his palm. He crouched so that he could get his face right up to the canvas. Finally, the man stood. He was over six feet high. Dressed in a light suit, his face was bland and formless like a worn coin, so that it was hard to gauge his age. But he also seemed rich enough for it not to matter what he looked like.

'The name's Scott. Hi.'

Scott's mid-American accent reminded David of shopping malls and neatly creased white socks, and of teenagers driving huge new cars – everything he'd envied when he'd been a teenager; everything he'd barely believed could exist somewhere in the world for someone his age.

'David.' They shook. Scott's hand was warm and sweaty. David concentrated hard on not wiping his palms on the side of his jeans.

'I love your country. I love that it's still Catholic.'

David made a 'huh?' face. *No one's Catholic any more.* But quickly he offered something that he thought a pious American tourist would like. 'So you're a man of strong faith, Scott?'

'Yes, sir,' he replied, as if David had asked him if he was human. 'Aren't you?'

Before David could reply, Scott added, 'I pray to Him and I want Him to hear me. But does He? The only thing I know for certain is that when you talk to God you don't expect miracles. And yet, here we are.'

'Here we are?' David glanced at the lobby doors. Where was Tara?

'A miracle occurred just a day ago. I was in Africa yesterday. We're doing the next Harvey Mac movie down there.'

'*The* Harvey Mac movies?'

'Uh-huh. Release has been put back till next year. Was supposed to be Christmas.'

'So what exactly is your line of work?'

'I'm Scott McCoy. Producer. And you?'

'David... History lecturer.' David suddenly felt a swell of free-floating anxiety. Scott oozed prosperity and refinement, and when confronted with great wealth, David experienced awe and revulsion: feelings as confusingly tangled as lust and disgust in the face of sex. David imagined the tasteful mansions this man must own all over the world, that would entertain bankers, lawyers and businessmen passing through from Vienna, Paris and New York.

Men worth tens of millions. More. He was probably the type of rich person who didn't throw parties – he would throw balls. No doubt he was only used to exceptional people.

Scott continued: 'So, a ten-seater Cessna does it on these trips, and we bounce around for a few days, landing at scratch airports. The kind where kids in shorts run beside the plane waving and throwing stones at the propeller – the crazy little turds. So we're coming in to land at Mufulira, where the crew are sleeping in tents next to the strip mine – you should smell the sulphur – the guys love that – makes them feel all rugged. And they're all gleaming with sweat – even at night it doesn't dip below eighty-two.'

'I don't know Fahrenheit.'

'It's no cooler in Celsius. So we're coming in to land and there's a bird strike. Believe me, David, nothing will scare you more than a bird strike in a Cessna. The propeller chops up some of them, but the engine sucks the rest right in and the bones twist the fan blades and that's it – game over. But we survived. Both wings broke off when we hit the runway. And the miracle is that we were all unharmed. Not even bruises. Just twelve hours ago, I was walking around the crash site, making my way between spilled suitcases, broken wing spans, a shattered propeller shaft and feeling the power of what it is to be alive – feeling *the gift* of it. I wish I could give it to you, David. I really do.'

David already detested Scott. The American was actually trying to imply that faith was the measurement of all things, when they both knew that money was how the world really measured things. If you were rich, it meant people liked you. It meant *God* liked you.

'So, you like this? The painting?' David was running out of small talk.

'I *love* this. It's great.'

'You're interested?'

'Am I interested?' Scott repeated, as if trying to get to grips with a curious type of street slang that David was speaking.

'It's for sale.'

'Everything's for sale. I come from America, buddy: the Land of the Free, where nothing's free. How much? A thousand euros?'

David glanced at the revolving door. He knew that Tara had stuck a €250 tag on the railings next to the painting. *Don't mess with this. It's not yours to gamble with,* he admonished himself – before gambling with: 'Scott, I'm genuinely surprised. Be more ambitious when valuing this work. It's not junk. Add a zero to your numbers and then we'll start talking.'

Scott took a step back. 'I'm driving out west to hike in Connemara. Just waiting for my car to pick me up.'

David offered a half-shrug. *So?*

'Well, if we're gonna make a deal, we better make it fast.'

'Oh – so *you are* interested?'

He smiled an 'of course I am' smile.

Just in time, a hand slipped around David's waist and Tara said, 'There you are.'

He wanted her arm to remain there. But it didn't.

'This is Scott McCoy. The producer. He likes your painting. He likes it *a lot.*' David inhaled deeply. He had no idea how to let Tara know that he had completely inflated her prices.

Scott smiled a white American smile. '*You're* the artist?'

'Uh-huh.' Tara placed two smaller paintings on the ground, their frames leaning against her knees.

'Well, label me surprised. So what are you like?'

'Smart, young and fabulous. Ask David, he'll tell you.' Tara unzipped her jacket and withdrew the bag of neon tetras, which she handed to David. 'Your babies – safe and sound.'

'Know what I like about your work?' Scott asked. 'It's straightforward.'

'Wow,' Tara said drily. 'Someone gets me at last.'

'Warren Buffett said never invest in something you don't understand. Now, the way I see it, with art of any kind it's easy to be complicated. It's much harder to be simple and clear. That painting of the world – it is perfect.'

'I wish. Nah – it's not perfect. None of them are. I'm never happy with them. All my paintings are ruined at the first stroke of my brush. It can never be exactly as I imagined it. I'm not good enough. Not accurate enough. But you know, it's this failure that drives me on.'

'You're honest. You probably think success in art is just selling your paintings.'

Tara's face straightened as if figuring out the final question of a long intelligence quotient test. 'Er, like, yeah?'

'But you're wrong. It's not just selling your paintings – it's selling them to the *right people*. Miss Artist – would you like to be a star?'

Tara smiled as if she was facing a child who had just asked an adorably naive question. 'No. Definitely not.'

In turn, Scott smiled at Tara like she'd just said the most stupid thing he'd heard all week. 'Yeah, you're right. I mean, who wants to be beautiful, rich and desired?'

Tara looked at David and made a 'who the hell is this nut?' expression.

Ignoring – or even enjoying – her insolence, Scott added, almost to himself, 'So much energy, you'll probably remain young until you're sixty. And so will your art. Therefore, young lady, I'd now like to speak to you about your existing and future oeuvre.'

'That's a good idea,' David said. 'But I've got to go, so just give me a second to say goodbye to her.' He nodded a farewell to Scott and walked halfway across the foyer with Tara. As they approached the exit, he leaned in and whispered, 'So far, ten grand. Go for it. You deserve this.' Before she could say anything, David pecked her on the cheek and drifted away through the revolving doors. It was time to let Tara get on with her great adventure and put an end to his ridiculous daydream. She may be single, but what could he offer a young woman like her? David told himself to be grateful for the taste of youth he'd just sipped from her. It had reminded him of what it was like to enjoy life, to feel that he wasn't wasting a moment. But of course, that was over now. Tara had plans, and as long as David's mother was ill, he had none. Tara had time to make mistakes. He didn't any more. She could even enjoy her mistakes, learn from them, while if he committed one, it could destroy him completely. The anxiety of his current stasis returned, alighting into him like disturbed sand settling back to the sea floor.

Beneath the hotel canopy, the pounding rain, tropics-like, hadn't slowed down or petered out – it had just ceased. The sun was again beaming, the marble patio of the smoking area already steaming itself dry. There was a smell in the air like the fresh chlorine bouquet of a suburban pool, as if the oxygen had been rinsed and then perfumed.

David's Trop Shop bag, weakened from being pressed from one person to another, suddenly burst. Water rushed down the steps until all that remained was the fresh stain on the concrete and three neon tetras flapping against their annihilation. David stomped on the nearest one. The second fell off the side of the step and the third vanished beneath the feet of the pedestrians. The sight of their obliteration almost winded David. He had accepted responsibility for the lives of these creatures – no matter how simple they were – and he had failed them completely, giving them no chance to take anything from their brief existence.

And then David saw the two men. Standing only feet away on the busy pavement, Ryan's hi-vis jacket and the architect's scroll of significance suggesting that nothing in their immediate surroundings could possibly be important enough to demand their attention, except each other. Immune to the outside world, they continued talking, Gordon's hand on Ryan's shoulder.

'Hey, Ryan,' David called from the second step of the Shelbourne. He knew that Ryan would have no idea who he was, but something within him needed to get a glimpse as to what this Ryan was like.

Both men looked stunned, as if someone had barged straight through them.

'I'm David.' He was surprised at how childish the sentence sounded. Most adults didn't give their name voluntarily. 'I'm Tara's friend. You two were with her across the road, right? Just about, what, five minutes ago?' *Why am I still talking?*

Ryan took off his hard hat and brushed a hand through thick brown hair.

'We met once before,' David continued. 'About eighteen months ago. Back when Tara was in Trinity. Very briefly.' *Why did I say that?* He hadn't met Ryan. He'd only watched him from a distance as he'd broken up with Tara in a burger joint.

'Who are you again?' Ryan asked.

'Tara's friend,' David replied, his smile straightening.

Gordon began texting on his phone. Without looking up, he asked, 'Who did he say he was?'

Ryan shrugged. Gordon looked at David again. When the moment for the expected 'hallo' came, he instead spoke to Ryan. 'The steel has to be sorted. Let's get to site.'

'Yeah, suppose…' Ryan looked up at David like he was about to say something, but just offered a bemused grin and nodded. It had taken so long for him to smile that when it finally arrived it felt like a gift.

David gazed after them as they merged with the faceless. There were many victories, defeats and wars which man must endure that are not recorded in history books. David just wasn't sure what that had been; had he discovered something about Ryan, or had he made a complete fool of himself for nothing? *What a pair of dicks.* David stepped down to the pavement. *But forget about them; it's not as if you'll ever see them again.*

'David! Where are you? Get your ass back up here.'

Tara stood beaming before the revolving doors and David forced himself not to run up to her, to just take two steps at a time, to be cool.

'Oh my god,' Tara gushed, waving a cheque. 'Ten grand. Ten *fucking* grand. And that's for a small one! He wants the big one, too. We just have to work out the price. And then he wants more, more, more!'

'Jesus.'

'*He* gets no credit. It was you. I mean, it'll probably bounce. But will it? I mean, he's staying in the Shelbourne, after all, and his secretary just took all my details. He's insane. A mentalist. But he's *my* mentalist. And he loves my stuff. He wants them for his offices in Los Angeles. Los *freak'n* Angeles. He says that if he pays that much, then that's what the market will decide they're worth. For him, like. And they'll only get more expensive as my name gets around. And he'll make sure my name gets around. Oh my god. This is it. This. Is. It!' She wrapped her arms around David and squeezed, like she meant it, like it was important, like it was a moment she – and not just David – would remember forever.

David prolonged the embrace for as long as he dared, relishing the cushiony softness of her cheek against his. He already knew that they belonged together. Then he said, 'Tara, is this for real, or is it just an excuse to talk to me again?'

'It's real – *and* it's an excuse to talk to you again.'

'Good. Cancel everything. You and me. Let's get hammered and tell each other all our secrets. Let's do this now. Here. In the Shelbourne bar.'

'A very fine idea, Prof.'

David looked beyond Tara at the traffic-jammed road, the bustling pavement, the city and the sky. He had challenged the world and it had backed down. He could see the future and it was stretched out in front of him. Nations would splinter, empires would fall, wars would begin and end and everywhere on the planet things would become undone – except for him and Tara. Their knot would persist and tighten.

# CHAPTER NINE

The wine glass exploded against the wall behind David, the splattered wine colouring the kitchen cupboards. Shards came to rest between his jacket collar and his neck. Slowly, he straightened and calmly observed Tara's fury as if through a reinforced window. David had rarely seen her cry before. It was like a new skill. Tears made her face settle in folds and creases that he didn't know it had. A shiver ran through him from the ground up, rippling through his head. Dora miaowed loudly, ran across the kitchen, out into the hall and disappeared upstairs.

There was a clock on the wall behind Tara. It hadn't been there that morning. Each sharp tick, every perfect stroke of the second hand, invaded the kitchen. The silence between them thickened like ice. Very slowly, 4.07 became 4.08. *She knows. But what does she know?* That he'd killed Ryan? That he was buried ten feet away under the travertine? Did she know about the money? Or did she know about it all? David glanced at the ceiling. Upstairs in the attic, his life had caught fire and had burned until reaching critical mass – before detonating, just now, in his brand-new kitchen.

'Our money. You're trying to take all our money.'

'It's not what you think.'

'Well, what the fuck should I think? I make one mistake and you punish and you punish and you punish. You're driving me insane. Voices in the head insane. Dark fucking thoughts insane.'

And suddenly it was all so clear to David. Of course he was going to the police. He had just been delaying and delaying and delaying because he didn't want it to ever end. The 'it' that was Tara: her presence, her voice, her warmth, her mind, her art, her body, her gaze – and that amazing thing they were making together – their baby.

David looked down at the destruction before moving towards the island counter, his shoes crunching dozens of glass diamonds. He sat on a metal stool and felt like an old man. Leaning over, he stared down into the black marble. *Can I kill myself?* His own death was something he'd found almost unfathomable when he was young. Now, it was a reassuring solve-all option; a gilt-edged opportunity to stop struggling. But all was not lost. It couldn't be. Not yet.

There was a sharp noise. *Click. Click.*

Tara was next to him, snapping her fingers like a hypnotist bringing her patient out of a trance. Her stare was so powerful it felt like a violation. 'Pay attention. Talk to me.'

'I just want... I just want you to know... that...'

'Complete the thought – what do you want me to know?'

'Ryan... He's... He's…' David would need to tell Tara gently, but there was nothing gentle about this news.

'I made a mistake. I can't unmake it. Fine – you're angry. But you need to deal with it rationally. You don't just take all our money. What the fuck is the matter with you?'

He tried to reply, but his mouth wouldn't open. Now that he was finally cornered, David's entire existence had become a singular emergency in which he was too paralysed to act. Choice was no longer an element of his world. No matter what he did from this moment on, it would make no difference.

'Why do we have to still talk about Ryan?' Tara continued. 'And even if Ryan is missing, I don't fucking care. People vanish all the time – it's one of their saving graces. I don't care where he is. The house is finished. We don't need him any more. We don't need to see or talk about him ever again.' She crouched to the maple boards and picked up the sharp, jagged stem of the wine glass and placed it next to David on the counter.

'I killed him. I killed Ryan.'

Tara made an expression as if someone had just splashed cold water on her face.

'I'll tell you everything. But you'll find it hard to believe.'

And she did find it hard to believe. To steady herself, she placed her hands over her stomach instead of the wall. They were about to lose it all. Their names would soon be abhorred. The tabloids would splash horrible pictures of them across their front pages. Those who trusted her would curse her. Her family would fall apart before it had even begun.

'David... I just need to know... Did he suffer?'

Silence. The pause lengthened and darkened. David stared at her, and she knew that she'd asked the wrong question.

'Did he suffer? Who cares? I hope so.' David looked shocked by his own words. But then his eyes widened, ready to unload what he'd been storing inside for two long, terrible days. 'He screwed my wife. He screwed *my* wife in *my* house. Well, he's paying for it now.'

Tara looked out to the neatly grouted slabs. *No one pays for anything when they're dead. That's when you stop paying for it.* But she nodded as if she agreed.

In the background, the radio switched to the news: a calm voice discussing the savagery of the last hour. Suicide bombers, apartment blocks shelled, people wailing in grief, American drones over Syria, a wedding party blasted to smithereens. Tara's lover was ten feet away, buried outside the window. Her husband was a murderer. Another man that she had trusted was blackmailing them. A fourth man who had pretended to be a policeman was threatening them. She was surrounded by man's atrocity, and it enraged her. But there was a greater horror, more intense and imminent than all the others: the possibility that David was close to being taken away from her, locked away, scrubbed from her life. The mere idea was as difficult to imagine as her own death. It was simply beyond her scope of experience.

'Look, it was an accident,' she said. '*You* know that. *I* know that. But it's happened. Irreversible. We can't bring Ryan back. The fact is, his death *was* an accident. So there's no point in you going to prison. It would be the most pointless thing in the world. And they'd sentence you for murder, not manslaughter. It would be insane. It would ruin our lives and the life of our child, and for what? For nothing! Nothing that can be changed. Nothing that could be helped. And once Gordon gets paid, it's all over. I mean, it's not as if Ryan left a note.' Tara thought of her father. Without a goodbye, death brings a silence with it.

'And Fenton is just desperate,' she carried on. 'A desperate bully who shapes around trying to get what he can't have. To think of that scumbag here in my kitchen, in my home. And then what he did to that guy in the car… But he did it to him and not you. Get me? He just wanted to scare you. Not harm you. Fenton can watch us all he wants, but he'll eventually accept that you and I have no idea where Ryan is. And then... Then he'll go away, too.'

Tara closed her eyes. Maybe Fenton would become solely Christine's problem. *Christine would tell him that I'd slept with Ryan. Maybe she has already. But so what? That doesn't mean I know where he is. Christine – telling me I'd get what I deserve. Is she some type of fucking witch? No, of course she isn't. She just knew Fenton was closing in on us because she's the one who sent him in our direction. Still, even she doesn't deserve Fenton in her life. Especially after what happened with Ryan. Would Fenton kill her? He can't. Things like that don't happen.*

Forcing aside mutinous thoughts, Tara tried to focus on what would happen after she and David paid off Gordon tomorrow.

The inescapable fact was that soon they would be just another couple with no money and a baby on the way. Their mortgage and bridging loan was supposed to be the doorway to all their finest dreams. Instead, it had ended up being their vow of poverty.

There had to be a way out of this. She almost felt ashamed for looking for it. *I just need to create another sure thing*. But what was a sure thing? *A sure thing is something that is guaranteed to impress everyone. A huge, rusty sculpture that millionaires will want on their lawns?* It was impossible. She wasn't a Banksy or an Emin or a McQueen. She'd simply had a baseline of raw talent, a singular very clever idea and amazing good luck: no one wins the lottery twice. Auction prices for her work in the secondary market had crumbled. Once the art magazines discovered her latest prices, they would announce the market's verdict and her name would never recover.

Still, Tara searched for a way out. But it was like trying to piece together a thousand-part jigsaw when most of the pieces were blue sky. And then, suddenly, she found an idea: 'We can tell Fenton. We can tell him what really happened. That'll make sure he backs off. And maybe he'll help us. Maybe he'll scare Gordon away, too. For money. For one hundred thousand. Two hundred. We can even afford three. He's a scumbag drug dealer. He'd jump at that.'

David shook his head and drained his glass. 'Know what happens if we tell Fenton? He'll just see me killing Ryan as me taking over Ryan's problems. We'd owe him whatever Ryan owed him. Then after he got that, he'd take the rest off us – because he can. He'll take all our money *and then* kill us. Because we'll be nothing to him but messy loose ends. That's the way people like him do business.'

*This is all my fault*, Tara thought. If she had not insisted on having her final fling, she and David would now be enjoying a celebratory drink, honouring their house, their soon-to-be child, all their good fortune. Instead, she had fucked Ryan. It was neither right nor just that her life with David was a single bad decision away from imploding.

'Look, Tara, even if I pay Gordon tomorrow—'

'*If?* You're paying him!'

'*If* I pay him tomorrow, our problem will still never go away, even if Fenton does. After we give all our money to Gordon and lose the house – know what happens then? The new owners dig up the patio. That's what happens. They dig up the patio because they extend this place further or they hate the travertine or whatever. But one day that patio will be dug up and—'

'Fine. Then we've a few months before the repossession to… deal with it. A few months is all the time in the world to… figure out what to do about *that*. So forget about it. Focus on the now. You're scared. Of course you are – you're sane. Look at our situation. There's nothing *not* to be scared of.'

David spoke in barely a mumble: 'You're better off without me. I've decided to go to the police. This is all on me. That way, you can hang onto the house and give our kid the life it deserves. And that way, Fenton can't touch you. Not if I'm arrested. Not with the whole world looking on. I'll say I fought with Ryan over money. Just money. And that I panicked and buried him. Gordon will have nothing, and he can hardly contradict me without implicating himself with what went on.'

Defeat seemed to be flowing out of David like ink, staining everything, ruining everything. It was as if, after all these years, Tara had suddenly lost the grip she'd had on him. And without that grip, they would both tumble and fall. Life had already taught her that the only way to know how much you love someone is when you lose them. And right now she felt a deep, essential hunger for her husband's return.

'I need another drink,' David muttered, and walked out to the bar.

Tara walked over to the fridge, opened it and grabbed the bottle of chilled tequila that was in there for the celebratory shots she'd planned to pour for her friends when they were due to visit later in the week. Slipping through the breach in the slider and out onto the patio, she stared down at the travertine. Where was her disgust? Where was her guilt? Were those emotions just postponed until after the crisis was dealt with? She sniffed at the air. The smell of new cement, drying paint and solidifying glue amalgamated into the single scent of Ryan. His aroma had stayed behind like a haunting.

She unscrewed the lid of the bottle. *You can't lose a baby with a single shot of tequila. It's a party drink. Sure, you've drank it since you were fifteen.* The doctor had assured her that everything was fine. The baby would keep growing, eating up all the clean space. David's child was inside and beginning to communicate with her. Soon she'd have to share it with the world.

She took a deep slug and winced. *There's too much going on. I can't deal with it. The baby will be fine. It'll be worse for the baby if I flip out for hours. It's medicinal. I can't fucking deal with anything right now.* She waited for that inherent, gut-wrenching response to stop her from taking more. But it didn't come. She took another gulp and, step by step, everything about her that had been fuzzy and grey was changing to bright Technicolor. It was like having her brain shaken out like a towel. Bit by bit her thoughts became uncrumpled, creaseless, simple and straightforward.

Taking a final deep slug, she shoved the bottle into the hedge and out of David's view. *There – baby is fine. I'm better. I can deal with this.* Tara returned to the kitchen with shoulders spread, running her hands through her hair. It was strange how the entire situation now seemed more distant – like a horrific news story unfolding live on TV rather than in her kitchen. But she also knew that soon the dreadful reality would collapse on her. So it was important to get David back onside now – to kill, once and for all, his crazy idea about going to the police and leaving her behind, alone, for years and years.

David was leaning against one of the supporting roof columns. Tara pretended not to notice that he had poured himself another triple measure. You don't punish each other for figuring out how to survive.

'You've given up?' she asked.

'There is no way out. I don't have any cards left to play.'

'Don't be a coward.'

'A coward? *A coward*? It's the right thing to do, Tara. The only thing to do. For you and the baby.'

'I'm looking at my husband and I don't see the man I married. This is not the guy that saved me in a bathroom. This is not the guy who took my going-nowhere life outside the Shelbourne Hotel and moments later made it into something amazing inside its lobby. This is not the guy who I chose to have a kid with.'

'Listen to me for a minute. You're always wondering what your father would think of your life. Well, what would he think of it now? Do you think he'd agree with your choices? That he'd want you to stick with the man who murdered Ryan and buried him right under his daughter's feet? The man who not only murdered Ryan, but then gave all your money away?'

Tara glared at him. 'My father's dead. He doesn't get a say in this any more. There's just us now.'

David straightened against the pillar. 'Tara, there's no "us" any more. There's just you and me. Tara and David. So you – you have to hold onto what you have, to make a life for yourself and the baby. Me, I murdered someone. There isn't anything worse a person can do. I'm screwed. The end.'

She could feel her heart pounding. 'In our current situation, a killer is not a bad thing to be. Killers are the type of people that survive these situations.'

Astonished, David stared at his wife. 'I'm not a killer. It was an accident. I didn't like Ryan, but I didn't hate him. I didn't hate him enough to kill him. I'm a university lecturer. I'm a historian. I am *not* a killer.'

'Act like a killer, or you'll never lecture again,' Tara said, justifying the unjustifiable. She knew that she and David now had to be above humanity's laws. In order to survive, they needed their own new moral code.

David was clearly stricken by the callousness of his wife's comments – their rashness. He took a step back and made a tent with his fingers. 'Where did *that* come from? What's wrong with you?'

'Nothing. Jesus. I just had a few shots of tequila.'

David increased the steepness of his tented fingers. He recognised the first phase of her tequila buzz – the phase he never liked, before it mellowed out into being affable and funny.

'You need to stay focused,' Tara continued, 'on what's important. We need a plan. Stop staring at me. Jesus. You can slam back half a bottle of Scotch and I can't have *one* drink? Is that all you've got to worry about? Can't we just sort this?'

He reached out and pushed her backwards until she was pressed up against the glass of the sliding door.

'You're hurting me.'

'No, I'm not.'

She looked to the ground. It was true, he wasn't hurting her. He wasn't even trying to demonstrate how angry he was. That had never been David's style. He was simply trying to get her to look at him.

'Jesus, if there was just one time in the history of the fucking world when a fucking few shots is justified then this is fucking it.'

'You're pregnant!'

'I know! I know! And Ryan is buried there!'

'First you have sex with Ryan. Now you throw back tequila while pregnant with my baby. Who are you? Jesus Christ.'

'Ryan is dead – DEAD – next to our kitchen. You fucking killed him and Gordon caught you. And Fenton's... And *then* I had fucking Christine here today.'

'Ryan's wife? Here? What the hell did she want?'

'She admired my shoes. I liked her dress. What *the fuck* do you mean "what does she want"? She was asking about her husband. She's in shock. She needs to be doing something but there's nothing she can do. And she fucking slapped me. In my own kitchen. I had to take ten minutes of abuse off her because she knows all about... She knew about Ryan and me.'

'How the hell does she know about that?'

'Haven't a clue. But believe it or not, that was about as good as my day got. And you, you just expect me to just... to just... I don't know what you expect me to do!'

'I don't expect you to lash into a bottle of tequila while pregnant with my child. Are you mad?' David held up his hands to show her that he was cooling down, that he was still in control, because he rarely raised his voice. He patted his breast pocket for the cigarettes he wasn't allowed to smoke, took them out and put one in his mouth. 'Tara, you can't hurt the kid. OK? No matter what happens to me or between us. Got that?'

She nodded. 'Of course I've got that. I'd never hurt the baby. Baby's fine.'

There was a twinge inside her womb. One of her college friends had a baby that had died when it was one year old. It was like it was just raptured out of the world; its entire life taken away at once – its schooldays, romances, its own children. Another of her school friends had miscarried last year, her body dumping the non-viable foetus like bad stocks. Tara pictured the image of *her own* baby on the doctor's monitor – a black stain just floating there, like an oil slick on an ocean.

'David, I need to sit down... No, I think I'm going to be sick.' And then she ran out to the toilet. But she didn't vomit. Instead, she locked the door, placed her hands over her stomach and wept. 'I'm sorry,' she whispered. 'I'm so sorry.'

The rest of the evening passed in a sweaty blur of anxiety and doomed resignation. Tara showered and drank herbal tea with Dora on her knees like a calming stress toy. All the while, she talked and talked, working herself around the same problem again and again, as if she was missing something, as if it would be obvious soon enough. She pleaded with David not to hand himself in, and while he could barely bring himself to talk to her, he eventually reassured her that he wouldn't, that he would meet Gordon as planned and transfer the money. He would've said anything to ease her stress. Finally, she crashed with the mental exhaustion of it all and David walked her to their bedroom at eleven thirty.

'Are you coming, David?'

He shook his head. Now that the alcohol was on the way out of her system he could barely bring himself to look at her again. *I can't believe what I've done to you, to us, to our future, to our child.*

'Are we going to be OK, David?'

'I have to lock up. I'll come to bed later.'

He shut the door, knowing that she'd be unconscious by the time he got back up. Sleeping for a straight ten hours was not unusual for Tara. He'd seen her sleep peacefully in a New York hotel with a dumpster screeching beneath the window. He'd watched her napping serenely on a Thai night train with all its windows open. But that was back when David's wife had been his. That was before Sunday night.

And yet he also took comfort from the fact that she was still there – that Tara hadn't left; that she was staying with him. The reality was, David loved her for who she was even as he hated her for what she'd done. And he knew his love for Tara was vastly more powerful than any smear of hate. That knowledge was reassuring because it meant that he could vent his anger, knowing that by venting he would diminish his umbrage rather than let it take root.

Going back downstairs, he walked through all the rooms, holding the purring lump of Dora to his chest, taking everything in, trying to imprint it all onto his brain because soon he'd never see it again. Despite having assured Tara that he wasn't going to the police, David was resigned to handing himself in. There was no alternative. If he met Gordon in the morning at the bank, then Tara would be implicated in covering up the murder of her lover. In fact, from the moment he'd told his wife the truth, she was implicated. Plus, sooner or later the *real* police would have to get involved with Ryan's disappearance. And when they did, Christine would tell them about Tara having slept with her husband – which would have been the last time anyone had seen him alive. From there it was just a matter of joining the dots before it was all over. If Tara and his child were to have the future they deserved, then David would have to take the blame for everything. By him going to the police, Tara would hang onto the house, have a few hundred thousand left over and a bright future once the inevitable hoopla from his trial blew over. She would eventually get used to him being in jail and then maybe move on. She mightn't want to at first – but he'd make her. He'd make her because he loved her utterly.

After letting Dora out, he sat at the kitchen counter, staring out into the garden, wondering if Fenton's men were going to return; if they'd already returned; if they were now down there in the woods, watching everything. Turning on the flexible spray tap, David filled a glass. For a moment, he marvelled at the water pressure. Then his eyes closed as he tried to examine the future in the darkness. Ahead, the tracks of their lives had been blown apart, and all they could do was sit tight and wait to see where their out-of-control carriage would land.

*

Later, David lay in bed, staring at the ceiling while listening to the fan. How could Tara sleep so peacefully beside him? Didn't she know that they were on the wrong side of a lost war? He closed his eyes and waited to fall asleep. Over the last few hours he'd drifted off here and there, but every ten minutes he'd awake with a fresh smear of sweat across his chest. Surely sleep would have to come soon? Proper sleep. Not this broken kind that merely teased him with moments of relief punctuated by depressing jolts back to reality. He'd endured many sleepless nights before Tara came into his life. Back then he'd often dress before strolling around the docklands, drifting by the apartment complexes, envying the darkened windows shielding the sleepers within from the tick-tock of night outside. But he'd also gained comfort from his nocturnal walks, because insomniacs tended eventually to stumble across one another; the world narrowed down significantly at 4 a.m.

He found Tara's fingers and enclosed them gently in his. Every man wants a woman who will lie for him no matter what he's done. *Why did you do it? Why did you have to do it? What was the point?* Despite what she'd done, Tara deserved the world – he'd always known that, from the moment he'd laid eyes on her as she took her seat at the back of his class.

At eight o'clock, after the bits of sleep he had managed to extract from the previous six hours, David stepped into the shower and let the water from the rainforest head drill his back. Then he shaved before the steam-covered mirror. Gradually, drops of condensation cut narrow paths of clarity through the mist; streaks of lucidity in which he could see his reflection. He felt no identity with the man who stared back. His dark, saturated hair had a haze about it from the light, giving him a vague, unfinished outline, as if his signal was weak. The bruise was still there on his forehead – but fading – and the skin beneath his eyes had become papery. He could even see the tracery of the blood vessels. *Five years older in twenty-four hours – thanks for that, too, Ryan.*

Outside on the landing, he looked up the stairs towards the attic. Intuitively he made a mental note to get Ryan to fix the stain on the wall before the absurd impossibility of that resolution dawned. He thought that he could smell a hint of stale smoke beneath the fresh paint, drifting down from his office. Ryan's molecules were still in the air. They would always be. He descended to the kitchen, where he opened several cupboards until he found the jar of instant that the builders had left behind. The coffee was so hard that he had to stab at it to loosen the granules before scraping them out.

He stood before the huge window. A trapped bluebottle bounced against the glass, rattling away. David caught it in his fist. For a moment he considered letting it go, but almost instinctively his thumb and forefinger pressed together, crushing the fly, its exoskeleton snapping like a popcorn hull.

As he pulled open the slider, he thought of how much his mother had been looking forward to sitting in the landscaped grounds, and how she was under the impression that Sundays in Lawrence Court would be a fact of life from now on. His mother: she had been so happy upon hearing that she was going to be a grandmother. '*You'll love being a da, Davy. You'll love seeing him learn things. You used to look at things, stare at 'em. There was a lot going on in there. You looked at bleed'n everything.*'

David imagined looking out over a blank page of snow in the garden from the heated luxury liner that would be his home in winter. *I'll never see that now.*

The smell of the cooling coffee curled up into his nostrils as the sun's rays pierced the fortification of leaves. It was a perfect city garden, because it hid the city. Standing on the patio, he closed his eyes and listened to the natural habitat. He pictured the cavernous hangar he had once worked in, jammed with crates and towering pallets of Chinese and South Korean hardware. He had never liked the way the warehouse smelled – damp, too warm, vaguely metallic. But what he *had* always liked was the almost magical magnificence of its grid storage system. The huge warehouse trafficked hundreds of tons of raw materials every week, and yet nothing ended up in the wrong place. It was unadorned, authentic precision. Maybe that was where he'd always belonged. If he'd stayed there, none of this would ever have happened.

*I never fitted here.* The environs of Lawrence Court were mostly an old-fashioned patriarchy – a home to the men who spent the day in their offices, spinning money out of their other money before returning home to relax with the women who had tastefully lined their nests with it. It was a luxurious sanctuary to city lawyers, actuaries and business professionals; the land where the Porsches, BMWs and Landrovers went to sleep at night when their fun day was over.

Over the years, David had taught many kids from this area, and had resented them. Their parents were busybodies who came to the university's open day as if their eighteen-year-old was joining a Montessori. These were the parents who raised their kids like racehorses, betting their futures on a winning pedigree; the children were their retirement packages. But even in his student days, when he'd only been there because of his scholarship, and when he'd never made the evening drinking sessions because he was working the warehouse nightshift, he'd never let them see that he felt excluded or slighted; he'd never let them see that he recognised the difference between him and them. His first class degree was better than any of theirs – and that was all that counted.

But despite having always resented the streamlined lives of the moneyed, David also drew comfort from the neatness of being able to divide the world into two like that. It was like reducing life to a simple and perfect map, portraying a clear and defined border between two very different and idiosyncratic land masses. Plus, he'd thoroughly enjoyed Tara's success. Despite himself, he'd thrilled at rubbing shoulders with the kind of men who had someone else shave them; the kind of men who got bored on their yachts. Like Scott, they'd all found Tara refreshing because she wasn't interested in critiques of the neo-Marxist, cyber-capitalist, post-human Manhattan variety. But in a few hours, those days would just be the fading memories of yet another banal, asinine loser from the Cawley Estates.

David looked to his feet. He was standing directly over Ryan. It was incredible to think that his wife's lover was beneath him, rotting, decaying into the structure of the house. He preferred to think of the body as miles below, in the earth's core. It was the human impulse to annihilate the corpse – burn it, bury it, sink it in the sea. The dead make the living uncomfortable.

There were footsteps on the decking next door – the irregular swish of slippered feet. It must be Stephanie, the quiet, unassuming housewife, who rarely talked to her husband in public. He could hear her clipping leaves from one of her many potted plants. Had Shay and Stephanie once been full of life and sex and love? The way Tara and he had been – before Sunday? It was impossible to imagine it. Shay and Stephanie's marriage seemed to be conducted in silence, with a grim determination on both their parts to get through it until the end.

'David?' The hedge quivered next to the wall and suddenly two hands shoved back the foliage just enough for Shay's face to peer through.

*No, no, no*. 'Good morning,' David said. *Why, dear nightmare? Why?*

Shay clearly resented the fact that some years ago he'd crossed a line where society no longer had any use for people of his age. Fifty was the new forty. Sixty the new fifty. But seventy? Seventy was just seventy. Shay was also immune to the disease of the suburbs – the desire to be liked – and he didn't believe in the natural ebb and flow of conversation. He wasn't the type of guy that David could simply mention the weather to and who in turn mentioned the weather back. Additionally, he was the worst type of pain in the neck – a know-it-all who was right all of the time.

David took a last pull from the cigarette before flicking it into the garden in a Catherine wheel of sparks.

'It's a disaster, David. An absolute disaster. It's soiled water.' Shay's head scanned about the stretch of patio, taking in the travertine, the glass slider, the lip of the roof with its spotlights, heater and stencilled ceiling. He looked at it the way some people look at modern sculpture: a hazy dislike turning to hatred when they see the price tag. 'The carpet has to go. The smell. I'm past breaking point.'

David, who only now remembered his brief exchange with Shay last night, said, 'You've had a flood?'

Shay's protruding head turned redder. 'Jesus Christ!'

'We're clear here.'

'That's. The. Point.' Shay tweaked the end of his nose. 'You're clear because nothing is getting from us into you. The drainage people said the blockage must be where you are standing. *Exactly* where you are standing.'

David felt a pulse in his feet. It was as if Ryan was banging on the underside of the travertine. *Act like the innocent man you once were.* 'When Ryan's next down, come in and talk to him.'

'Me? Go and talk to him? I wouldn't waste boot leather. Ryan would talk the rain out of wetting him. I've dealt with Maximum's management pyramid over this and that for the last two months. Did I say "management pyramid"? Chain of complaint, more like. Sure, your architect was even in here recently about your garden levels. When was that?'

'Last week, I think.' David had no idea.

Shay shook his head, making it clear that once again David had lived down to his expectations. 'I can see you nodding and making all the right noises. But I can tell that you're done with it. "Not my circus, not my monkey". It radiates off you.'

'Shay, it's terrible what you're going through. I genuinely understand. And I'm not trying to palm it off. I just can't do anything about it right now. You've got to trust me on that.'

'You think that I, for one minute, even imagined that you would do anything about it? Look David, *I* got my hands on some rods. So, *I* want to get into your drains.'

David's feet felt hot. *Ryan can't be causing the blockage. It's not possible.* David, trying to phrase it diplomatically, said, 'Look, when the guys are here snagging, I'll have them lift our drains and stick the rods down. And I'll even send them in to you to take another look at your drains.' Being nice was exhausting. Suddenly he spotted something at the end of the lawn, just before the spread of trees. It looked like a bunched grey T-shirt.

David drifted by Shay's protruding head and approached the steps to the grass. What was that at the end of the garden? Where had it come from?

'Are you... Are you even listening to me? That's it, David. You're rubbish. A terrible neighbour. If I'd known…' But his sentence was never finished, as his wife reached through the hedge and pulled Shay back to his own decking.

David descended to the grass. Something had been missing that morning, and he suddenly realised what it was. He continued on down the lawn, and as the football-sized lump came into sight, his heart plunged. He quickened his pace, wishing he was wrong but knowing that he was right. Dora's decapitated head lay on its side, her eyes serenely closed.

# CHAPTER TEN

Tara had slept through for eight hours after the tequila's speediness had finally worn off. At nine o'clock, she took her time beneath the hot pins of the rainforest showerhead. The only lingering effect of her drinking was a pounding pulse. But she couldn't be sure whether that was the remnants of the alcohol or because of the anxiety throbbing through her. While rubbing her belly in the shower, she muttered, 'I'm sorry. So sorry. I don't deserve you.'

Now Tara sat at the edge of the bed as steam and the scent of honey shampoo escaped through the closed en-suite door. She turned off the blow-dryer's roar of air. *David killed Ryan. He's buried in front of my kitchen.* A trail of her wet footprints led all the way across the maple floorboards. *Is the fact that he killed Ryan the only reason why David has stayed with me in the house? And is that all I fucking care about? I am a bad person. I am utterly self-centred. I am rotten.*

Next to Tara's make-up table was an antique rose-pink upholstered dressing screen. Hanging from the side of it was a gorgeous linen Vuitton raincoat and a chestnut crocodile Prada tote that she'd bought when the real money had begun to arrive. She saw herself selling them on eBay. *Only yesterday I was face-to-face with Ryan's wife. Now I know she's a widow. And who knows what Fenton will do to her. Can I really deal with all this shit?* And yet the moment she thought those words, Tara knew that she could. She had to. She didn't want to wake up alone for the rest of her life.

Tara again wondered where David was. She'd called out for him earlier, but there'd been no reply. That hadn't surprised her. What had surprised her was that he wasn't in the house, even though his BMW was still on the driveway. She'd been surprised when David had bought that car. It was the only glimpse he'd given the world of his base nature – but it was a very public glimpse, even if a brand-new BMW 5 Series saloon was nothing special in this neighbourhood. Tara looked down at her own car next to David's. It was six months old and had a sunroof – a sunroof that she never opened because of the sun. They would have to sell them both now, to be replaced with a single second-hand, low-emissions car.

She entered the kitchen and as she started the blender whirring, suddenly noticed an absence. Making a *pssch-pssch* sound, she scanned the kitchen for Dora. *David must have fed her and then let her out.* Usually, Dora waited for Tara to get up before wanting to be fed. The cat would be so pleased to see her that she'd try to nose her way into Tara's torso. *The move must have thrown the poor thing off kilter*. Tara looked down the garden, expecting to see Dora squaring the land, marking her territory. She drifted towards the kitchen door, watching as the peaks of the trees came into view beneath the lip of the roof. Miles above the tallest branches, a commercial jetliner crossed the cobalt blue like a tiny dart, chalking out a fattening contrail. And then something moved in her peripheral vision.

Tara turned, expecting to see David on the patio. But it was Shay. With his back to Tara, he was holding the long pole of a drainage rod and moving towards the bordering hedge in a tense, jerky type of walk. There, he accepted another pole being passed through the branches. Tara could see the shape of Shay's wife through the hedge.

The manhole at the edge of the patio was uncovered, the metal lid resting upright against the bordering wall. Shay stared down into the void, looking imperious and sombre. He already had two poles connected. He screwed on the third one, his face red and creased, beads of sweat on his forehead. It was like watching an animated Lucian Freud. Then he fed the elongated rod into the darkness as if he was sweeping a chimney from the top down. Just feet away – in the direction that he was thrusting the rods – was Ryan's body.

Tara's eyes looked to the left and the right as if a clue as to what to do next was somewhere in the kitchen. She wished David was home. He'd know what to say to defuse the situation calmly and efficiently. It was usually a positive characteristic of his that in times of crisis he inevitably solidified into an automaton of practicality.

She opened the door, stepped outside and said, 'Shay, what are you doing?'

He looked up, and then with pigeon darts of his head towards the hedge and back again, blanched. 'Tara? Oh, I thought no one was in... I called in ten minutes ago but there wasn't an answer.'

'I was in the shower.'

'Well... This morning I told David I was going to unblock the drains.'

Tara could see right through him. He was that transparent, like tracing paper. 'And David said this was OK?'

'I didn't realise you were in. Sorry to frighten you.'

'You didn't frighten me. Did David tell you that this was OK?'

'I told David that the drain needs unblocking.'

'*Once again* – did he give you permission to come in, through the hedge, without either of us being here?'

Each sensed the other's nervousness – which was good – as it meant neither of them had the power. Shay released the elongated pole. It remained sticking out of the sewer at a forty-five-degree angle. 'Enough is enough,' he said. 'If *you're* not going to help us fix the problem that *you* caused in the first place, then I'll take care of it myself.'

'Where do you think you're living? Beirut? You can't just squeeze through the hedge and lift—'

'There was *human excrement* on the downstairs toilet floor this morning. There's now a smell coming from the kitchen sink drain. It has to be fixed *now*. The drainage people can do no more. They said that the local council are powerless without your cooperation. And without it, we have to go to court. Which we will. Oh, yes. But are you really going to force us out of our home? It's a blockage. You understand that? Just a simple blockage. It's not right to cause that and do nothing about it and leave us to stew in it. And that's what we're doing – *literally* stewing in it. So I've only put two rods down and it's hit something solid. Something that won't budge. I can feel the blockage. And it's directly there.'

He pointed to the slab that was, in essence, Ryan's gravestone. For a moment, Tara was paralysed with fear. The smooth travertine surface appeared like the placid water of a lake: too still, too calm and far too indifferent to have wanted her lover's body in the first place. Could the body actually be *in* the sewage waste pipe?

'Jesus, Shay, David will talk to you later. This is *not* the fucking time.'

Shay paled, as if he'd never heard such language outside of when he'd accidentally come across it on television. On the other side of the hedge, Tara could make out Stephanie pacing in her slippers, impatient for her husband's return.

Trying to plant an obvious idea into his head, Tara said, 'David will have the guys back snagging, so…' She looked away. She felt genuinely sorry for Shay. But she had to remain focused, ruthless. She took a step towards him. 'Leave my property, or I'll…' She considered saying 'scream', but settled for, 'Call the police.'

Shay left the rods stubbornly poking out of the manhole. As he backed away towards the hedge, his head shook in disgust, as if helplessly watching a man beat a dog. From the other side, Stephanie spread the undergrowth wide to help his return. He muttered, 'They can't do this to us. We've always lived here. They haven't even unpacked. It's not right.'

For the first time, Tara felt isolated rather than secluded in her dream house – as if she was the only astronaut left on a space station. The future suddenly terrified her. She was an hour away from losing everything she'd ever wished for, and months away from gaining something precious that she could no longer afford. Soon she'd be alone in some rented apartment with their child. She'd watch the front door close, leaving her at home with the baby. She pictured David returning at the end of the day and reluctantly asking if she'd any news, and she'd have to craft an anecdote out of nothing. At night she'd be exhausted and silent until they wrapped the day up by whisper-fighting in the dark of their bed.

David appeared from the woodland at the end of the garden with a shovel. He marched up the lawn and climbed the steps to the patio. He dropped the shovel with a clatter onto the travertine and continued past Tara, stalking off into the kitchen. Tara waited a moment, trying to come up with the right thing to say, before retreating inside to the central control room of their unfolding catastrophe. Inside the kitchen, David was leaning against the island.

Abruptly, Tara felt a burning resentment towards her husband – as if she'd expected him to come up with the impossible solution overnight. 'What the hell were you doing down the garden?'

David toyed with his packet of cigarettes, clearly wondering whether it was still OK to smoke indoors. He decided that it wasn't and pushed the pack across the countertop.

'Is that meant to be an answer?' Tara said. 'While you were doing something really clever and useful like – what? *Gardening*? – I've been chasing Shay off our patio. He wants to get down to our drains. He wants to get down to…'

Rubbing his hands through his hair, David said, 'I was talking with him this morning. I think we've fallen out.'

'Who fucking cares? Right now, *that's* the least of our problems. Are you ready to meet Gordon when he calls?'

David offered confirmation by looking down at his phone. But there was a peculiar vibe shimmering about him – as if he was only acting concerned; as if there was something else on his mind, something more important to do that morning than meet their architect.

Tara said, 'I can live without the money. I can live without the house. The one thing I can't live without is you. Do you understand that? If you keep talking about giving in, then I'll... I'll... I swear I'll kill myself.' Sometimes it seemed that the whole point of life was not to die the same death as her father.

Silence expanded around them. Usually they were comfortable with the absence of words: that telepathic marital communication that is often misconstrued by outsiders as awkward silence. But this time it was different. This time it *was* awkward silence.

Tara broke it: 'I'm serious. And I'm not going to say it again. I want you and I want our child. Fuck the house. Fuck the money. I don't care if we end up in a bedsit in some shithole down the country. As long as there's you and me. Got it?' She leaned forward, and with both hands clutched David's fist like a prayer book. 'I can't deal with this unless you accept that we are in this together. I *really* need you to stop thinking about giving in and leaving me alone for the rest of my life. This is about *us*. Got it? Tell me you've got it.'

'I told you last night. And I'm saying it again. I'll meet Gordon this morning and I'll do the transfer.'

Tara only half-smiled; she doubted his honesty. She knew that David was wary of her now, as he was suddenly unable to read the future that he had so meticulously nurtured over the last few years. It was as if he saw Tara as a malfunctioning satellite, spinning away from its safe orbit and out into the blackness of the abyss.

'You need to be crystal clear,' she said. 'In the zone. You've got to realise that Ryan is irrelevant now. We can only deal with what's left.' Tara looked through the glass to the corner of the patio. 'It's no longer anything to do with Ryan. And nothing will ever be about him again.'

'Tara, remember when we began drinking at four on Fridays? All those mojitos… After we have the baby, we'll do that again. They were good times.'

Feeling that her words were finally landing here and there, sticking like snow on dry land, she said, 'And there will be more good times. I need my man back. The man who, from a windowless office at the back of the Arts building, managed to get Leo Di-fucking-Caprio on the phone after hearing that Scott McCoy had gifted him one of my paintings. It's because of you that we had features in the *Chicago Tribune*, the *Toronto Star*, the *Miami Herald*, the *Guardian*, *Le Monde*. You dealt with it all *and* basically ran a fucking history department *and* worked on your PhD. Now you're going to deal with this. We'll figure out what to do. Together. We always do. This type of thing – pressure – we thrive on it.'

David placed his hands on her shoulders. He spoke softly: 'I think that I did something really, *really* wrong to you somewhere, at some time, and I don't know what. Why were you so unhappy that you had to go and—'

She kissed him, briefly, inexpertly, and said, 'I told you why I did it. It was barely a reason. I know that. And if I could rewind, I'd rewind. But I can't.'

'I love you.' The few times David had ever said that sentence – he had only ever said it to Tara – she had sensed his discomfort. Not because it was untrue, but because he was saying something that the world would hear a million times that day in cinemas and on TV. The world would read it in a million books and hear it on the radio in a million songs. David had simply not been able say it without being embarrassed. Until now.

'Do you love me?' he asked.

'Of course I do. I love you as much as it's humanly possible to love someone.' Tara stared at him, feeling his desire to believe.

'You look different,' David said.

'I took a shower.'

'Some shower.'

Tara knew what he was doing, but couldn't dissipate the 'Last Supper' ambience; the feeling that destiny would soon take hold and that there was nothing they could do but fulfil their roles in it.

They tried again, this time kissing long and deep, Tara feeling the press of his hand against her breast – possessive, confident. But then David broke away and asked, 'Did you think of me during it?'

'No. Of course I didn't. I mean... Yes. Jesus, I don't know.'

'Did you compare him to me?'

*Jesus.* She folded her arms. 'I'm not doing this. Do you want to make things worse?' And yet, simultaneously, she could feel his anger slacken further.

'How much effort did you put into it?' She could tell that David was thinking while speaking. 'I saw the underwear you had on.'

'They were black.'

His eyes widened a little.

'Lace.' In the past, she'd told him all about her previous lovers. He'd liked to hear about their lusts, their secret fantasies, what she'd done with them and what she hadn't. It had been like foreplay. David pressed himself tighter to her now, his hands under her blouse, his knuckles grazing across her stomach, gliding over her smooth skin. She felt the pulse in his fingers.

Tara, her attention hooked like a fish, whispered, 'Tell me what you want.'

'You've the psychology degree. Whatever you give me, I'll like.'

She watched as a lovely, preoccupied kind of look fell over his dark eyes. They kissed again, as if it was the first time, like they had both been waiting months for someone to make the first move. With Tara's blouse pulled down past her elbows and one leg removed from her lowered jeans, she sat astride him on the kitchen floorboards and they finally made love in their new house.

Afterwards, as she lay still on the floor, her cheeks were flushed and reddened. So was that it? Was everything OK now? She looked down at her nakedness, taking in the vague rosy imprint of her husband's fingerprints on her skin. She kissed the fading bruise on David's forehead and then sank back into her nicely fucked mood.

David stood, and as he pulled up his jeans, Tara checked her blouse for stains. She put it back on, adjusting her breasts beneath it. David lit a post-coital cigarette and she watched him smoke it. 'Don't look so pleased.'

'Why? I take pride in my work.'

Tara couldn't help smiling. Did sex have the power to make everything between them better again? She felt a shudder of excitement. A mistress is a private thing, a meal to be eaten alone. But her husband had ripped it from Ryan's jaws.

The arrival of a text sounded. Immediately Tara stood and they both stared at David's phone. 'Gordon' flashed on the display. David opened it.

*The corner of Vern and Sobal Hill. In front of your bank. I'll be parked there. Be here in 30 minutes. Let's finish this and get on with our lives.*

'Thirty minutes,' David muttered, and looked at the clock as if he didn't know what to do with himself until then. 'Right, I'm having a quick shower. You OK?'

'No, I'm not OK. You're having *a shower*? You had a shower already.'

'I was digging down the garden.' Tara detected a flash of melancholy in his gaze as it turned towards the window. But then he added more cheerfully, 'The landscapers missed something. And just now, after that, I *need* a shower.' Unable to offer anything else, David left the kitchen. She listened to him climb the stairs. A dresser drawer slid shut above. He was undressing. The shoe rack creaked; wooden hangers clattered against one another. The water pump in the control room began its low drone.

She muttered, 'A fucking shower…' She didn't know how she'd wanted him to respond to their conditional surrender – but this was not it. Obviously, there was nothing normal about their situation, but David was acting abnormally abnormal. She picked up his phone to reread the message.

*He doesn't care about the text because he's still going to the police – not to Gordon.* She suddenly had no doubt – Tara trusted her intuition. He'd lied to her. She'd believed that together they were indomitable, and that the world would always be theirs to explore, experience and use.

She moved towards the hall, intending to race upstairs and scream, cry and rage at him. But that wouldn't be enough. He'd made his mind up. The next time David left the house, it would be to go to the police. Or maybe he would just phone them? Tara knew what she had to do, and it had to be done quickly. *She* would meet Gordon and do the transfer. Then she, too, would be guilty – of covering up Ryan's murder. She would be an accomplice. If David went to the police after that, he would be condemning them both.

As if the idea was a diamond, she turned it round and round in her head, looking for a flaw or crack, examining it from every perspective, looking for regret. She found none. Quickly, she tapped out a text.

*Fuck 30 mins. I'm coming NOW. Be there.*

She waited, counting silently in her head. *I shouldn't have cursed. David doesn't curse.* But when she reached fifteen, Gordon replied:

*K*

Tara left the house. As she drove to Sobal Hill, she sipped on her lukewarm breakfast smoothie. It was a dismal disappointment. She yearned for something sweeter than sugar and honey: her life from forty-eight hours ago.

Tara stopped at the lights. Across the intersection was the row of shops with their bank in the centre. In front of it was Gordon's Saab. A feeling of amazement fell on her. It was as if she couldn't quite believe that she still had no plan to get out of this. The lights changed, and she pulled up onto the span of pavement beside her architect. Climbing out, she opened the Saab passenger door and slipped in beside him.

Immediately, Gordon said, 'What do you want? Actually, let me rephrase that – what *the fuck* do you want?' With his shades on, he looked past Tara to her car. 'Where's Dave? Is his mother on the way too?'

'David's not coming. You're stuck with me. Deal with it.' Tara took a deep breath, trying to sharpen herself. The heat in the airless car felt like a physical weight.

Gordon nodded to himself, making a decision. 'Fine. Whatever. Let's leave Dave at home, pondering all the ways in which his wife has failed him. So you're doing the transfer?'

She nodded, but then said, 'Please don't take it all. Leave us enough to cover the loan. You're not just doing this to David and me. You're doing this... to three of us.'

Gordon's face took on a veneer of sincerity. 'I'm sorry.' He lowered his shades a few centimetres, lending her a granule of eye contact in the process.

'You're *sorry*?'

'Oh, I just automatically say that when I hear "whine whine whine".' He painted inverted comas in the air. 'I just assume that there's something to be *sorry* about.'

Tara opened her mouth to respond, but the space where the words should have been just filled with the bleakness of loss. Her eyes watered and she swallowed back wretchedness. Placing her hands on her stomach, she said, 'We have a child coming. We just want to get on with our lives. Why can't you just take two hundred k? Three hundred k?'

'Can we establish right away that I'm much smarter than you are?' Gordon removed his shades, placed them on the dashboard and continued, 'We're not bargaining. We're not scratching each other's backs. This ended two days ago, in David's office.'

'But Gordon, it's our house. For our family. We'll lose everything.'

'Tara, save me the Flower of the Earth bullshit. Jesus, I know what you are. I know how you work. Look at you. Even *you're* fucking embarrassed.' Gordon looked tired and pale. His skin had loosened from his face, as if too exhausted to cling to his jawline any longer. 'But I tell you this – you do know how to cause a scene. I mean, I'm old school. I'm of the vintage when marriages crashed and burned from lipstick on the collar. These days it's a carelessly undeleted text or email. But where's the fucking drama? I'll tell you where it is – it's when a husband catches his wife with his builder's balls in her mouth in his attic office. Now *that's* drama, Tara. That's class. Respect.'

Tara had heard Gordon being crude before, but only in terms of cracking the whip in the direction of builders, suppliers and subcontractors. With her, he'd always played the role of gentleman knight, ready to defend her cause with his pitiless perfection. When they'd toured the site together, Gordon would often ask her to pop outside for some air, and from there, she'd hear him dressing down Ryan and his men with venomous sarcasm in a naturally booming voice that would have reached the last row of a concert hall. She'd even come to consider Gordon as a friend – but your friend is your friend until suddenly he's not. Life had shown Tara again and again that good people aren't particularly interesting, but that people could be bad in so many remarkable ways.

'You're not a psychopath, Gordon,' she said. 'You're many things, but you're not that. You knew Ryan, and you can't just dismiss his death like you're pretending to.' She'd surprised herself. It felt like she was talking about herself. 'I'd looked Ryan up just because he was the only builder I'd ever known, and the first thing he told me was to talk to you. "You need Gordon." That's what he said.'

Gordon raised his head, as if Tara had slightly interested him. Then he sighed. 'Fine, we worked well together, and since I'm a perfectionist, that's a rare thing. "Perfectionist" is the scariest word a builder can hear when meeting an architect. It means missed deadlines and stupid demands. And I won't deny it – Ryan was a decent man. He didn't deserve what happened. Of course not. But what happened, happened. And in the end, like with most of us, it turns out that Ryan is totally replaceable in every aspect of his life. In other words, he was the average man. And the death of the average man is nothing more than a shift of a number from one column to another; from the list of the living to the list of the dead. That might sound cold. But reality *is* fucking cold.'

Tara pictured Ryan so clearly now: laughing, charming, funny, filling every room with his presence and humour. 'After you get your money, what do we do about Fenton?'

Gordon reddened. He checked the rear-view mirror, pretending to fix his fringe but really checking behind his car, almost as if he expected Fenton to be approaching. 'Who?'

'Stop dicking around. Fenton – the guy who pretended to be a fucking detective.' Tara felt her heartbeat against her blouse. 'The guy who *you* let us believe was a detective. The guy who pointed a fucking gun at my husband.'

'I don't know what you're talking about or who you're talking about. Got it?'

*He's lying. He has to be lying. Gordon and Fenton* have *to be connected. Somehow. And not just through their association with Ryan.* If only David and she had more time to work things out, to figure out what was really going on. She thought of one of David's lines back in college: 'To understand the meaning of history is to understand that where secrecy begins, power begins.' She had no power, because men like Gordon and Fenton had all the secrets. Or maybe they had been buried with Ryan.

Tara said, 'Fenton was Ryan's problem. Now he's ours. David's and mine.'

Gordon didn't seem surprised to hear this. 'Then deal with it. I. Am not. Ryan. Now, we're getting off point. You need to stop opinionating and calm down. So let's go into the bank and finally put all this behind you. They're expecting us.' He licked his lip, not in a sordid manner, but in a man-lost-in-a-desert way.

*Wait. Something's wrong.* Tara noticed a yellow sauce stain next to Gordon's tie knot. It was an uncharacteristic blemish; Gordon was always so perfectly turned out. Tara turned towards him, her knees banging into the automatic gear shift. 'I'm not done yet.'

'Jesus. You are. Trust me.'

Tara suddenly saw him anew: as something stupid and repellent. She looked out the passenger window and, coughing into the hollow of her fist, said, 'Know what I think, Gordon?'

'Tell me – my pulse is pounding.'

'You're just a trust-funded, overprivileged, weak, measly prick.'

'Fuck you, Tara Brown – you're just a washed-up painter whose true success story is managing to get knocked up by her teacher.

Now enough! This conversation is finished. We're getting the fuck out of this car and doing the transfer. Now!'

*Something's not right. Something's off.* Tara shook her head and folded her arms tightly across her chest. She had never seen Gordon act like this before. She could see it in his eyes: a fearful desperation, a rising panic.

'You don't have the balls for this. None of your type do.'

'Tara. Come with me into the bank and do the transfer.'

She stared at the dashboard. A voice in her head pleaded with her, begged her, to just go with him, to give him what he wanted.

'What is the matter with you, Tara? Are you totally fucking stupid? I will ruin your life. I will send your husband to jail. I will—'

She pushed the passenger door open. As she stepped out, she looked back into the car and said, 'Fuck you, Gordon.' She slammed the door, and a moment later was sitting in her own car, staring through the windscreen. *Trust your intuition. Trust your instinct. You've done the right thing.*

Next to her, Gordon's Saab reversed quickly into the intersection.

*Oh my god. Where's he going?*

The Saab disappeared through the lights before the waiting cars had a chance to move.

*Oh Christ, what have I done?* Was he going to the police? *He* is *going to the police.* Should she go back to David? Spend their last few minutes of freedom together? *I fucked up. I fucked up. I fucked up.* No. She mustn't think like that. She had to follow him. If he was going to the police, then she would catch him before he went into the station and give him what he wanted. *I've ruined everything. Or maybe he's not going to the police. I DON'T FUCKING KNOW!*

Her car was already out onto the street. The lights were orange. She stomped on the accelerator. The needle leapt up to sixty. Then seventy. Eighty. She was through the lights, ploughing through a puddle from a broken water main, sending a satisfying fan of water hissing up into the warm summer air. *Breathe.* She breathed. The windscreen wipers beat back and forth.

# CHAPTER ELEVEN

After showering, David stood before the wardrobe, studying the plain white shirt on the hanger. He didn't want to dress, because then he'd have to get on with the worst day of his life. He wondered how Tara must feel. She'd had less than twenty-four hours to soak it all up – how her husband had killed a man; how he'd seemingly conspired to lose all their money, their house, all their dreams. And yet she'd never wavered in battling for them both. Her enthusiasm for the fight was infectious, and when threatened, her mind was like a switchblade. But David knew it was pointless. Soon, she would have to deal with the fact that he had handed himself in, that her future would no longer involve her husband. David had no choice. He *had* to provide Tara and his child with a roof and a future.

Besides that, there was Fenton. After what had been done in his garden last night, David realised that Fenton posed a greater risk to his wife than even losing their home and money did. But once David went to the law and admitted killing Ryan, Fenton would never be able to go near Lawrence Court again with all its attendant media scandals and police attention.

He pictured Dora's sleeping face; how she would nullify a bad day by purring it away on his lap. David had found the remainder of the poor creature's body about twenty feet away, in the middle of the trees. It had been a clean decapitation – perhaps a single swing with a machete rather than a serrated-edged blade. Had Fenton's guy beheaded her because he'd been instructed to, or simply because he'd wanted to? David considered the underappreciated fact that SS commanders had only defied their Führer when he wasn't cruel enough – and yet at the end, they'd all claimed to be just following orders. If all was fair in the world, David would get a chance to take at least two of Fenton's fingers – enough to make him regret for the rest of his life what one of his men had done to a defenceless animal. But life was not fair.

After dressing, David entered the kitchen. He shouted Tara's name. *Where the hell was she?* A moment later, he opened the front door and saw that Tara's car was gone. His pulse began to hammer. He felt like a child whose mother had gone to the supermarket, leaving him alone with a feeling that everything in the world he knew and understood was about to be blasted to pieces. Quickly, he returned to the kitchen, where his phone was on the counter. He looked at his texts, and with disbelief read the exchange between Gordon and apparently himself.

'No, no, no!' he exclaimed, rubbing his hand frantically back and forth through his hair. He phoned Tara, but she didn't answer. Pulling on his jacket, he left the house with a premonition that his wife would never return.

If he hurried, they'd still be there. They *had* to be still there. As he sped out of the cul-de-sac, his anger began to rise. *She knew that I was going to hand myself in. I was never any good at lying to her*. He punched the horn a few times, broke a red light and entered the final stretch to Sobal Hill. But they were gone. So had Tara done it? Had she transferred all their money to Gordon's account and implicated herself? Parking in front of the bank, his phone started ringing. 'Gordon' flashed up on the dial. *Don't think. Answer.*

'Yeah?'

'Are you under the impression that this is a game? Do you think murdering your wife's boyfriend is acceptable in modern society? Your life is over. You. Are. Done.'

'Calm down. Tell me exactly what's happened.' David needed to think fast, figure out what was going on. *Tara hasn't paid him?*

Gordon wasn't listening. 'And you send Tara up to do your dirty work? What the fuck is that about? She's "your gang" now? I thought you were a hard man. But you're a pussy. Well, that's it. I promise you, you have one last chance to—'

'Gordon, if you've touched a hair on her head, I'll kill you. I will rip out your heart.' David pictured Tara with her eyes closed. He pictured her having walked into something that she couldn't get herself out of; something that was too big, too dark, too discordant. He pictured her alone. 'I will slit your throat.'

Gordon was finally listening. 'Zip up your dick, Dave. This isn't a pissing match. Control your fucking wife and you get to decide your immediate future. Do you want to live in a cage for the rest of your life, or do you want the luxury of being allowed to start again? You, Dave, have the freedom of choice.'

'You're talking about freedom of choice now? This isn't civics class.'

'And you're not a figure from your history class. You're not a crusader, or a revolutionary. You're just something close to being shit beneath my shoe. But I'm going to give you one last chance; you and that crazy bitch. So rethink your idiocy, or I—'

David hung up. That was all he needed to hear – Gordon wasn't on his way to the cops. What was Tara up to? Where was she now? He took out a cigarette and called her again. It rang and rang, and finally she picked up.

'Tara, what the hell—'

'It's cool. I'm on top of it.'

'You're OK? Gordon didn't—'

'I don't have time to explain.'

'Yes, you do. But first, where are you?'

'I'll call back in a few minutes. *Trust* me.'

David didn't like the emphasis on 'trust'. He lit the cigarette. 'Tara, I need you to take a few seconds to step back from whatever is going on and then we'll—'

She hung up. She hung up before he could do his usual thing: offer advice or issue a warning – the male habit.

'Goddammit!' He called her back. It went straight to her message box. He turned the ignition, levered into reverse and waited. He had nowhere to go. He didn't want to be at home in the empty house. He pushed the lever back into park and turned off the engine.

He felt utterly useless, as if he was a spectator of his own life rather than living it. Everything was now out of his control. He caught himself in the rear-view mirror, looking tired and drawn. A wave of exhaustion crashed down on him and he leaned forward over the steering wheel, closing his eyes, letting the leather cool his forehead. The BMW was drowsily, luxuriously warm. He tried to straighten, to sit tall, but his body didn't respond. It was as if everything had ended; as if the battery of his life had suddenly, inexplicably, failed. He couldn't breathe properly. Each inhalation stopped midway, as if there was something plugging his windpipe. As he gasped for air, his fingers gripped the steering wheel. Then he released it and instead clutched his chest, as if it were possible to rein in his heartbeat.

But he knew it would pass. *It's just a panic attack.* He'd experienced it once before, during his first year exams. David took a deep breath now – he would not lose his mind. His phone started ringing again. With miserable resignation, he looked down to that oracle of doom and then answered.

'Bruno, this is not a good time.'

'Good time? No, very bad time, Dave. You need to come. I am at your house.'

'What are you talking about? Why are you at my house?'

'Police. Sirens. There will be an arrest made. It is insane, Dave. All in your house and no one home. Big problem here. The police looking for you. Back patio – all the travertine – it's wrecked to hell. Get home now. The police looking for you.'

David looked through the bank window, where Sandra was walking by with a file. She smiled at him and David smiled back. He wished that this was America. Because if this was America, then he'd own a gun. And if he owned a gun, then this would be the moment to blow his brains out.

# CHAPTER TWELVE

Tara was three cars behind Gordon's Saab. She could make this better. After all, he'd just passed a police station without stopping. That had to be a good thing. *You've been given another chance. A last chance. Don't fuck it up this time.* Part of her wanted to chase him down, blow the horn, flash her lights, nudge him into the pavement and then bring him back to the bank. But another part of her – the more adamant part – told her to wait and see.

Gordon finally turned off the seafront to press on into Cawley, an area that consisted mostly of industrial parks, council flats and run-down estates. Tara looked out at the depressing vista as her car wound by petrol stations, billboards and warehouses. In an area where the recession had never ended, four tower blocks stood against the high sun like megaliths that had survived a failed civilisation. It was a glum panorama of sensory deprivation; a place where supermarket trolleys came to die.

She recognised one of the roads that whizzed past – the street that David had grown up on. He had given her a guided tour a few years ago. Back then, she'd wondered if the houses were as bad on the inside as they were on the outside. Everywhere she looked, there were modern terraces tacked onto whatever land was available, the most recent blocks being uniform bunkers with small windows, built for people who lacked the money to complain. *Me, David and baby – we'll be happy anywhere together.* Was it actually possible to maximise a child's potential here without having to fight as hard as David had had to for a better life? She didn't like the idea of all those kids growing up as if they were mushrooms in the dark. *The countryside. We'll live in the countryside.*

Gordon turned into a shopping centre car park built for a hundred motors but home to about twelve. As Tara kept her distance, he exited out the far side and parked on a road of pebble-dashed terraced homes with tiny front lawns, no driveways and tablecloth-sized backyards. Gordon exited his Saab, a conspicuous presence among the ageing family hatchbacks and the empty driveways. Flinging open the garden gate of one of the houses, he hurried up the narrow path and disappeared through the front door.

Tara parked before the low wall that separated the car park and the pavement. An old woman pulled her wheelie bag as she hobbled away from the shopping centre. Summer didn't suit this area. Everything was parched. Dog piss dried to yellow stains, while the unbagged shit just hardened and crumbled.

Tara stepped over the low wall, crossed the road and pushed open the creaky gate. No shadows moved behind the bubbled glass of the front door. There was no bell or knocker. A letter box was nailed to the pebble-dash like a birdhouse. She took out her phone and quickly wrote a text. Pressing 'send', her mind could almost see the message shooting off to David.

Tara attempted to bang her fist against the door, but instead of making a pounding noise, the door just swung inwards.

'Gordon?' she announced – not quite as loudly as she'd intended, as if she was in a crowded room and dreaded attention. The narrow hall stretched past a slim staircase. The walls were papered in a white B&Q-type plastic flock design with a few hanging pictures – nothing personal or noteworthy, just the type of stuff that would adorn a two-star hotel room. There was a small side table clogging up the narrow hall. On it was a coffee mug. Above, on the small landing, nothing moved.

As Tara stepped into the hallway, she almost doubted having seen Gordon enter this house. The rules of the universe seemed to forbid his very presence in an estate like this. She heard the rumble of a boiling kettle coming from behind the kitchen door. *Gordon must be in there.* The urge to retreat was like gravity pulling her backwards, sucking her out to the street. *You're a coward.* She forced herself to go on.

The front door clicked shut. Tara spun round. Christine stood in the hall, one hand on her hip, her head slightly back, prepared to tackle anything before her. She was holding a wrapped sandwich roll.

'Christine!' Tara said. 'I followed Gordon. I need to see him. Why are you here?'

Christine advanced, picking up the coffee mug on the sideboard. Even as it cracked against Tara's skull and white light exploded behind her eyes, her thoughts were, *There's been a terrible mistake.*

She knew she had stopped falling because she could feel the carpet against her hands. She hadn't felt the rest of her body hit the floor.

She opened her eyes. The ceiling was spinning and listing, as if the entire house was sinking in a storm. *Am I about to die?* Tara had a flash of memory of her teen years, sitting by the window in school, staring out to the fields, losing herself in her favourite daydream – planning her own funeral in great detail: the music, the readings, the flowers. And only now did she realise that this had been silly, because it wasn't as if she was going to be at it.

Tara moved her arms, and her hands rested on something new. It took her a moment to realise that it was her stomach. As she fell away from the world, she told the baby to be good. *Stay with me*, she urged. 'Stay with me.'

'I should sew your lips shut,' Christine said from above. 'Each time you open them, you sound like an imbecile.'

# CHAPTER THIRTEEN

David parked in the road because there were two squad cars in his driveway, one with its blue lights still flashing. He felt shamed by the police, remembering how their presence had been an almost daily feature on the street he'd grown up on. Crossing the circle of the cul-de-sac, he tried to ignore the neighbours opposite, who were standing in their porch pretending not to look. David wondered what they were thinking. Security was a favourite topic in this neighbourhood.

*I hate Lawrence Court. I always did. Good riddance.* But even as those thoughts flashed across his mind, he knew that they were just murmurs of self-deceit. *It's my fault that our child isn't going to grow up here, isn't going to attend the local schools and make the special connections. It's my fault that the kid will be banished to a foster home, probably in some provincial town held together by burgers and booze.*

He passed the empty patrol cars, climbed the steps and entered the hallway. Through the kitchen door, he saw two uniformed men outside on the patio. He turned into the living room and made straight to the bar. One last slug. He unscrewed the bottle and poured. *Remember the good times.* The two of them, backpackers, lying on a double hammock, drinking, looking at the Andaman Sea. *My favourite thing.* Getting quickly drunk on an oriental beach at dusk; like shooting up on heroin and slowly, luxuriously dying.

David poured a second double and glugged it back. It seemed a long time ago that he'd used to drink just to maximise pleasure rather than to minimise pain. And then it occurred to him: Tara was already slipping from his life into his memory. Soon those memories would splinter into fragments, until the only real thing left of his wife would be the picture of her that he would keep hidden in his cell.

'What are you doing, Dave?' Bruno asked from the hallway.

David poured another large glass, raised it and said, '*In vino veritas*.'

Bruno put out his hand for a shake, as he did every time he met David. David took the hand and forgot to squeeze, letting his limp fingers be engulfed by Bruno's thick, calloused digits, rippled with soil-filled cracks. 'Do you not think you've had enough?'

David took another sip. 'I certainly don't. No.'

'Perhaps you've had too much.'

David threw back the remainder. 'Perhaps you should have one. Make it a double. Loosen you up for once.'

'I am sorry, Dave. A terrible thing is outside. They are waiting. But look, out where I come from there's always a nearby war on the way – that is life. So you must come and face it. Then, maybe, finally, things will get good.'

'When you're reduced to relying on miracles, things will not "get good". In fact, things will never "get good" again.' But despite saying this, David followed Bruno into the kitchen, hands locked professorially behind his back. As his throat burned and the booze warmed his blood, he thought of how this would all be recorded, how his story would be twisted and shaped by the tabloids, neighbours and the chattering classes. History was the lies of the victors and the delusions of the defeated. It was something that never happened, written by someone who wasn't there.

Bruno stopped at the kitchen door and stepped aside, letting David exit the house first. The fresh smell of a recent mowing filled the air. There was a police officer standing by a hole in the travertine, directly over where Ryan's body was buried. A pickaxe and a shovel lay against the wall, having been used to smash through the slabs and dig up the foundation.

The officer tore his gaze away from what lay in the hole and looked at David. Tall and slender in a uniform usually worn by bulky men, he somehow managed to make the police look cool. The peaked cap was tipped low over his forehead and his pale face was baby-smooth, as if he'd just had a cut-throat shave. His hands gripped his leather belt, which contained mace, a mobile phone and handcuffs.

'David? David Miller?'

David lit up a cigarette and breathed out smoke to the beauty of his garden. He didn't want to finish the cigarette – because when he did, everything would have changed, forever. But he took a final pull and dropped it to the undamaged travertine at his feet. Slowly, he approached the hole, his hands automatically joining together as if following a coffin. It seemed the right thing to do, in the way that even an atheist genuflects before an altar.

# CHAPTER FOURTEEN

Tara was draped over someone's arms, as if being carried by a fireman from a burning building. But she was being brought up the stairs, deeper into the house. Her eyesight was blurry and the voices in the hall sounded like gibberish. The door to the back bedroom opened and Tara was deposited onto a mattress. Her head lolled to the side and she saw enough of the room to understand that it was mostly unfurnished, with a bare light bulb hanging from the ceiling. Stacked along the skirting were cardboard boxes and paint tins. Protruding from the wall about four feet above her head was a brass bedside assist bar, the type used by disabled or elderly people.

Tara tried to sit up but could barely lift herself with her elbows. Her hands slipped against the grimy cheap plastic of a blow-up bed. She lay on the synthetic spread like a germ about to be bleached clean. A man – Gordon? – was in the room, closing the door, shutting them both inside. Then he turned to face her.

*It can't be.*

*It is.*

Ryan – not Gordon – shoulder-slouched against the wall, one boot pressed against the old wallpaper, his other knee bent forward. He smiled and said, 'Howdy, T,' just like he'd always called her.

'You. Are. Dead,' said Tara.

'Alive and kick'n, T. Back from the grave. Kinda like... Actually – *just like* – our lord and saviour Jesus Christ.'

Tara took a moment to look at Ryan, confirming to herself that he was actually there, in the room, and not about to vanish back to the afterlife. She took in his expression: the liar's lookalike states of innocence and deception. His cheek was bruised and there was a bloody gash across the side of his forehead. But he also seemed older than the last time she'd seen him – as if he had gained years rather than a few stressful days. She'd noticed him losing weight over the last few months and now that was suddenly very apparent. However, it didn't suit him. Instead of making him thinner, it just made him look emptier.

Finally she said, 'You're alive! And you're not hurt. Not really. Look at you!'

'Yeah, *now* I'm fine. Though no thanks to your husband. He threw me out of a window, you know?' Ryan turned to exhibit a shaved patch at the back of his head where a makeshift bandage had been placed. 'If that cup slammed against your head hurts, imagine how I felt. Your bruise…' He squinted over at her upper cheekbone. 'Nothing but a hickey. Tell you this, T, as I lay there, not sure if I'm dying or just fuck'n paralysed, and feeling the clay against my head, seeing every pebble in the dirt and soil, wondering if anyone was going to come and get me, I decided one thing – I'm putting into my will that they're not to lower me down into the earth till I've been dead at least three days. No exceptions.'

'We've got to tell David,' Tara said, her pulse banging along at the sight of the miracle before her; the living, breathing ticket that would collect on all her problems. 'You need to get me out of here.'

'Come on, T, you know that's not going to happen. Just make yourself comfortable. Hey – does this bed remind you of my bedsit back in the day? Back when I was good enough?'

Tara's mind was blowing up. *He's alive, but it isn't over.* Her thought processes were a stream of questions: Where's Gordon?

Where's Christine? What are they all doing here? And all the why's, why's, why's. But she couldn't get one word out.

Ryan's laugh was deep and spoke of cigarettes. 'Calm down. Get it under control. If you stay alive, then the chances are I will, too.'

Tara stared into the brilliance of the ceiling light bulb. She forced her eyes wide as if the harsh glow could literally illuminate her mind. 'You couldn't have planned it. You couldn't have known that David would follow us to the house that night and that he'd try to kill you. You couldn't have planned to be thrown out of the fucking window. So, what happened – you and Gordon just leapt on the opportunity to blackmail us? Why? Because… Oh my god, because you need the money for Fenton?'

'Uh-huh.'

'*All of it* for Fenton?'

'All of it.'

'Fenton told David you owed him over some drug deal. But we assumed it was fifty or maybe a hundred thousand. Not one point four million!'

'It's one and a half million actually. But I already have a hundred k. I need everything you have for the balance. Tara, I used to *truly* believe that the man I was scared of was not born yet. But then I met Fenton.' Ryan had started off calm, but gradually his eyes widened, his speech quickening. 'The last guy who disappointed him, Fenton bashed his head with a hammer. Put him down. In front of the guy's wife and two daughters, in their own living room. Then he prised open the back of the skull with the claw part. I mean, can you *imagine* what it took to do that? The daughters were five and seven. They saw it all.'

'And knowing this, you what? Decided to do a deal with him?'

Ryan walked over to the window, limping slightly. '*Me*? Jesus, the whole thing with Fenton was Christine's idea. I'm a builder. I built myself up from a man-with-van to a thriving business. I work. I like to earn my crust. It's the natural state of things.'

'That's what I said the moment I heard you'd got yourself into this mess. I said that you weren't a gangster. You were never a thug.'

Resting his elbow on the sill, Ryan said, 'Fuck'n right I'm not. But... Things went south in the bust. Way south. Our savings disappeared with the banks – Jesus, they bent us over one desk after another and fucked us every which way they could.'

Tara wanted to sit up, but she still felt woozy from Christine's assault. Instead, she pulled herself backwards and rested her head against the wall. 'Ryan, you roll with the bad in business. You know? Like everyone else has to?'

'Rolling with the bad? Yeah – that would be easy.' Ryan's laugh was false, bitter. 'That would be straightforward. But life isn't like that for me and Christine. We're not allowed to waltz through the years. That's not in Christine's DNA. She fucks up her life time and again and blames me, blames the weather, blames me again.'

'Did it occur to you that you just weren't capable of giving her what she wanted? What she needed?' Tara pressed her hands against the mattress and finally managed to get herself into a sitting position, her legs stretched out before her.

'You've met her twice. The second time, she smashed a mug over your head. You think *you* know her?'

Tara, blinded by the spotlight of Ryan's full attention, remained silent.

'Christine continued to push me into piling on the debt because she needs to spend. She doesn't know how not to. And yeah, we should've split up back then, but we couldn't afford to. And so we live separate lives in our big, flash, negative-equity house, where we scrape something together for the mortgage arrears. But one day Christine thought she'd found a way out. We could make an easy lump sum, divide it and split up.'

'Yeah, I know this story too,' Tara said, rubbing her head. 'She used one of her clients to get to Fenton and make a deal, right?'

'*Client*?' Ryan crossed the room to the door and turned. 'The kid was what? Fourteen? Can a fourteen-year-old be anyone's *client*?'

Ryan began pacing, as if trying to iron out the remnants of his limp. 'My wife's meant to be some type of social worker! And she uses some slow kid to do a deal with his master? Jesus – *that's* what I married.'

Nonchalantly, Tara scanned her immediate surroundings for a weapon. There was nothing but paint cans. 'Fenton told David that you sold the drugs. Why would you do something as stupid as that? You're not "street".'

'Fenton has it wrong.'

'So just give them back to him.'

Ryan shouted, '*They're fuck'n gone.*'

'How?'

He stood still and ran a hand through his thick, sandy hair, but he may as well have been punching the wall. Clearly, the mere memory of what had happened set his adrenaline pumping. 'After the truck crossed Eastern Europe where shit *could* go wrong, it ends up at the gates to civilisation, where there's a charge on the border crossing by Syrian 'fugees. Mayhem. They climb all over the truck while it's *still* moving. The driver panics and the truck topples. It lies there on its side for two days. At some stage during those forty-eight hours, the steel is stolen – and therefore the drugs are too.' Ryan sighed, as if still not believing it.

For a moment, Tara thought he was about to cry, and almost felt sorry for him.

'So, the only thing to do was jump town. When we were with each other at Lawrence Court – that was my goodbye to Dublin. I was splitting a few hours later on the morn'n ferry.'

Tara was thinking about the nearest paint can. She could make a dive on it and throw it through the window. Then she could scream.

'You were just going to leave Christine to Fenton? How could you do that? You may hate her, but she doesn't hate you. She slapped me in my own kitchen and just broke a coffee mug over my head. Because of you, apparently. No one's that good a fake.'

Ryan leaned against the wall and softly knocked the back of his head rhythmically against the exposed plasterboard. 'Oh yeah? Christine is faker than fake.' A glare of disdain crossed his features. 'Anyway, I wasn't leaving her behind. She knew I was going. She was running herself on Sunday night. But not with me. I'm sure she was good at pretending that she was in bits when she popped out to visit you yesterday. But she was just keeping up appearances. Making sure you didn't suspect anything. Here's a deep thing I came up with all on my own: she might've been taking her hatred of me out on you – *you* being the picture of every sane woman I've managed to have a second of pleasure with since the day I married that bitch. But the bottom line is that if I'd died on your patio, she wouldn't have given a shit. As a married couple – no, as human beings capable of being in the same room as each other for more than five minutes – we were finished years ago.'

Tara moved to get up to her feet.

'Stay – the fuck – down.'

Tara blinked slowly and stayed where she was, sitting against the wall. 'And so once you survived the fall, your new master plan was to get David and me to pay off your debt?'

Ryan stepped forward to the end of the mattress, patting the bandage at the back of his head. 'Not *my* master plan. I've no say in anything that's going on. Never had. It's Gordon's. Once your husband nearly killed me, Gordon took over. Hate to say it, but I owe him my life. All this – me playing dead, the bank transfer, the blackmail – it's all his. He came up with it, spur of the moment. He puts me into hiding in this shithole street he's renovating, pretends to you and Dave that I'm dead, pretends to Fenton that

I'm missing – and then we wait. We wait for the transfer. But you decided to be mental. Fuck you very much for that.'

For a moment, Ryan turned his back on her and Tara had a clear view of his shaved skull wound. *Forget about breaking the window.* She could get the small paint tin and smash it down onto his bandage. *Tackle the problem at the core.* 'But why did Gordon arrive at Lawrence Court on Sunday night when he did? And why would he get involved in this – your mess? It doesn't make any sense.'

'We're not going to talk about Gordon. OK?'

'But I don't understand!' Despite Ryan's previous order, Tara tried to stand on the mattress but only made it to her knees. 'What is Gordon doing *here*? Why is *he* involved? How did he... But if he knew... What the fuck is going on?!'

'Lie down!'

'Just let me go, Ryan. It's over now. This is all insane.'

Ryan's expression had changed. The rising panic that had cast a damp, filmy sheen over his face had hardened into a calm glower. 'Just give me my fuck'n money. That's your role in this. That's it. Nothing else. I need it today. I need it *now*.'

'Ryan, this is *not* you. Whatever you've done, it's not too late—'

'It *is* too late!' he shouted. Crossing the room, Ryan raised his foot, and with the flat of its sole, shoved her back down to the mattress. He then stomped up onto the plastic bed until he stood over the top half of her body. 'I'm dead if I don't sort this out. Christine's dead, too. My time was up three days ago.'

Tara glanced over at the tin of paint. It was out of reach. 'Tell the police. I won't say anything about what you've done. Neither will David. Just leave us out of your mess.' The words were bits of broken glass in her throat.

'If the police find out what I did with Fenton, they'll lock me up for a decade. And what would his guys do to me in there?'

There was now nothing available to Tara but words – so she used them. 'Ryan, think for a minute. Even if the money is transferred and you give it to Fenton, you reckon it'll be over then? After we go to the police, you'll go to jail anyway. You'll be done for robbery, for kidnapping. But it can all end without you hurting innocent people. It's just a choice you have to make.'

Ryan's boot pressed against Tara's shoulder, forcing her onto her back. His knees then slammed onto the plastic on either side of her hips, the fulcrum of his weight pressing down on her groin. She gasped as her lungs emptied of air.

'Let me spell it out. You were always going to discover that I'm alive. But if Fenton realises where I've got his money from, then he will have no choice but to make sure that you, Dave and your kid are dead in case you decide to do something insane like go to the cops. So I won't tell him where the money came from, and you won't go to the cops. Understand now? Am I making fuck'n English to you?'

Ryan yanked her hands above her head. Tara caught the gleam of metal before hearing the *snick* of the stainless steel bracelets as they ratcheted into place. He'd handcuffed her hands together, the chain passing behind the bedside assist bar, shackling her to the wall. Ryan continued, 'Fenton just wants his money. He doesn't care where it comes from – you, me, anyone. He gets his money: I live, you live. He gets his money and you go to the cops: I live – you die. It's not really a choice, is it? So let's do this the easy way and get me my money right fuck'n now.'

Tara stared up at him. Ryan was supposed to be dead – now he's not. That was all that mattered. The fact was, no matter what he now said, she didn't have to give him what he wanted. 'Oh my god, I'd rather rip my eyes out and eat them before I'd give you my money. David would too. So you *lose*, you dumb, sad, stupid piece of shit. It's over. So fuck you, fuck you, fuck you.'

Ryan's bulk shifted and the fulcrum of his weight moved to the base of her stomach.

*My child.* 'You're hurting me. You're hurting the baby.'

'I'm not hurting you. Not yet.' From his pocket, Ryan withdrew a box-cutter. Click by click, he exposed the blade.

# CHAPTER FIFTEEN

David stared into the hole. It was about three feet deep. The travertine around the rim was splintered and cracked from the repeated blows that had rained down from the anger of the pickaxe. The loose soil and foundation mix had been shovelled out into a neat pile next to the lawn. Running through the centre of the hole was an orange sewage pipe, the core of its exposed portion blasted open as if something inside had hatched. Through that breach, crushed limestone had spilled into the pipe, effectively plugging the internal waste flow at that point.

'I used to be a builder,' the uniformed officer said. 'Five years ago. And I've never seen such a complete shambles as that.'

David's concentration remained focused into the hole, as if at any moment he'd spot a finger in the rubble, a shoe, a toe. *He's not there. He's absolutely, one hundred per cent, not there*. David stepped down into the hole and crouched, his fingers scraping against the loose soil, reassuring himself, proving Ryan's absence to his own brain. Digging his fingers into the clay, he half-expected to touch clothing and rotting flesh. But there was nothing there but more clay.

'Who's your builders? Who did this?' the uniform asked.

'Ryan... Maximum Building Services.'

'Judging by this mess, they need to do a refresher course on the basics of the screwdriver, never mind plumbing. I mean, just look at that...'

*He was dead. I saw him*. David pictured what he'd seen: Ryan, handsome Ryan, lying on his back over that very pipe, trying to lift his arm, the arm then falling lifeless to his side; a glaze forming on the blood across his lips, like sealing wax; his last breath, his eyes already with a thin, cloudy, filmy appearance. *Wait.* He couldn't have seen that. David had been on the second floor. Ryan had been thirty feet below. *I couldn't have seen his eyes. His hand rising and falling, maybe... But not his eyes.* David didn't know what he'd seen, what he'd imagined.

The uniform observed the facade of the house as if looking into a great, glass pleasure-liner. 'Incredible they did that, considering the quality of the rest of it.'

David batted away the compliment with a nod. There was definitely no corpse there. But Ryan had landed in that hole, smashing the pipe and then... What? Gordon wouldn't have moved the body. A body is heavy, and the risk involved would have been multiple times higher than burying Ryan where he lay. Had Ryan survived? Had Gordon helped him leave the house, and then... then had Bruno arrived in the morning and just filled in the patio like he was supposed to do?

David pictured Ryan arriving at his house three nights ago, waiting to meet his wife, strolling through the hallway that was soon to be Tara's personal gallery. He saw him in the downstairs toilet, blasting yellow urine against the porcelain, shaking his cock dry, drops splattering across the maple wood floor. *I'm going to find him. Wherever he is. Then I'll beat him until he's bleeding out of every hole.*

Bruno spoke up: 'Dave, I find that I am in some way responsible. I visit yesterday to apologise about football match, but your car not here so I leave it. Then meet your neighbour out on road. He ask to borrow pickaxe and shovel and rods from my van. Paid me one hundred euro. But I swear to you, Dave, he never said for what. Never.'

'Don't sweat the small stuff, Bruno.'

'Then I call back today to collect them. His wife brings me in and says, "Thank god", and "Stop him from getting himself arrested".

Only when I hear a *ka-thunk* and a *ka-thunk* coming through hedge do I realise that he is in your beautiful house destroying it. This time you *and* Tara's car not there. So I call police. Straight away, Dave. I let them in with key you left for snagging jobs.'

'I know, Bruno. Thanks.'

Shay's wife was pacing back and forth on the other side of the hedge, muttering into a phone as if praying. She was recounting in a panicked voice everything that her husband had done that morning, presumably to one of her grown-up children; who, no doubt, was delighted to be on the other side of the planet.

The uniform asked, 'So you're what? A history teacher?'

David stepped out of the hole. 'Why?'

The officer reddened. 'That's what your neighbour said when we stopped him from wrecking your house.'

*Remember where you live. The filth* are *your friend.* 'Yeah, I'm a history lecturer.'

'Wow,' the officer said, scanning the back of the house and then the sprawl of garden. 'I should've paid more attention to history in school. I mean, what's it good for, really? When you look at the world, like, the state it's in, what does it teach you?'

David stared into the uniform's face. 'It teaches you that you're better off winning a war than losing it.'

The officer returned David's stare, trying to make up his mind about him, when a second officer appeared from the woodland with Shay.

'My colleague took your neighbour for a chat as he was getting upset,' the first officer explained. 'Especially when we tried to explain to him that the existence of the blocked pipe did not legalise his actions in any way. Honestly, I thought we'd have to Taser him.' He chuckled, and David knew that he was supposed to chuckle too, but he'd forgotten how to laugh.

Shay and the second officer stepped up to the shattered travertine and joined the rest of them. David watched Bruno watching Shay, who was watching the police, and for a moment felt like he was partaking in some ridiculous caper. Finally, Shay spoke: 'David, you drove me to this. You left me with no choice. I told you what we were going through in there. So fine, have me arrested. Throw the book at me. I have nothing to be ashamed about.'

'I'm not pressing charges.'

'What?' the first officer said. 'He broke into your property and caused about a grand's worth of damage. I *urge* you to reconsider.'

'Seriously, man, it's fine. I'm sorry for the time you've wasted here.'

'If he entered here without your permission, then I have a duty to—'

'He had my permission.'

Shay, who had been holding out both wrists as if expecting to be cuffed, looked to David and then back to the police, like he was choosing his moment at a busy intersection. Then he asked, 'So what's going to happen now? It needs fixing.'

David said, 'You think that's an original observation? Jesus, Shay, I'm not going to have you arrested. And I'm not going to sue you. *And* I'm going to fix it. Today. So what else do you want from me? Bruno, can you get going on repairing the pipe and patio? I'll sort you for two days' work. No, three days. Whatever you want. Shay – off my property. Right now.' Then, turning to the two officers, he said, 'I'm sorry that police time and resources have been wasted. But everything is now fine.'

After Shay was helped back through the hedge by his wife, David walked the police out to the driveway and made a big deal of cheerfully thanking them in front of the neighbours, who were still watching the show. As Bruno departed in his van for the wholesaler's, David's phone began to vibrate. He took it out and looked at his architect's flashing name. Fighting the urge to slam it mindlessly on the driveway, he answered with, 'Ryan's alive.'

Whatever Gordon was about to say, he replaced it with silence.

David continued, 'See, Ryan broke the sewage pipe when he fell. And then you failed to fix it before filling it in. It's over. You don't have any cards left to play.'

'We have Tara.'

Slowly, David withdrew the phone from his head as if it was a dangerous animal that didn't like him and never would. Steeling himself, he put it back to his ear.

'The fact that you know about Ryan just saves me a whole lot of explaining. So pay attention, because *this* is the new situation: Tara followed me. And then she ran into our good friend, Ryan. The first rule of the observer: never be a witness. Your wife just broke it. She's now with Ryan, and she's not happy about it. But she's not as upset as Ryan is about not getting his money. Let's hope he doesn't lose his temper. After all, her husband did throw him out of a fucking window.'

'Look, whatever Tara said or did, that wasn't part of what I'd planned.' Across the road, a neighbour was getting into her SUV. She waved over at David. He waved back. 'Gordon, you are going to get your money. Tara just went off on one.'

'I was just listening at the door to the lovebirds reacquainting themselves. You know, Dave, the difference between men and women only comes down to our use of verbs and adjectives. For example, when women show their worst selves – such as how Tara reacted to Ryan being still alive – we call it "passionate" or "mental" – depending on how hot or ugly they are. But when men do their worst – such as what Ryan is threatening to do right now – it doesn't matter what they look like. We just call it "psychotic, cold-blooded, preconceived mayhem".'

David closed his eyes, locking himself into the blitzkrieg of his brain.

'So I hope you understand how delicate the current situation is?'

'What do you want me to do?' But David was talking to dead air – Gordon had hung up.

He turned away from the world of Lawrence Court and the smell of freshly cut grass that carried on the breeze. *Situations like this do not happen to ordinary men. This doesn't happen to regular everyday good husbands*. He – David – had to be fundamentally flawed. Why could he not protect his wife? Why had he failed her? And if he couldn't protect his wife, how could he have ever believed that he could protect his child?

At the steps to the house, just as he was about to put away the phone, David noticed a text from Tara sent less than an hour ago.

*61 Heffernan Place. Gonna sort it with Gordon here. Call you after if you don't come.*

Before David had a chance to process this information, the phone buzzed the arrival of a picture: a close-up of Tara's frightened face, the extended blade of a box-cutter pressed against her throat. The text read:

*Meet you at bank in fifty minutes. As planned. Then Tara is released.*

David quickly replied:
*I'll be there. You'll get your money.*

He waited, staring down the road, as second by second the quiet, warm summer slipped away. David thought of today's date. As a student of history, dates were important to him. The ones he remembered, the dates he cared about, were either glorious victories or terrible defeats. What would he eventually remember this date as?

David reread Tara's last message. He knew the address well.

# CHAPTER SIXTEEN

Tara was alone in the room. *Remember, there are two of you now. Start thinking like a mother.* Her gag was tied too tightly, so she sucked panicked inhalations through her nose. Then she found that if she focused on the stiff pain of her raised, handcuffed arms, she could calm down and breathe normally.

Her mind was exploding. The same thought was spiralling around: *You have lost all control.* That one-off intimate coupling with Ryan was meant to have been the perfect bookend to all that had happened before life got captivatingly serious with a husband, money and pregnancy. Even when they had parted that night, there had been an adult casualness about it – as if there was no drama left lingering; as if it would all be just a memory of something naughty that had happened and would never happen again.

The door opened now and Ryan returned. He pulled the gag from her mouth and said, 'Dave knows I'm alive. And after he saw the pics of his beautiful wife, he's about to do the transfer. And I'm sorry – really sorry – cos you're the last person on the planet I'd want to hurt. Does that tell you how much I need the money? You're the only one... the only one that, I suppose, was real.'

Ryan sucked in his lip, preparing to move the conversation to safer, shallower waters. But Tara knew that she needed to keep him talking. He'd let his guard down. He was giving her a chance. Part of him must care for her. What she had to concentrate on was her face. What she had to put all her work into was her expression, and the business of what she had to do with her mouth – smile, breathe; and her eyes – widen them, fill them full of brightness. Show none of the mayhem that was inside.

Her eyes watered and she swallowed. 'I was lonely when I came to the city. I thought you were nice. And you know? You *were* nice. You were *nice* to me. That's what I saw in you. That was our bond.' She needed Ryan to like her all over again. She needed him to remember that they had something – a spark, a connection, chemistry. Though it occurred to her that their type of chemistry tended to blow things up: a chain reaction.

'You tell yourself that, T. But I remember it all. You're the same person now. Sure, there was once a healthy farm-girl quality about you. But you got rid of that real quick. You wanted cocktail parties, spinning classes and all that shite. I'd never have fitted. That was the one thing Christine has that you never did and will never have – feet firmly planted on the ground. No interest in all the bullshit airs and graces. Not wanting to be something she isn't. Even if Christine had got all her family's money, she wouldn't have wasted it on all the crap that you do. Tara and a builder? Nah. You're too fake for that.'

It took a mental effort to suppress the anger flaming beneath her watering eyes. She needed to *not* antagonise him. He had to feel something for her besides sex. Tears formed, but not enough to fall. 'Ryan, don't hurt me. Please…'

'Ah, T, leave it out. You can't wrap me around your finger now. After a certain age it doesn't really work any more. I mean, at least in the past you sounded like you believed yourself. Wow, you were so good at getting what you wanted. You always had that look about you – like you didn't know what you were doing. Remember back when I was playing lead with The Hunger and you danced in front of the stage, trying to sing along, keeping your eyes on mine, and you looked so innocent – yet *so* fuckable? It was like you hadn't a clue that every man you met was thinking manky things about you within two minutes. But fuck that – you *knew*. Oh yeah. Well, that's over now. That power, that skill, it only belongs to the young ones. You just can't pull it off.'

It took an actual physical effort to swallow back her anger and suppress the urgent itch to strike back with her own vicious words. She swallowed, caught her breath and said, 'I know you don't mean that. Let me go, Ryan. Let me go and I swear I'll forget all about it. David will, too. I'll make him.'

'What do you see in Dave, anyway? I hate him. Always have.'

And just like that, something snapped inside her and Tara sprang upwards before the handcuffs yanked her back. 'You hate David? Yeah, I get that. Some men can't help but hate a guy who's better-looking than them, smarter than them and more successful than they'll ever be.'

Ryan reddened, but as he was about to speak, Tara continued, 'And he's tougher than you. I mean, when he wanted you to leave his house, he literally threw you out the window. Christ, how humiliating is that? But don't answer. Your face is already doing a roaster. Oh yeah – and I forgot to add a crucial character trait of David's. My husband is a good man.'

'Don't make me laugh, T. When did *you* like "good men"?' Ryan let his question hang in the air, letting the complex truth it contained further murk the room. 'So, when you thought that your morally upright, principled, hard-working husband had murdered a man, did you still think that he was your cool, clean hero? Cos – newsflash – most people would see him as a villain.'

'Really, Ryan? Everything in the world is still that black and white for you? Wow – you're so emotionally stunted, you've still to learn that your adolescent days of "either/or" are long over. Adulthood is more complicated, Ryan. Jesus, you really are a fucking idiot.'

'Yeah, well once you saw a future with this fucking idiot.'

'Time for a reality check, you dull, stupid animal. I don't remember those days. I never think of them. But it's nothing personal. It's only because you're a nonentity.'

'So what are you saying? That me and you was nothing much? That you and me—'

'My days hanging out in uni were more important to me. When I think back to that time, *that's* what I remember. You were something in the background – a dude in a crap band. Obviously I knew I was going to quickly outgrow you, like anybody with a drop of ambition or talent would.'

'Bullshit. I remember—'

'Remember the letters you sent me? I threw them all out after we split up. And you know why? Because sending them back to you just seemed too theatrical, and I just didn't care that much about you.' Tara laughed, before promptly switching from mirthful to bored, hoping that Ryan wouldn't guess that she was lying about throwing out his letters. 'I mean, think about it – what girl doesn't hang onto her lover's letters? I've hung onto others. But not yours.' Already Tara's thoughts were refocusing on her dilemma. 'David's *not* going to give you the money. He's just going to kick your head in. *Again*.' For a moment, Tara was back in that downstairs toilet half a decade ago, replaying David's fist smashing into that guy's short snout and slow, chimpanzee eyes. How she wanted to see David do that to Ryan.

Ryan's face darkened and his shoulders spread, tightening his shirt against his chest, making his strength abundantly clear – demonstrating how much of him was pure muscle, how much of him was all outside and not inside. 'Bring it on. Dave's punch was cheap. A mosquito bite. I *fell* out that fuck'n window.'

The door opened and Gordon joined them. He passed Ryan like he wasn't there, just like he'd strolled around Tara's house, treating it like something he had conjured up from nothing. Then he said, 'I have to meet Dave at the bank. So you stay *the fuck* away from Tara. Get Christine to mind her while I get the money. I'll give it to Fenton. Then we all move forward with our individual lives and our remarkable new realities. *Comprende*, Ryan?'

Tara was crying. She hadn't even felt the emotion building. It just happened – a brief shudder, tears and two quick sobs.

Somewhat reluctantly, Ryan handed the key of the cuffs to Gordon and said, 'Tara, you're the one chained to a bed. Not me. So who's the stupid animal now? Huh? Nah – forget that. Look, I'm sorry. I was just... Well, none of this was supposed to happen. I was going to just split the country. But what happened, happened and... It is what it is, right? I mean... What the fuck do you want me to say?'

He slammed the door closed as he left.

'What he's trying to say,' Gordon said, 'is that we all have problems. I have lots of my own. Ryan has lots of his own. But this one – our big one – it's now yours.'

Tara squeezed her eyes, as if that would wring them dry. *Get your shit together*, she admonished herself, suddenly realising that by breaking down she had ceded an important advantage. 'You're going to take our money and then feed us to Fenton?'

Gordon was suddenly irate. 'You'll survive. You have Dave. Vermin doesn't die. He burrowed his way out of *this* hole, all the way up to Lawrence Court. You two will figure something out. Jesus, I'll even arrange for you to be top of the housing list for one of these refurbished beauties. A goodwill gesture. David would love it up here. No more having to act like a real person. He could just relax back into the scummer he is beneath the Hugo Boss suit and the Beamer. It'll be good for you, too. He'll be a happy husband for a change. So you won't have to commit adultery every six months just to feel alive.'

Tara craved to defend David, but she wasn't in the right frame of mind to match Gordon's cruel intelligence. 'And Fenton? You know what he's capable of.'

'All I know is what you know. Fenton's a degenerate. And Christine made a grave error to get involved with him. Yes, you're right to be scared. A man like Fenton will put a few bags under your eyes, a few more notches around your mouth. I'm sure he was once just an everyday adolescent cum-stain with a long future on the dole ahead of him – or a short one wearing a uniform in some desert. But then he decided, "Nah, I'll use my aggression and wiles for myself and become a considerable danger to anyone who displeases me". He does terrible things to people because he is ruthless. Or maybe he does terrible things to people because he's evil. It's not *that* uncommon, apparently.'

'Why don't you just kill us yourself?'

Gordon sighed, and then spoke almost sympathetically: 'Fenton won't hurt you as long as you don't try and hurt him by going to the police. You'll have signed a contract with me – your money will be legally mine. And then the money will be his. I'll convince him that you and Dave will be good kids. I'll promise him that you'll behave. I'm sure he'll leave you alone.'

Tara felt like they were playing chess – except Gordon was the only one who could see all the pieces. 'Gordon, why are you involved in this? Why were you at Lawrence Court on Sunday night?'

Gordon laughed, but not unpleasantly. 'To stop Ryan from leaving.'

'But what difference would it have made to you? He's just a nobody builder, in way over his head.'

Before she could push him further, footsteps sounded outside on the landing and Christine entered. She was holding the now mostly eaten breakfast roll on a napkin, fried egg and brown sauce oozing out the sides. Looking down on Tara, she made a face like she'd spotted a stubborn stain on the floor. 'Gordon, you let that slut follow you. She doesn't work for Mossad. She's a pregnant housewife. And you allowed her to mess everything up *twice* in less than an hour. You should've parked in the back estate like me, and only come into the house through the laneway entrance. They're watching us.'

'They're watching *you*.'

Christine kneaded her temples with her spare hand. 'If I hadn't just got back with this gross sandwich, she'd have found Ryan in the kitchen.' She threw the last piece of the sandwich into her mouth and allowed about five seconds of chewing with her eyes closed before continuing. 'And then she would have run and told the police, or worse – she'd have told Fenton where we are.'

Gordon blinked once, slowly, as if deleting everything he'd just heard.

Christine ran her hands through her hair. 'This has all gone mental, Gordon. This is *not* going to work and I'm going to die in this shithole. It really has all gone wrong.'

Gordon placed his hands on Christine's cheeks. 'I know precisely what I'm doing.'

'No, Gordon. It's out of control. It's all gone to—'

Gordon's lips landed on Christine's and they kissed, embracing tightly. Tara was as shocked as when she'd first set eyes on Ryan in this room.

*What. The. Jesus?*

When they parted, Gordon held the sides of Christine's face. He said, 'By tomorrow, Fenton will be gone from your life. Ryan will be gone too. Then it's just us. You and me. So keep it together and do exactly what I say. OK?'

'OK,' Christine whispered.

'And you know what? After Fenton's gone, I have a contract lined up. Not just these council houses. I'm talking about a *serious* job. Yes, Christine – I got it. I'm designing and building the church; a church the size of a shopping mall, all bankrolled by American biblical interests. Wait till you see my plans and drawings. Then after I invest twenty grand here, twenty grand there, soon we'll be talking about real money again.'

The revelation that Gordon and Christine were lovers *had* thrown Tara. But she needed to concentrate on her survival. She said, 'You didn't want Ryan to get the ferry on Sunday night because Christine would have had to leave, too?'

'You looked pretty, gagged,' Christine said. 'You want it back on?'

Almost gleefully, Tara persisted, 'And how were you going to get Ryan to stay? Did you expect him to just come round to the idea of taking one for "Team Gordon and Christine", his estranged fucking wife and her fella? Did you actually think Ryan would do the honourable thing and die for the woman he hates? What is the matter with you, Gordon? I mean, Jesus, I didn't hire an imbecile to design my house.'

Christine said, 'Oh, just spell it out for her, Gordon. At least it'll shut her up. Or maybe we'll just gag her again.'

Gordon turned from Tara and looked out the window.

Christine sighed. 'Fine, then. Tara, remember when your husband was hit on the head with a hammer on Sunday night?'

'Yes. *Gordon* hit him with it. From behind. Real brave.'

'But why do you think Gordon was holding a hammer?'

Tara lay down flat on the mattress, her arms dangling above her head from the handcuffs. In a low voice she said, 'Gordon, you were going to *kill* Ryan?'

Gordon turned from the window. 'What else could I do? If he got the ferry, then Christine would have had to leave and hide until Fenton found her. Just like he'd find Ryan. Fenton has a long reach, and Europe is just another short little continent. By running, Ryan was killing them both. But with Ryan found dead, the police would be involved. They might discover something about importing drugs, but they would never be able to prove anything. They never can with guys like Fenton. But there would be enough attention to make Fenton go away. He'd probably assume a rival had killed Ryan instead of paying him for the stolen drugs. No honour among thieves, et cetera.'

'But then your husband almost did the job for him,' Christine said.

Gordon rolled a cufflink between his fingers. 'I wasn't expecting Dave in the house. So I hit him with the hammer before he saw me. It was a hard thing to do. I'm a normal person. Normal people can't do those types of things just like that. And then when I found Ryan in the pit, I stood over him, wishing he was dead – but when he wasn't, I had to try to force myself to smash his skull in. But no chance. Even with him unconscious. And that's when I realised that I didn't have to kill anyone. And so, thanks to Dave, no one had to die and no one *has* to die. A house is lost. A fortune is squandered. But—'

'*Our* house. *Our* money. Gordon, if you're doing all this for Christine, it is, unquestionably, the most stupid mistake of your life.'

Christine said, 'Do you think Gordon and me happened, like, this morning? We've been seeing each other for years.'

'Once all this is over, we're moving to America together,' said Gordon. 'It would be a real treat if Dave and you could come over for the house-warming.'

'Christine loves the fact that you'll kill for her,' Tara said. 'But she also loves the fact that you'll die for her. Because that's what could happen, *if* you don't go to jail.'

'I'm curious, Tara, what would you have done if Dave was in Christine's situation?'

'Don't you dare compare that woman and you to David and me.'

'I know what you were prepared to do for Dave. You thought he'd killed an innocent man and buried him under your patio. And yet you snuggled up to him and pondered all the ways that you could help him get away with it.'

Tara wanted to say something that would illuminate what she'd been prepared to do for her husband in a different light. But if it had come to it, she'd have taken a hammer to both Gordon and Fenton's skulls. *Unlike you, I wouldn't have hesitated.*

Gordon's demeanour suddenly reverted back to the competent alpha male that had made the building of Tara's house so stress-free. 'Right, I have to meet Dave and do the transfer. Christine, keep her quiet until I've spoken to Fenton. Gag her if needs be. Let's keep this smooth and simple, the way I like it. OK?' He placed the key to the cuffs on a paint tin.

Christine leaned against the wall looking at her feet as the architect's shoes pounded down the stairs. Then she sighed and said, 'This would never have happened to you if you hadn't slept with a married man.' She adjusted her gaze to the mattress. 'I hope you understand that. If you were just an innocent party, just a client of Gordon's down on Lawrence Court, then I would never have agreed to any of this.' Christine gave a walrus snort. 'But you're just a slut. So, like, whatever.'

Tara's raised, handcuffed arms felt a subtle jolt against the constant weight of her hanging limbs. The support bar had loosened a few centimetres. Tara pretended to shuffle her body into a more comfortable position, but was really taking her weight back from the metal bracelets, giving the chain slack, preparing herself for one big tug to free herself from the wall. But she needed to get Christine close to her. And so she started laughing, wheezing as if she was a teenager at the back of class.

'What?' Christine demanded. Her eyes narrowed into mascara-clotted slits.

'Ryan really did a job on you, didn't he? Like, even with all that heavy, disgusting make-up I can still tell that you were once very beautiful.'

Christine dropped the stained napkin onto the floor. She walked over to the mattress and hunched down. 'Don't try and do cynicism. You can't do it very well.'

Tara lunged forward – but her handcuffs snapped backwards. Christine scrambled away from the mattress, which gave Tara enough time for a second tug – ripping the support bar out of the plasterboard.

'Stay down!' Christine ordered.

Tara jumped up and swung the bar blindly towards her captor. It whacked against the side of Christine's head and she promptly buckled to her knees. Tara dropped the bar onto the mattress, and with handcuffed fists clenched together whacked the metal bracelets against Christine's forehead. Christine hit the floor, face down.

Tara stood still for a moment, listening. Was anyone coming? There was the muffled sound of voices arguing coming from somewhere downstairs. *Good. They're distracted with their own shit.* She snapped up the key from the paint tin. *Don't drop it.* Her panicked movements meant it took three attempts to get the key into direct contact with the lock. *Don't fuck up.* She tried to turn it, straining her wrist, bending her limbs. *Got it.* She pulled her hands from the bracelets and threw them to the mattress. She went for the window, where she could see her car across the road. She could break the window and scream. Would anyone hear? Would anyone care?

She left the bedroom, entered the grubby bathroom at the back of the house and opened the frosted window. Below was the yard, and beyond that, a wall bordering a laneway. She stepped out onto the window ledge. In the neighbouring garden, right up against the border wall, was a small shed. It was a fifty-fifty chance whether or not the structure would support her weight crashing down on top of it. As Tara leaned out, she felt a surety of pride: that it was she who was keeping the baby alive – her alone. Then she jumped.

She landed on the felt roof and waited for it to give way. It didn't, and she lowered herself to the neighbouring yard. For a second she considered banging on the back window, but then remembered that Gordon was supervising the renovation of the entire street, so there was nobody living there either. Instead, she hauled herself up on a bin and scrambled over the back wall to the lane. *Keep going. Keep going.*

The road was up ahead. *Twenty feet away*. An army of pigeons charged with her down the concrete canyon like a spooked shoal. *Ten feet away*. She sprinted past heaped bin bags, broken glass and a rusty washing machine. *Almost there*.

A white van screeched to a halt. Tara stopped just before slamming into the side of it. The side door opened. A tall skinhead, the size and shape of an industrial refrigerator, glared at her. Tara looked at his tattoos, his tracksuit, the cruelty that poured into the vacancy of his expression. In what sounded like a Russian accent, he said, 'Good day, Tara. I'm Viktor. Nice to meet you at last. Mr Fenton will see you now.'

Tara covered her face with her hands as if she'd just turned over an exam sheet and immediately knew that she couldn't answer a single question. Her life's dream was getting away from her like something slippery and alive that did not want to leave the water, gliding away again every time she thought she'd grasped it.

Viktor reached forward and grabbed her, but he was surprisingly gentle as he nudged her into the back seat of the van. Fenton was sitting in front of her, on a toolbox in the middle of the floor.

Tara swallowed. *It's just like going over the edge on that Busch Gardens rollercoaster. You can't get off. You take a deep breath. You open your eyes. You stare down at the height and the speed. You face it. It's like what David shouted beside you: 'Open your eyes, or you'll miss it all.'*

As Viktor scrambled back into the driver's seat, Tara remembered when, as a little girl, her father had brought her to work one Saturday. They had been in the forest to check on the seedlings when they'd come across a gang of drunk teenagers from the nearby town. The young men had tried to frighten her father, but he had been so brave. She remembered a little of what he'd said – shaming the gang for acting so crass as to frighten a little girl.

Tara glared at Fenton. 'I'm not frightened of you. You're pathetic. Two big tough men, alone with a pregnant woman, trying to bully her. Wow – if I was a man and I got to that point in my life, I'd kill myself.'

'I heard watching your kitty die was fascinating,' Fenton said. 'See, Tara, animals die different to people. Prey becomes so still in the jaws of the predator. According to Viktor, it was as if the poor thing felt no pain. It was as if there really is a God, and at the end He felt sympathy for it.'

*Dora?* Tara was suddenly aware of the relevance of the cat's absence that morning. She thought of David in the woodland with a shovel. *Fenton is waiting for emotion.* She tried to shake the image of her loyal, friendly pet from her head. *Never give them what they want.* Calmly, Tara said, 'You're psychotic, Fenton. And you can't see it *because* you're psychotic.'

Up front, Viktor moved the driver's seat further back and lowered its backrest, giving him a clearer view of the van's hull. Tara had impressed him.

'Psychotic?' Fenton said, his expression stiffening, for the first time not liking what he was hearing. 'Like a serial killer, or a pervert like Fred West or something? Or like that doctor with the beard in England?'

'No,' Tara said with an air of boredom. 'They're all interesting. You're just the run-of-the-mill sociopathic kind. The kind that tortures animals. But then, how else would a loser like you get respect in a world that only rewards ambition, talent and hard work?'

'Very ballsy, Tara. But I work hard. Just like your husband. Except I didn't have the learning potential that Davy had. And yet, at the end of the day, I still have the cash to move to your area – yeah, to Lawrence Court. But I never would. Cos I'm not a fake cunt.' Fenton raised his head, as if by even indirectly complimenting Cawley, he was complimenting himself. 'I'm proud I come from here. I hate it, too, but I never want to fully leave. Probably the same for Davy. I bet every so often he creeps by in his BMW just to reassure himself that all the shit is still here. So don't you judge me when you come from the type of lucky background that allows you to pick a bleed'n Indian jewellery-making course or arty path, so that your career can reflect the one long group hug that your fucking life is.'

'My father cut down trees for a living. My mother worked in a bar.'

'So? You think you know what it's like growing up in a place like this just cos you're working-class? There's a difference between being working-class and being scum-class. You haven't a clue. I'd be a virtuous cunt, too, if I'd arrived onto the earth with a perfect body, born of loving parents in a town that didn't know violence and gear.'

Up front, Viktor had become disinterested, like a young man in the back row of a lecture. Tapping his watch, he said, 'Boss. There is our business we need to do.'

Fenton nodded. Then he said, 'Tara, you're a smart girl. You know what I'm capable of. I'm not going to play games with you. I don't have the time.' He lifted himself off the toolbox, undid the catches and flipped the lip open. Reaching inside, he withdrew a large black metal handgun.

'Oh Jesus, you can't be serious.'

Fenton began screwing on the silencer. 'This big boy holds the barrel axis close to your hand. Makes the Glock more comfortable to shoot by reducing muzzle rise. If you screw up and only maim your kill – which is not liable to happen – it allows for faster aim recovery in rapid shooting sequence. But best of all, Glock rhymes with cock. Granted, it doesn't have much stopping power, but I'm not being asked to level an elephant. Just a pretty little pregnant girl who is really getting on my fucking nerves right now – which are frayed, because I'm not used to *not* getting what I want, whenever the fuck I want it. *Capiche*?'

'This can't be happening. I didn't jump from a first-storey window onto a garden shed just to be stuck here with you. I could've hurt my baby.'

Fenton shrugged, turning the Glock's weight over as if one side was preferable to the other. 'So, Viktor was following Christine this morning. She left her house in Sutton and parked Ryan's white SUV deep into this estate. The good news is that there's only one way in and out of the estate. The laneways and roads just twist and come right back out here. Which means she's in there somewhere, hiding. And I can only speculate that Ryan is with her. Which leads me to conclude that you were just in there with your pals. Am I getting warm?'

Tara's brain was moving fast now. Even though the mess had become messier, the situation had, paradoxically, become clearer.

'Where's Ryan, Tara? You have ten seconds to volunteer the information. Otherwise I'll just take it, like I take everything I want.'

Tara realised she could free David and herself from this mess forever. She could hang onto her money, her house, her future. All she had to do was give Fenton exactly what he wanted. 'If I give you Ryan and Christine right now... Then I walk away? And David walks away?'

'You and Davy mean nothing to me. I want Ryan. There's no money in hurting you. There's no connections to make by hurting you. There's no territory to be gained by hurting you. If I hurt you, then I just get complications. When rich people get hurt, cops care.'

'You leave David and me and our baby alone forever, and scum like him' – she pointed to Viktor – 'never go near our house again. You forget us and we forget you.'

'You have my word, and my word is my bond. Otherwise why would anyone do business with me? Ryan had no doubt that he'd get paid. Just as he had no doubt that he was fucked when he failed to deliver. *Because* my word is my bond. Tara, you're out of time. It's your call.'

She closed her eyes. *It's nature. You don't want to get in the way of nature.* She had to think of the baby, her husband, their future; the money. *Let nature take its course.* Tara nodded at Viktor. 'Start it up; I'll bring you there now.'

Viktor turned the key and pulled away from the pavement. Fenton rested the silenced Glock on his lap.

'Turn right,' Tara said. 'It's about five houses along.'

'Good girl,' Fenton muttered. He opened the toolbox again and this time brought out a small pair of binoculars. He leaned over the passenger seat and glassed the front of the terraced house. Then he lowered them and chin-pointed towards the front room. 'Why's your husband in there, Tara?'

'What?' *Oh my god.* 'He can't be. He isn't. That's impossible.'

Viktor said, 'I can get extra muscle here in five minutes. We can get every last one. No mess.'

Fenton checked the silencer on the Glock. 'I don't need no extra fucking muscle. In fact, I'll do them myself. It'll be a pleasure. Keep her here. We'll do her in the woods after.'

Viktor's hand roughly smacked down over Tara's mouth and a huge arm locked into place beneath her neck. Tara closed her eyes and hoped that somehow it would be relief that awaited her in the darkness. She would like to find her father there, put her head on his chest and feel the heat and the strong pumping of his heart.

# CHAPTER SEVENTEEN

Just ten minutes before Tara jumped from the bathroom window, David's BMW, heavy and powerful, was speeding along the coast road. He couldn't stop picturing the blade at Tara's throat. He saw his child inside her belly. Whenever it came out of there, it would be just a murmuring weight in his hands, helpless and needing their protection.

David sped past his childhood road without even glancing at it. Then, as the blocks depopulated, the shopping centre appeared before him. He swung off to the right and pulled up in front of number 61. Getting out of the car, he felt both the security of familiarity and the diffidence of the misplaced. He remembered how it was a twenty-minute walk to here from his old house – a walk that he'd hated, because of the shopping bags pulling his arms from their sockets on the return trip.

Opening the garden gate, he scanned the windows. The net curtains didn't twitch, shadows didn't retreat. *Am I afraid?* It didn't matter. There was nothing shameful about it; one cannot be courageous unless there is something to be frightened of. He pressed his hand against the door to test its heaviness and it clicked open. *Too easy.* He stepped into the hall. The only sound came from the kitchen – a running tap. He moved forward, past the side table and turned the handle. And there was Ryan – alive and well before the kitchen sink – his eyes wide, confusion parting his lips into a half-smile.

Ryan withdrew the box-cutter from his pocket and extracted the blade. 'How's it hanging, bud?' Then his eyes widened, registering a great injustice. 'You almost killed me, you fuck'n prick.'

David looked affronted. 'It was an accident. If I'd known how much of a pussy you were, I wouldn't have bitch-slapped you so hard.'

'Don't know why you blamed me. I just finished what your wife started with those tits.'

David lunged forward, his hand grabbing Ryan's wrist, knocking it against the sink and forcing Ryan to drop the box-cutter. They crashed into each other, arms and legs flailing. Almost immediately, a stalemate was reached with both men doubled over, side by side, braced in headlocks. Ryan punched David in the side of the head. David punched him back.

'Enough!' Gordon shouted like a parliamentarian from the hallway. He entered the kitchen and stretched for something on top of the fridge – a black pistol. It looked very real and yet very unreal. It was something David had seen too often on TV. 'Dave, you can't outpunch a bullet, and I can't unpull a trigger.'

David's face tensed, willing himself to take the risk.

Gordon saw it. 'Think about it, Dave. Long and hard.'

'Where'd *you* get a gun?'

'Jesus, what do you think I spent my formative years doing? Hanging around street corners? My father worked for the RAF – remember? He made sure I could shoot before I could ride a bike. I've being hunting since I was ten.'

David released Ryan and shoved him back towards the kitchen door. Ryan's head wound was bleeding again through the ripped bandage.

Ryan shook his head like an animal awakening. 'You're a dead man, Dave. *Fuck'n* dead.' The tendons on his neck bulged, his teeth exposed and gritted.

Gordon snapped, 'Stay where you are, Ryan. This is not the time for that shit.' The gun wavered in his hand as he struggled to make a decision. He gestured to David. 'Into the front room. Where there's no knives. Where you can't fuck up my life any more than you already have.' Gordon retreated into the hall, keeping the gun trained on David as he entered the living room. It had a coffee table, a three-seater sofa, a grubby carpet and net curtains.

'Now what do we do?' Ryan shouted from the hall. 'You were meant to be meeting him at the fucking bank! Jesus. Can't anything go right? It's like... It's like God has just decided that I am fucked.'

Gordon reddened. 'It's OK. We're still going to the bank. It's going to be fine.'

David laughed. 'What? You're going to walk in holding a gun to my head?'

'No. Ryan's going to stay here, holding a gun to Tara's head.' Gordon didn't even sound as if he believed himself. He sounded as if he'd had enough.

David sensed that it was all coming to an end. Suddenly, Christine appeared on the staircase, moving slowly, holding her head. She stopped halfway down and looked over the banisters into the front room. The side of her face was bruised, and blood trickled from the corner of her mouth. But even more noticeable was the smudged eyeshadow and lipstick, giving her an air of decay.

'Tara's gone,' she said, her tone flat and dead, full of the inevitability of the day.

Ryan covered his face with his hands. 'That's it. It's done. It's over. I'm dead. We both are.'

Christine stared down at Gordon before beginning to sob. Gordon had paled. He blinked rapidly a few times, as if a coding error was occurring in his brain.

'Where's my wife?' David said.

'Did you not hear me?' Christine screamed. 'Are you fucking deaf? She's gone. Out the bathroom window. She's gone and—'

'I'm getting my passport,' Ryan said, climbing the stairs and squeezing by his wife as if he didn't know her.

Gordon said, 'It can't end like this. Not after everything…'

David took a small step forward. 'It's over. You know it is.' He needed his architect to put down the pistol. Gordon looked tense and scared. And when people were scared, they were stupid. And stupid didn't go well with guns.

'He's right, Gordon,' Christine said. 'It's over. We have to leave now. We have to run.'

Gordon looked up at her, smiled wistfully and said, 'Whatever happens, I love you.'

David straightened when he heard that. Which meant that the bullet hit the wall next to his face instead of going through his skull. Powdered plaster and flecks of paint fell onto the shoulder of his suit. He looked round to see where it had come from: it had first passed through the window in a perfect round hole. The rest of the glass had cobwebbed.

The front door whacked against the wall. Fenton's footsteps moved towards the living room. There was the sound of a single *pop* and on the stairs, Christine recoiled backwards, clutching her face. Ryan turned to catch her and both of them sprawled across the steps. David looked at Gordon, waiting for him to raise the pistol, to do the smart thing: let off a burst of rounds, make a spider line of bullet holes along that shitty internal wall and take Fenton down before he reached the living room door. But the architect seemed paralysed.

'Shoot him!' David shouted as Fenton rounded the corner. He slammed into Gordon's back and, as if slipping into a suit, reached round him, fitting his hand over Gordon's fingers, raising his arm to point the weapon at Fenton. As Fenton entered the room, David pressed on Gordon's trigger. He squinted just in time for the noise and the flash – but all that happened was a single, measly *click*.

'It's fake,' Gordon said, terror raising the timbre of his voice. 'Of course I don't own a fucking real gun.'

Fenton pointed his Glock at both men and pulled his very real trigger. It fired – a deep bass concussion that David felt in his chest. The brief blaze from the silencer barrel was woven through with strange green sparks. It was something David could still see as he shut his eyes. More bullets came, the rounds hacking off pieces from Gordon like chips from axe blows. Gordon wasn't a hostage. More a human shield; a thick mound of bullet-absorbing flesh. And then, just as David opened his eyes again, Gordon took a direct hit to the side of the head and a chunk of his forehead blasted across the room, landing on the old sofa.

The architect's weight pushed David backwards until his legs hit the coffee table. Both men crumpled to the floor. Lying on his back, David stared into Gordon's devastated face, which had been blown open like a ruined jigsaw. Gordon's lips moved, saying something. Then his eyes glazed over, staring up to the ceiling at the final mystery. There was little blood – the insides of Gordon's head remained static, as if he'd been refrigerated.

Over the years, the terrifying idea had remained with David that his mother was right, and that God really existed. And if He did exist, then He might become aware of David's existence and *lay His hand* on him, and then he'd be stricken with religion and waste his entire life with everything that accompanied it. Now, for the first time, he wished that there really was a God, and that he believed in Him, because then he could pray.

Fenton turned and pointed the Glock up at the huddled Ryan, who was muttering, 'Jesus, Jesus,' as he rolled his dead wife off him.

Fenton said, 'Ryan, apologise.'

Ryan shouted, 'Sorry!'

'Again.'

'Sorry.'

'One more time.'

'I said, I'm fuck'n sorry.'

'Apology *not* accepted.' Fenton closed one eye. David, back on his feet, lunged into him from behind, grabbing Fenton's arm, raising the Glock to the ceiling, his other hand seeking out every hard man's weakness – the eyes.

'Why are you fucking alive?' Fenton muttered as he shoved backwards, his bulk pinning David to the living room wall. Suddenly, from behind, Ryan's right arm arced through the air and the box-cutter blade plunged into Fenton's neck. Fenton dropped the Glock, clutching his throat, the tips of his fingers burying themselves in the gaping, seeping wound. Within the red moisture David could see loose, soaking tendons.

Fenton staggered into the centre of the room, clearly horrified by the feel of his blood oozing between his fingers, pumping hard with each pulse. Ryan dropped his arm and attacked again, low, straight into Fenton's stomach. The blade passed through his shirt and seemed to confront, for a moment, stiffer resistance. But then that too gave way and the blade continued on, scraping by bone and cleaving through internal organs with a squelch. Fenton remained standing, staring wide-eyed. Ryan had to tug the box-cutter a few times to free it. It made a moist *pop* sound as the tip reappeared.

Fenton fell backwards onto the carpet. Down there, his eyes remained stubbornly alive as his body thrashed about – a dying shark. Then his eyes widened, as whatever he had been left the world in a second. With the blood drooling from his neck and smeared over his face, it seemed that the only part of Fenton remaining human was his mask of pure fear.

Ryan, his face rained-on with blood, staggered backwards until his back hit the fireplace. He then sank towards the floor, the mantelpiece propping him upright in a sitting position, his legs splayed out.

David stepped over Fenton's body. With assured, steady movements, he took hold of Ryan's hand and tossed the blade across the room. Then he grabbed Ryan by the hair and twisted him onto his back. Ryan was too finished, too traumatised, to fight, to resist. Sitting on the builder's chest, David stared down. He was stunned at how much he suddenly hated Ryan. Those dark, unanalysed forces disengaged him from his fear of consequences and provoked him to new levels of recklessness. He placed his hands on Ryan's blood-greased neck and felt the knotty Adam's apple beneath his thumbs. He began to press. His feelings were now beyond language. Ryan had tried to destroy everything David had believed he was worthy of – his wife, his child, his house. Ryan was a nightmare totem to David's unworthiness. A part of David knew he was doing the worst possible thing – but something within drove him on, told him it was for the best, that he would regret it forever if he didn't finish this now.

He began to squeeze. Ryan's eyes bulged. They watered. Blood vessels burst. *He tried to take everything you've ever wanted, everything you have.* History didn't just affect nations. It affected the individual, in the most private way. History demanded a debt from the world and it insisted that people pay in blood. History was this very moment.

Tara looked up the staircase. Christine was lying there, face down, her head towards the hall. Tara entered the living room. There was Gordon, his life of plenty blown away to nothing. She glanced down at Fenton. A damp pool of burgundy was expanding around his abdomen. He'd only left the van a few minutes ago. Viktor had been watching through the binoculars before cursing in Russian and starting up the engine. He hadn't even tried to stop

Tara when she'd jumped out. She'd shouted over to a woman in the car park to call the police; that there was an emergency; that there had been a shooting.

Tara stood over her husband as he squeezed the life from Ryan. The whine and howl of emergency vehicles came ever nearer. Already, blue lights stained the room. She placed a hand on his shoulder. 'David, I need you. The baby needs a dad, too. Let him go.'

People were already in the hallway. Tara didn't look to see if they were police or not. A woman screamed, over and over, like a siren.

# CHAPTER EIGHTEEN

It was late on Saturday afternoon, and the house-warming party on Lawrence Court was three hours old. There was an outdoor bar set up along the line of the hedge. The guests mingled and circulated through the opened slider to the kitchen and the library, and on to the front room, where a DJ played Tara's favourite songs. Catering staff worked the crowd.

Tara, alone for once on the patio, scanned her friends, neighbours, art dealers and fellow artists. When she'd first come to Dublin in her twenties, with no money and an uncertain future, it had been enough to have a great coke connection at your party. A decade later and you *had* to have someone famous – which thankfully Scott McCoy had provided, by bringing along a Hollywood star in the middle of his European publicity jaunt.

Tara had already given five guided tours around her home. The house was perfect now – even the stain at the top of the stairs had been painted over. As her guests had 'oohed' and 'aahed' at each new architectural flourish, it was interesting to see the many ingenious ways they found to ask how much something cost. Tara had hung out long enough on the art scene to realise that just because a person was an intellectual, didn't mean that they didn't care what sort of car someone drove.

From her corner on the patio, she spotted Shay in the kitchen, filling another glass of water for Stephanie – who was 'resting' in the library with David's mother. Shay seemed shocked, almost alarmed, at any conversation he happened to overhear, while the dress sense of the artists – especially the female ones – left him wandering around with the expression of a teenager at a party for the first time. But Shay and Stephanie were getting on surprisingly well with David's mother, with whom they had swapped anecdotes about growing up on opposite sides of Dublin.

'Tara!' Someone had spotted her alone. 'I am pleased it work out so well in the end of it all.'

'Bruno? Oh, hi.' Tara couldn't help but look him up and down. She'd never seen him in a suit before. It was almost impossible to recognise him without his uniform of blue overalls or paint-stained jeans. She waited for him to say something more, but he didn't, preferring to just stand, smile and shift awkwardly. He then looked at his wrist as if checking the time, but there was no watch present.

Trying to muster up some enthusiasm, Tara suggested, 'Go and get a drink. Go. Go. Lots of cocktails while they last. And David's looking for you, I'm sure.'

Excited at the prospect of examining the wares of a free bar, Bruno drifted off. Tara scanned her party again. And there was the star of the show: Scott McCoy, roving by, his all-American face marred by vagueness, but willing to talk to anyone – which was just as well, because everyone wanted to talk to him. Of course, he always dictated the conversation, spinning it quickly to his favourite topic – God – and he was too rich and too famous for anyone to tell him to shut up. But Tara understood Scott's unrelenting self-righteousness. He had no doubt that the next life contained even greater riches for him than the vast amount he'd already collected in this one.

Tara was flattered that so many distinguished figures of the art world – some so distinguished she'd thought they were dead – had turned up. But she knew that the reinvigoration of her reputation had everything to do with the headlines of the past month. Because of the incessant attention, she'd worn shades every time she'd gone out. She had been like a widow in sunglasses, seemingly wearing them to hide her tears when, in fact, the dark lenses served to hide her relief.

And still the stories kept coming in. The papers loved the drama. Especially the tabloids, who followed the gangland scene like it was a soap opera. Just a few weeks ago, Viktor had been arrested at the airport with a false passport as he tried to make his way back to his own corner of the world.

Then there was Ryan: he'd been attacked in jail while awaiting trial. Two Russian prisoners, associates of Fenton's, had tried to kill him by shoving a bar of soap down his throat. So he was now in a secure wing for his own safety. Tara couldn't help feeling sorry for him. She also felt some gratitude: despite everything else he'd done, Ryan hadn't mentioned their fling to the police. According to Ryan, he'd fought with David over money that Sunday night in the attic – a story which David had been only too happy to corroborate.

But where had Ryan's unsolicited loyalty sprung from? Did he feel that he owed both of them his life? Privately, she wondered if it was because he had nothing left now but reminiscences. Unsurprisingly, David maintained that it was because the only sympathy Ryan could evoke in his trial was from the fact that Christine had been an unfaithful wife – which evidence of his own adultery would nullify.

Of course, David had been on hand to make sure that Tara's career capitalised on their great newsworthiness. In the last few weeks, he'd already secured a London retrospective at Brick Lane, despite the fact that the markets were depressed. But Tara knew what to expect once this second flurry of interest died off: they'd discard her as quickly as she'd risen in the first place. But that harsh fact wasn't so demoralising to her any more. At first she had assumed this was because of her forthcoming child. But then she had realised that it was because she had actually felt the old hunger return; that luxurious exhilaration from the great potential of a new idea for another series of artworks. She was still wary about it at this point, though, feeling that she mustn't yet talk about it, as if it might benefit from secrecy.

There was also the fact that Tara *needed* the added distraction of making art. Her pregnancy wasn't enough to keep away what she'd seen. And even as she thought that, the vision of the bloodied mayhem in the Cawley Estates returned to her – as it did twenty times a day. But she was trying to be philosophical about it: life was just trying to tell her something, and wasn't it her job as an artist to hear it?

Thankfully, most of her guests had been tactful enough not to ask Tara about what had happened, instead focusing on her house, or the fact that she was due in four months. One gallery owner and divorcée had said, 'I hope you have a boy – because girls are utter little bitches. They always take *Daddy's* side.'

Tara spotted David on the other side of the patio. He was rakishly handsome in his suit as he waited for people to approach him rather than work the gathering himself. The setting sun caught his profile, stressing the speckles of grey in his hair, yet highlighting its thickness. Tara felt sure that he would be around forever. She needed him to be. The world now scared her. Her life had briefly become a horror story full of violent people, and it seemed that all she could do to keep herself safe was fixate on her love for one of them.

It occurred to Tara that the world she had briefly stepped into was just an example of what David had taught her in his tutorials, and what he was now teaching his new students: that it was always the same people in power everywhere. Sometimes they called themselves communists; sometimes capitalists, popes or ayatollahs. But they were just the people who had always owned the industries. And this time, drugs had been the industry.

Tara looked down the lush garden that had begun to turn golden in the late summer sun. It made her feel that God and magic had made the house, and not East European labourers and money. *Lots* of money. But her father had always told her that a house does not make a home. It was a fact he'd experienced when his wife had died. And it was a lesson he'd passed on to Tara when he'd put a gun in his mouth and pulled the trigger. After all that had happened, David had demonstrated that he was not a man who would ever walk away. He would be there for the long haul, giving Tara exactly what she wanted, keeping her and the baby sheltered, no matter where. David was her home.

Suddenly, two women grabbed Tara's hands – one each. Her friends had travelled up from her home town. They dragged her inside, where the DJ was playing one of the seminal songs of their youth. They pulled her through the library and into the front room, where they joined about ten others, dancing and laughing. With the music washing over her, Tara spun around, moved her hips, caught herself in the mirror and wryly smiled.

*Fuck – when did I start to dance like an old person?*

A caterer drifted by David on the patio with a tray of mini spanakopitas. He grabbed one, while wishing there was a TV in Ryan's cell that could relay a live feed from the party. Even though Ryan had saved David the ordeal of the world discovering that his wife had cheated on him – an ordeal that he would've found as cutting as the betrayal itself – he still felt no gratitude, and was not remotely unsettled by the fact that only Tara's arrival had stopped him from committing cold-blooded murder.

David picked up his Bushmills and Coke and swirled the ice about. The party was a success, and was unravelling itself just like he'd thought it would. When millionaires got together, they wanted to talk about art. When artists got together, they wanted to talk about money. And so it went. The only thing they all seemed to have in common was that the louder they were, the funnier they weren't. But the important thing was that David had already laid the groundwork for a few major retrospective exhibitions for Tara. One or two more, and they'd never have to do anything they didn't want to again.

David was talked out. He'd been lured into too many difficult conversations this evening that had left him wishing he'd actually read an issue of *Modern Painters* rather than just telling people he had. Already, he'd had what amounted to three business meetings on the patio with London dealers. Only ten minutes ago, he'd been obliged to give a personal tour of the house to one very important Bostonian collector who was in Dublin for the week. Now he just wanted to be alone with Tara.

'Shit, boy – you're meant to drink that. Not romance it.'

David raised the glass in a brief salute and took the expected sip.

The man who'd spoken cocked his thumb and pretended to fire at David's head. Then he said, 'I don't know why I did that. After all, you've had a real one aimed at you, haven't you?'

David let silence be his reply.

'I know about guns, actually. I have an antique Sten. Belonged to my grandfather.'

'Sten machine guns – that English piece of crap from the Second World War.'

'Well, I'm not going to argue with an historian. It's George, by the way. You were talking to my wife earlier. Samantha.'

These type of people – the ones who owned country houses with many acres – would always make David anxious. He both despised and was in awe of their show-pony sheen that came from generations of money.

George offered his hand now, and David gave him the type of handshake where he made sure the other person was aware that he was only using about ten per cent of his available strength. George said, 'I see Scott McCoy is here with a movie star to excite the ladies. Very impressive. The only thing I know about Hollywood is that McCoy's insanely rich; rich, as in wipe-out-the-deficit rich. I mean, compared to him, we're poor. Literally.'

'You haven't travelled enough,' David deadpanned.

A group of men that David had yet to speak to were huddled together around one of the patio tables. The alpha of the group tapped out some cigars and handed them round. A whiff of the smoke blew by David's nostrils – bitter and black.

George, his eyes narrowing as he thought of a way to take control of the conversation, said, 'My wife loves Tara's work. Now, I'm no expert but I do like paintings. I have a Picasso and two Gauguins at home.'

*Jesus*. 'That's cool.'

'It's such a pity that painting doesn't seem enough for Tara, that she's not sufficiently fascinated by that struggle towards mastery that was so absorbing for Klee, Bacon, Rothko.'

David hated it when assholes like George had a point.

'So Dave, you're teaching at uni, eh? As well as managing Tara, of course.'

'Yep. Just a few classes while I finally finish the PhD. Wrapping that up is my present to me.' Automatically his mind began flipping through the pages of 'Discovering Resistant Opposition: World War Two in the Savage'.

'Very good, Dave. The university obviously thinks very highly of you.'

'Ah, they just need a few people like me around to inflate the grades of each new disappointing generation.'

'Huh?'

'You know? To banish their mediocrity from the national psyche.'

'Ah, I can understand that. My kids intend going there.'

'Well then, it'll be first class honours all round.' David thought of how his future parties would have kids at them. Their friends would be allowed to bring their own, if just to play with his –

because the odds were that his child would be just like theirs, which would mean that he and Tara would raise the type of teenager who would never scratch a lottery ticket, and for whom therapy would be as required as inoculations and preventative dentistry.

David shook George's hand again and moved on, aiming for the space and peace down the garden. He strolled across the lawn, past the garden table and towards the woodland. With Tara away dancing inside, he lit up a cigarette. Tara thought he'd given them up again, and he almost had – except for three or four secret ones every day.

Through a break in the trees, he could see the mound of clay that covered Dora's body. Above the highest branches, the sky fought against approaching night, slowly turning the colour of a bruised fingernail. It seemed only last week that the heavenly summer had been stretching before him like a broad, slow river. He took in the lawn and the green of the trees and was amazed that he had yet to enjoy it, use it, soak it all up. September was slipping away, and David found himself nostalgic for the summer even before it had passed. That morning on his early walk, the park hadn't been as densely crowded as the week before. Already he felt a new, slight pinch in the air. There was a change ahead.

And then he spotted her. Tara was back on the patio, standing in the corner where he'd thought Ryan had been buried. He gazed up at her, appreciating how, through her pregnancy, she had recently become an even more mysterious creature. Despite her bump finally showing, most of the men still eyed her hungrily as she mingled with the guests.

As David approached, he felt the familiar sensation from her gaze that he'd first felt as her teacher, then later outside the Shelbourne Hotel, and a great many times since: divine providence. Tara was stunning in a full-length Marc Jacobs shift with minuscule spaghetti straps. If he reached to unclasp the strap at the back of her neck, the dress would slip by her hips, down to the floor, where it would pool at her feet like spilled water. David pressed into her side, enjoying the feel of the violin curve of her body from hip to shoulder as it fitted against his.

They kissed, and the luxury prize of their house vanished into nothing. Now they finally had what they wanted: to be able to stand together in their own space, their voices growing quieter, as if huddled together on a life raft, gaining warmth and assurance off each other – and not particularly looking for rescue.

# LETTER TO THE READER

Dear Reader,

Thank you so much for choosing my novel and swapping your real world for that of *The Accident*. For those who would like to join a mailing list for alerts on my future novels, please sign up here. You can unsubscribe at any time, and your email address will never be shared.

www.bookouture.com/sd-monaghan/?title=the-accident

I hope you enjoyed it, and if so, I would be very grateful if you could leave a review. First, because I'd love to hear my readers' thoughts, since they've spent hours of their life, in some sense, in my company. Secondly, because it is via the recommendations of like-minded readers that others may discover my work for the first time.

Emerging from the isolation of writing a novel to receive so much interest and positivity from readers across all social media platforms has being truly heartening. Thank you to all those who have messaged and been supportive so far.

Until the next chapter begins, take care.

S. D. Monaghan.

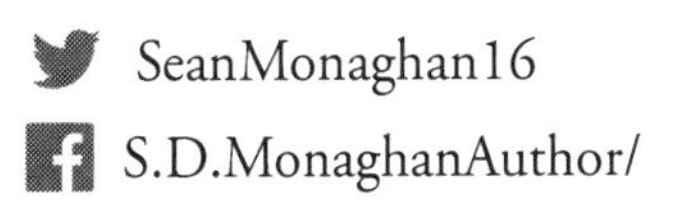

# ACKNOWLEDGEMENTS

I would like to thank:

My wife, Anne Hughes, the sounding board for every idea and my initial editor, who took 500 pages down to 300.

My agent, Zoe Ross at United Agents, who had faith in *The Accident* and championed it tirelessly.

The brilliant team at Bookouture, who have all been a pleasure to work with. In particular, I'd like to thank Abigail Fenton, my exceptional editor, who has such a sharpness of vision that it makes working with her a privilege. It was also great to have the support and advice of Kim Nash.

My parents, Carmel and John, and my sisters, Pat and Teri.

And finally, for advice and encouragement of various kinds, I'd like to thank Deirdre Madden, George O'Brien, Michael O'Loughlin, Thomas Kilroy and Richard Ford.

Made in the USA
Lexington, KY
13 September 2017